Captivating Captains

THE CAPTAIN
AND THE SQUIRE

CATHERINE CURZON &
ELEANOR HARKSTEAD

The Captain and the Squire
ISBN # 978-1-83943-846-2
©Copyright Catherine Curzon and Eleanor Harkstead 2020
Cover Art by Cherith Vaughan ©Copyright January 2020
Interior text design by Claire Siemaszkiewicz
Pride Publishing

THE CAPTAIN
AND THE SQUIRE

Dedication

CC – to EH. How is it 2am already?!?
EH – to CC. Marzipan balls!

Chapter One

Tarquin yawned and stretched in his deckchair. Although most of the blossom had gone from the orchard, blown away by the storms in late spring, it was still a beautiful place to sit in the evening. He took a mouthful of brandy and scratched the head of the pig who was snuffling at the grass beside his chair.

"Now look here, Oracle!" Tarquin held up the length of carved wood that he had been nursing on his lap. "The craftsmanship is second to none."

The Oracle seemed to be listening, even if she was still busy hunting for truffles. But over the contented snorts of the pig, Tarquin heard the music from next door rise in volume and yet another car revved in the private lane outside his house.

His new neighbor had arrived.

The bastard.

The car doors slammed and the sound of braying laughter carried on the breeze as yet more visitors arrived to greet — who? Who was it who was moving into the Hardacre house anyway? Who was it who'd had removal vans and tradespeople coming and going for weeks to the empty house? Who was responsible for the smell of fresh paint and the sound of hammering and drilling from that tottering, crumbling pile where the late Beardsley Hardacre had lived for his one hundred and three years? Who had landscaped that wild garden?

Who was it who had arrived by nightfall not quite twenty-four hours earlier and was apparently already throwing a party?

And why had this interloper made no effort to claim the Oracle of Delphi?

"Your new mummy and daddy have arrived, my friend," Tarquin told the pig, his voice soft. But as another toot and another bray of laughter reached him in his formerly tranquil orchard, he rose from the chair, fire in his tone as he declared, "And I'm going to have words!"

Tarquin ran across the orchard and, his brandy in one hand and the carved wooden length in the other, took the fence in a single bound like a steeplechaser.

The evening air was torn by that most dreadful of sounds — the cry of ripped corduroy trousers.

Now in the Hardacre garden, Tarquin cast a glance back at the fence, where a ragged square of golden-colored corduroy waved back at him like a tiny flag. It must've caught on a nail, but instead of going home to change, Tarquin was too inflamed with rage to turn back, and instead plunged on through the garden.

And what an improvement it is!

What had once been a tangle of brambles amid a sea of grass that would have hidden an army was now a manicured lawn so flat that it could have been a golf course. Bright bursts of color sprang from well-tended borders and for the first time in years Tarquin could actually see the banks of the river that ran along the bottom of their neighboring gardens. How strange it was to think that such a beautiful view had been hidden all these years, but the cantankerous old gentleman who had lived here far longer than Tarquin had even been alive'd had little time for gardening. He had been too busy with wine, women and song for that.

And whoever was now in his house seemed to be of similar appetites, Tarquin realized, as he rounded the corner and froze on the edge of the patio.

Everyone appeared to be in swimwear, or something resembling it. Tall, elegant women wearing sarongs and high heels with their jewelry chatted with handsome young men in shorts and little more, each of them holding a fizzing glass of champagne, each of them exuding money and confidence and…*the city*.

A huge hot tub that bubbled on the patio contained yet more of the incomers, tan and braying and so bloody *loud* and one of them, he knew, must be the new master of Hardacre Grange.

It had to be the man whose braying laughter was louder than anyone else's. The man who seemed to be holding court in that absurdly overstated hot tub.

The only one wearing sunglasses on an evening that required no such thing.

Tarquin strode straight up to the hot tub and bellowed, "Which of you ruddy coves is in charge here?"

The chatter fell silent but the thump of the music, of course, did not. The man in sunglasses took a leisurely sip from his glass of champagne and said, "That would be me, squire. Why don't you grab a glass and hop on in?"

Tarquin shook with fury, the brandy slopping up against the brim of his glass. "Hop in? Hop bloody in? The bally cheek of it—I don't bathe in public with strangers!"

"Oh, you've brought your own booze, I like it!" He lowered his sunglasses just a little and peered closely at Tarquin's *other* hand. "And you appear to have also brought a large wooden penis. Is that a traditional welcome in Bough Bottoms? *Hello, old man, here's a penis from all of us on the parish council!*"

The partygoers guffawed that braying laugh, every eye now focused on Tarquin's hand.

"Penis?" Tarquin thundered. Then he recalled the antique object in his hand. "This? This is a Tudor dildo! It belonged to Her Majesty Queen Elizabeth I herself!" Tarquin wagged it under the nose of the man in sunglasses, because surely the man couldn't see properly wearing Ray-Bans in the dusk.

Although Tarquin could see his new neighbor very well, smarmily grinning at Tarquin from under his arrogant flop of blond hair. Tarquin wasn't going to admit it, but the fellow was in exquisite form, with swimmer's shoulders and toned arms that Tarquin would have happily spent hours squeezing like a shopper deciding on a grapefruit. And that angular jaw was worthy of a statue, finished off with a square chin that Tarquin would never tire of nibbling on.

Not that he would. Tarquin threw a furious glance at the woman chortling at his new neighbor's side.

Married. Has to be. Bugger it.
Or sadly not.

"A Tudor dil— oh, just a minute!" The man pushed his sunglasses up into his hair, his welcoming smile evaporating. "You're Bough! You're the man who did Great-Uncle Beardsley out of Prince Albert's ceremonial Prince Albert!"

"No, I bloody didn't! It's *mine!*" Tarquin stamped his foot. *Oh, my dander's most definitely getting up!* "And besides which, you could at least extend the courtesy of pronouncing my surname properly. It's *Boff*, to rhyme with *cough*, not *Bow* as in *bough* as in part of a tree! It's bloody Anglo-Saxon and if my ancestors weren't conquered by the Normans, I won't be conquered by a bloody blow-in Yuppie like you, accusing me of theft, who's got a bath on his patio like a peasant!"

A collective intake of breath sounded around the patio. And where had the patio come from anyway? The last time Tarquin had glimpsed the back of the neighboring house before the brambles had claimed it, this had been a mud pit.

An eyesore.

But the man who now rose from the water of the hot tub was certainly not an eyesore.

Bloody hell, he's no old Uncle Beardsley.

"Uncle Bea said you were a *Bow,*" he said in a plummy sneer. Then he grinned and held out his hand, as though Tarquin weren't juggling a glass of French brandy and Queen Elizabeth's favorite dildo. "Christopher Hardacre. You can *only* be my new next-door neighbor. You're exactly like Bea said you were in his letters. I feel like I already know you!"

Tarquin shoved the dildo into his pocket, its curved end poking out like a rhino horn. He held out his hand. "Your Uncle Beardsley was a dreadful old git—never got on with him, and he always pronounced my name wrong just to rile me. I'm Tarquin Bough, as in *cough*, and that's the end of it. Christopher Hardacre, eh? My new neighbor!"

As Tarquin shook Christopher's square hand, his gaze wandered down the planes of Christopher's dripping chest, down to his muscular stomach and those wet shorts that clung to his every contour.

My other dander's up now, blast it.

Tarquin cleared his throat and forced himself to look Christopher in the eye. *Why did he have to have such cloudless blue eyes? So large, so beguiling, so* – oh, there was a sarcastic glint, Tarquin could see that all too clearly. Another Beardsley, although this one was younger and therefore could be infinitely more annoying.

"He was a great old bird!" Christopher released Tarquin's hand and climbed out of the tub, a drizzle of water falling onto the patio around him. Then he put his arm around Tarquin's shoulders, soaking his tweed jacket through to his skin. "I've heard *all* about you from Bea. Do you know what his dying wish was, Tarkers?"

Gritting his teeth, Tarquin managed to hiss, "*It's bloody Tarquin!* And no, I don't know what that grumpy old bastard's last wish was. If it concerned me, he was wasting his breath."

"Well, this comes second-hand via his lawyer, but according to his last lady friend – he got through several, as you probably know – with his dying breath he said" – he tightened his arm around Tarquin's shoulders, tensing his muscle just enough for it to be deliberate – "'I wanted to give you Prince Albert's Prince Albert.'"

Tarquin forced himself to relax his grasp on his glass or the stem would've shattered. "It was never his. I bought it at auction, and I beat him. I don't even think the old devil wanted it — he bid against me to force up the price, and all because I very politely asked him if he wouldn't mind clipping back his trees that were overhanging my land. I would even have done the clipping myself, but he threatened to sue me for damaging his property if I even laid a finger on his trees, the litigious, wrinkly old gonad!"

"Oh, I've heard all about that too. About you making his poor old life a misery, putting the squeeze on a defenseless little old man!"

A defenseless little old man? A monstrous, portly nightmare, more like, with more girlfriends than you could shake a stick at. And none of them older than thirty-five.

"He couldn't manage a place this big on his own, poor old fellow, and to make matters worse, you storm in and start telling him to hack down his trees! I was all for giving you what for, but he was always the peacekeeper. Lucky for you I'm not the sort to carry a grudge."

"He was never *on his own* — he had a parade of women tripping in and out of his house! It's amazing he's left the place to you and not one of them!"

"I think you should leave," Christopher decided, steering Tarquin toward the fence once more. Only then, as he heard a collective *whoop* of amused cheers from the partygoers, did he remember the tear in his trousers.

"I can see your arse," a woman called in a voice so high-pitched it was a wonder that the champagne glasses didn't break.

Tarquin's hand shot to his bottom. He could feel the hem of his paisley boxer shorts through the hole and just beneath it the firm, fleshy curve of his buttock.

"Lucky old you!" Tarquin quipped, with rather more of a camp purr than he intended. Returning to his usual timbre, Tarquin told Christopher, "We need to talk. There's unfinished business."

But his neighbor didn't seem to be listening. He had taken the slightest hint of a step back and was peering down at Tarquin's bottom. His gaze glittered with mischief, but he made no comment.

At least, not for a moment.

"Starkers Tarkers," he finally said. Then his hand slapped Tarquin's shoulder. "Showing off the goods, eh?"

"You — don't you — how dare you — ! Goods? My fine rump is *goods*?" Tarquin's lip quivered with fury. But by god, how long had it been since someone had even remembered that Tarquin had a bottom, let alone remarked on it? But he'd be damned if he let a Hardacre charm him. "You've really got my dander up, you bounder, you!"

"Then it's probably a not good thing that the tear is now on the front of your trousers too!"

"It never bloody is!" Tarquin glanced down, only to discover that the split had spread from back to front, revealing a couple of inches of his thigh. "A fine pair of corduroys like these, ruined! And ruined, I might add, by a poorly kept fence, which is the all the fault of your ruddy Uncle Beardsley!"

"I'll add the fence to the list," was the smooth response. "Now, what else can I do for a man like you on a fine night like this?"

"You can collect the Oracle of Delphi, for one thing, although I have no idea where you'll keep her!"

"Ah, yes! That's all a bit of a mystery." He took his arm from around Tarquin's shoulders. "That was in the will too, along with the house. *Take care of the Oracle of Delphi.* What is it? Statue? Painting?"

Tarquin chuckled and patted Christopher's arm. Perhaps he lingered a little longer than he should have, but he patted it again, just to make sure that those biceps really did feel like mahogany. "I can show you right now if you'd like. The Oracle is in my orchard — I'm babysitting."

"*Babysitting*?" He emptied the champagne from his glass in one gulp. "Do I need to put some more clothes on before I'm introduced?"

"Oh, she won't mind you turning up in a state of near-nudity." *And nor shall I.* "Though you might want some shoes, perhaps?"

"Give me a minute to find my trainers and I'll be right with you." Mr. Hardacre the Younger made a fist of his hand and knocked it playfully against Tarquin's biceps. "We can talk about Prince Albert's Prince Albert at the same time!"

Tarquin raised an eyebrow. "Let's not," he replied.

"Let's," Christopher corrected, then turned and made his way toward the house. *In those clinging damned shorts.*

Tarquin glowered after him. No one would think he was staring at Christopher's fine arse instead. *Damned cheek of it, a Hardacre having a body like that.* It was a far cry from the stooped old man with his malicious sneer and his raucous girlfriends. The old man who had taken so much pleasure in tormenting the farmer next door and who had now apparently appointed his great nephew to do the same.

But there the similarities ended, because this was no seemingly permanent nonagenarian. No, this new agent of chaos was young enough to make Tarquin's life hell for decades.

Oh, sod it.

Tarquin had his dogs, though, and, tormented though he may be, with them he would never be lonely. Even now, they would be padding across the veranda in search of biscuits or snoring in the hallway.

And there was his collection, too, inherited by dint of Tarquin's descendancy from many a royal Groom of the Stool, and Tarquin's own careful perusal of auction sales catalogues from across the globe.

Prince Albert's Prince Albert was most definitely *his*.

"I really *can* see your arse," a plummy voice called from over his shoulder. "Sorry about the fence, perhaps you should use the driveway next time? You know, seeing as you're not a racehorse and all."

Tarquin swallowed the remains of his brandy in one gulp and turned to face him. "At least, unlike you, I'm wearing more than a mere scrap. There used to be a gate between the two gardens, I'll have you know, until your uncle got rid of it."

"And instead, gazelle-like, you leap the fence." Christopher laughed, drawing level with him. "So, I'm ready to meet the mysterious Oracle."

I bet he thinks it's a statue. A glorious marble nude standing majestically in a columned folly.

Tarquin would've rubbed his hands together with glee if he hadn't been holding an empty glass. He gestured toward the boundary of Christopher's garden. "Follow me. You can hop over the fence, can't you?"

"I think I can probably manage it," he deadpanned. "Without tearing my clothes, I daresay."

An image of those swimming shorts tearing straight down the cleft of Christopher's buttocks filled Tarquin's mind, and he inhaled raggedly. "Would...would hate you to tear your shorts, old bean."

"Your dander would *really* be up then, wouldn't it?"

The last thing Tarquin needed was anyone knowing about his personal tastes. Especially a Hardacre. "I'm engaged, I'll have you know, to the lovely and fragrant Petunia. If you're insinuating that I'm some sort of...some sort of...*Grecian*, then I'll have you know that I most certainly am not. I have no need to find out how toned or otherwise your behind might be, and I have certainly no desire to see your tilly-tadger!"

"My *what*? Toned I'll take, guilty as charged, but...*tilly-tadger*?" He chuckled, then asked, "Wasn't that a character in *The Wind in the Willows*?"

And Christopher Hardacre vaulted the fence.

My God.

"Rhymes with badger," Tarquin mumbled. How the hell was he going to live next door to an arse like that without going insane? But, importantly, it was a Hardacre arse, and a Bough had no business mooning over it. Mooning being the appropriate term, of course.

Tarquin wedged his empty glass into his pocket and clambered over the fence. He plucked the torn piece of fabric from the nail, but wasn't quite sure what to do with it. "Welcome to Bough Towers, Christopher."

"Chris, please, we're not in church." He put his hands on his hips and surveyed the garden. "This is nice, not at all how Uncle Bea made it sound. I was expecting a herd of cows and a manure pile three stories high!"

Bloody Beardsley.

"Yes, well, that's your uncle for you. Truth was always slippery with him." Tarquin led Christopher through the trees. Now that his new neighbor was here, he decided to give him a tour. "There's apples here, and pears. Quinces and some impressive plums, too!"

Chris nodded, peering up into the trees as he said, "Do you come down hard on scrumpers, squire?"

"I believe in good, firm punishment." Tarquin picked up a stick and swished it through the air. "Anyone found scrumping will receive the full weight of my ire, and a good thrashing to boot!"

His infuriating neighbor raised his eyebrow, then reached up and plucked a ripe, juicy plum from the tree. "That's me in trouble then."

Tarquin planted his feet firmly and swished his stick. The bloody man was playing with him, he knew that only too well, but how could Tarquin not follow through on a promise? In a low murmur he said, "Oh, so you *want* a swipe across your bottom?"

"I'm only human, squire."

The insufferable cur.

Tarquin *could* have laughed it off, but there was something about those wide blue eyes and, admittedly, that delightful rear, that spurred Tarquin on. He swished his stick again.

"Up against the tree. Hands firm on the trunk. Feet shoulder width apart. Hop to it, Hardacre!"

"What would the fragrant Petunia say if she heard that?" His tormentor winked, then dropped the sunglasses again and bit decadently into the plum. "Show me the Oracle, before I decide to take you seriously."

Tarquin didn't reply. He'd made a fool of himself. Outed himself, and to a Hardacre! He hurled the stick aside and strode on through the orchard, not caring that the undignified tear in his trousers was on full view to his new enemy, until they finally reached his abandoned deckchair and the contented pig.

"Right, here we are then." Tarquin flopped down in his deckchair and mussed the pig's bristly head. And when Chris lifted the sunglasses again, Tarquin felt an unmistakable thrill of triumph. The expression on that handsome face was no longer one of self-assured smugness—instead, there was only confusion. Confusion that was swiftly giving way to disbelief.

"It's a pig," he muttered finally.

"Yes, the Oracle of Delphi is a prize-winning Gloucester Old Spot!" Tarquin rubbed her head with renewed vigor and fussed her leathery ears until the pig squealed gleefully. "Did your dear, lamented uncle neglect to mention you'd inherit a sow who'd won rosettes at the Sussex County Fair?"

"It's a pig," Chris said again, then he lifted his sunglasses. "Is this a joke, I mean—it's an actual *pig*. With a curly tail!"

"Yes! Well done, City Slicker!" Tarquin chortled. "What else do you think this delightful creature is? She's not a frog, nor a salmon either for that matter. She's a gorgeous pig!"

The Oracle grunted deep in her throat, clearly enjoying Tarquin's compliments.

"I don't... How..." He fell silent again, his mouth gaping. Had the man never seen a pig before?

"She's all yours! I've got a harness for her here, but she's not overly fond of it—are you, Orry?" Tarquin blew her a kiss. "I've been looking after her since

Beardsley passed on to the Great Big Gin Palace in the sky."

"*Mine*?" Chris pressed his hand to his all-too naked chest. "I don't know what to do with a pig! Do you know about pigs?"

"Oh, yes. I've had them before. Orry was in a pen in the cowshed for a couple of weeks, but she's as friendly as a dog and she managed to get out—I found her sprawled on the veranda with Mabel, my old spaniel. So after that, she lived in the house." Tarquin quirked his eyebrow. "Petunia was not happy about that at all! Hahaha!"

"Well, it doesn't seem fair to take her away from her friends," he replied. "Wouldn't she be happier here?"

Would you like to be the one who tells Petunia?

"But she's *yours*, Chris! I'm sure she'd *love* to have a wallow in that hot tub of yours!" *With all those braying Hooray Henrys tipping champagne down their throats.* Tarquin chuckled at the thought.

"My gift to you?" Chris asked hopefully. "She looks very cozy."

"You haven't even said hello to her. You can't yield up your uncle's pig without giving her a fuss!"

The pig seemed to be smiling at Chris. Was she pleased to see him, or was she mocking him? Tarquin had no idea.

"Oh, you're enjoying this, Tarkers, aren't you?" He looked down at the Oracle of Delphi then extended one hand before he snatched it back again, as though she were a flame rather than a pig.

Tarquin grinned. "As I said, she's as friendly as a dog. You've stroked one of *those* before, haven't you? Just do it. On her back."

The pig peered up at the two men, that little expression of amusement still on her face. How anyone could be afraid of her, Tarquin couldn't imagine. She was soft as a kitten, after all.

Tarquin kissed the top of her head. "Look, it's your new daddy! He's come to take you home!"

"But won't you miss her?"

Nice try.

"She'll only be next door!" Tarquin chuckled. "Come on, let me get her into her harness, and you can take her home. She loves a party—and all those nubile young women crowding your patio will remind her of your uncle's heyday!"

"Don't get too excited, you won't see too many good-looking ladies on my watch." He quirked his eyebrow. "Good-looking guys, on the other hand…"

Tarquin tugged down the hem of his jacket. *Good-looking guys. Cavorting in the hot tub. And only on the other side of the fence.*

"Right. Yes. Well. You're not Bough Bottoms' first chap of a gay persuasion. We're surprisingly modern here, I think you'll find!"

"Well, I *am* on the market." Chris grinned. "Anyway, I'll leave you and the Oracle to enjoy your evening. I'll turn the music down a little too, it's a bit bassy over here, isn't it?"

Tarquin winced. *Hot, single gay man right next door. And I can't tell him I'm gay.* "A tad, yes. That would be kind of you. I enjoy a power ballad as much as the next man, but possibly not when I'm sitting in my orchard. Anyway, you must take the Oracle with you."

Tarquin rose from his deckchair and picked up the Oracle's harness. He started to buckle her into it, and she unleashed an annoyed squeal. "Shh… Your new daddy will take you home! Lovely Chris! And just you wait until you see Daddy's hot tub!"

"What does she eat?" His voice had taken on a somewhat panicky timbre. "Oh, come on, squire, at least give me a pointer. I'm sorry about the plum!"

"There should be a sack of her food in your garage, but apples are her favorite if you're in a jam." Tarquin handed the lead to Chris. The Oracle snorted.

"Apples," he repeated nervously, closing his fist around the lead. "Got it. What else?"

"Make sure she has access to water, and remember to let her out for a…y'know, a widdle." Tarquin narrowed his eyes at Chris. "You do understand all that, don't you? You're living in the countryside now!"

"I know, I know. I'm not in Canary Wharf now," Chris murmured.

Oh, you would be from somewhere like that. Somewhere showy. Somewhere where it was hot tubs ahead of orchards.

"Early retirement, or are you a DFT?" Tarquin asked, as he absentmindedly fingered Good Queen Bess' special toy. "Y'know, Down From Town, only gracing us with your presence at weekends?"

"What?" Chris blinked, looking for all the world like a man who was about to face the firing squad. His gaze traveled from the Oracle of Delphi back to Tarquin and he said, "I've got a pig."

The pig seemed to know when she was being talked about. She looked up at Chris and snorted, then tugged on her lead.

"You have indeed got a pig!"

How wonderful it is to get one up on a Hardacre for once.

"Right." He nodded firmly and squared those wonderful shoulders, apparently girding himself to become a pig parent. Tarquin would miss the old girl, in a funny sort of way. She had a quiet dignity about her. "Nice to meet you, Tarkers. We'll discuss the dying wish another time, I think. Come on, Mr. Pig, time to go home."

Mister?

"She's a *Mrs.* Pig!" Tarquin shook his head. *Bloody Canary Wharf canary!* "Mother of several prize-winning litters, no less!"

Chris nodded again, then gave a sharp tug on the lead, which earned him nothing from the Oracle but a careless twitch of her ear. With a rather withering glance at Tarquin Chris pulled on the lead again, putting a little more force into this time. *Twitch,* went the cheeky ear, but the majestic sow didn't move.

Tarquin leaned back against the trunk of an old, gnarled apple tree, enjoying the sight before him. To think that he was the source of a Hardacre's woes, *and* he had the bonus of a very nice view of those biceps and pectorals straining with effort. *Who would've thought the day would end so well?*

"Come — on —" His neighbor planted his feet, pulling at the lead like he was taking part in the annual tug-of-war on the village green. He gritted his teeth, every muscle taut with the wasted effort of trying to coax the Oracle to move.

But what a marvelous sight it is.

How could a creature like this be a Hardacre?

Tarquin patted the Oracle's rump. "Off you go with Daddy! There's a good girl!"

Only then did she move from her spot and turn toward Tarquin like an obedient puppy seeking her master's favor. She gave a happy snort then showed Mr. Hardacre exactly how one should handle a lead and, with a sharp toss of her magnificent head, pulled him off his feet and onto the grass.

Christopher presented a fine figure even face down in the grass, it seemed, his shapely bottom on display. Accidental display, of course. Tarquin roared with mirth. "Need a hand, old chap?"

"You're bloody nuts!" Chris exclaimed, blinking up at him. "A pig on a lead? A dildo in your pocket as though it's your mobile? Baring your arse at a housewarming? You're not right in the head!"

"*I'm* not? You're the one lying on the ground in the middle of my orchard in his swimming trunks!"

Tarquin took a step toward his new neighbor, but couldn't go any farther as he was bent double by a new gale of laughter sweeping through him. He wiped away the tears in his eyes and finally controlled his hilarity for long enough to hold his hand out to Chris.

"I can get up on my own, thanks," he snapped. And perhaps he could, had he not still been holding the lead and had the lead not still been attached to the Oracle's harness. No sooner was he halfway to his feet than she gave another flamboyant shake, sending Christopher Hardacre sprawling on the grass again.

Tarquin took hold of Chris' hand that was holding the lead, and looped his other arm around Chris' waist. It was the neighborly thing to do, of course. "Ready? Let me pull you up!"

"So long as you keep your royal dildo safely in your pocket," was the carping reply. How ungracious he was, considering his pig had been Tarquin's honored and rather spoiled guest since the demise of Hardacre the elder.

Tarquin tightened his arm around Chris. A rather tortured sigh escaped him as he pulled him to his feet.

Oh, what a joy to hold a muscled fellow in his arms. Even if it was only for a matter of seconds.

Even if the muscled fellow in question was a bloody Hardacre.

"Right. Well." Chris nodded, brushing a few blades of grass from his chest. "Thanks, I suppose. For the hand up, I mean."

Tarquin retreated, but he couldn't look away from Chris. He wanted him, with a pull so visceral that Tarquin wondered how he could ever return to his old life without being tormented by the thought of that man—*that exquisite man*—being only next door. "Any pig-husbandry issues, you know where I am. Just knock me up."

"She's not going to come, Mr. *Bow*. Look at her, nothing's going to shift her!" The unruffled Canary Wharf Canary was *very* ruffled by now, and it made him even more delicious. "Are you sure you wouldn't rather keep her?"

"Mr. *Boff*." Tarquin patted the Oracle's rump again. "Go on, piggy-wig! Off with Daddy!"

She lay down in the grass and closed her eyes, apparently done with such tomfoolery for one day.

"Mr. *Boff*." Chris widened his eyes and said, "I already have a pig-husbandry issue and I've not even been here twenty-four hours. She doesn't like me, she *loves* you. She wants to stay."

"Loved by Hardacre livestock, eh?" Tarquin crouched down and fussed the Oracle. "Very well, then, it would appear the lady has voted with her trotters. But...I well remember how litigious your uncle was. I want you to write a letter on headed paper signing this pig over to me until such a time as she will go willingly to your house. I won't be sued on account of a sow!"

"Bloody hell, you *are* crazy." He pushed his hand back through his infuriatingly floppy hair. "Fine. I'll do better than that. Uncle's lawyer is coming over tomorrow to go through a few last bits. I'll ask *him* to draw up something if that keeps you off my back. I'll also ask him where we stand on the Prince Albert's Prince Albert question, if we're making it official."

"Do your worst, canary!" Tarquin chuckled as he fussed the pig, who grunted contentedly. "I have my paperwork for the Prince Albert, and your uncle's hot air died with him! Good. Send over the lawyer and we can have this hammered out once and for all."

"Oh, I will. Expect us at noon," his new nemesis told him sternly, wagging his finger. "And I'll be fully dressed too!"

"Good. Glad to hear it." Tarquin tried his best not to sound disappointed. The thought of Chris, wearing nothing but his swimming shorts, in Tarquin's drawing room, was dangerously exciting. *If he weren't a Hardacre.* "Bough Bottoms is not the place for wanton displays of semi-nudity."

"I was in a hot tub." Chris said it slowly, as though Tarquin was an idiot. "I wear a suit all week, I'm not wearing one in a hot tub, am I? That lane between the houses, by the way… Mine or yours? I told my guests to park wherever they like, so I'm assuming it's mine."

"Mine," Tarquin replied. "But you have right of way over it. Which basically means that it's *not* a ruddy car park because we both need it for access. I won't leave my combine harvester parked in it, and you can't have your matey chums leaving their Beamers there."

"I'm living in the bloody *Archers*! I'll tell you what." The finger wagged again. "You don't leave your tractor in it, and I won't leave my Aston in it. How's that, *squire*?"

"Sounds fair to me." Tarquin got back to his feet and held out his hand to shake. "Gentlemen's agreement?"

"Before I shake that hand... You haven't been *using* Queen Elizabeth's wooden friend, have you?"

"What? It's an antique, for heaven's sake!" Tarquin shook his head, incredulous. "No, I haven't been using it. I've been admiring the craftsmanship whilst sipping a brandy in my orchard. It only arrived today—I won it in an auction just the other week."

"Bit of a funny hobby, collecting dildos." Chris offered his hand. "I always thought farmers were a bit weird, now I know they are."

"I can't help it if Canary Wharf is devoid of culture. A wasteland of the vulgar and the new." Tarquin took the dildo from his pocket again and smiled as the last rays of the sun blushed the polished wood. He caught the barest hint of an amused grin from his neighbor before he resumed his stern demeanor.

"Well, I shall leave you and your sovereign sex toy to get to know each other. Goodnight, Squire Starkers Tarkers. Your arse is *still* showing."

"Oh blow it, I'd bloody forgotten!" Tarquin nearly dropped the dildo in his haste to cover the rip in his trousers. "Night, then, Canary Christopher! Enjoy your terrible party, won't you?"

"Count on it." He stooped and patted the pig's back. "Goodnight, Mrs. Pig. See you tomorrow."

The Oracle raised one of her ears and gave Chris a searching look, then closed her eyes and grunted. And with one last look—was it a knowing look, even?—the canary strolled back across the garden toward his party.

Tarquin stood for a moment in the gathering gloom of the approaching night. So he'd met his new neighbor. His new nemesis. As handsome as the day was long, and all the more dangerous for it.

Chapter Two

The Oracle of Delphi grunted with delight as Tarquin topped her trough up with her pellet feed. He put the scoop back in the sack and lobbed pieces of carrot and apple in too.

"You've got a bally banquet, old girl!"

From the boot room, which he had turned into the Oracle's quarters, Tarquin heard the sound of Petunia's high heels clattering downstairs, her voice loud as she bellowed into her mobile about a consignment of Meissen. There was money to be made, it seemed.

As ever.

Without pausing in his task, Tarquin called over his shoulder to her. "You off out, then?"

"I'm going in to the sale room to keep an eye on things." She appeared in the doorway, now tapping out a message on the screen of her phone. She dropped it into her bag and looked at him. "And Bryan's got a buyer coming in to talk PA first editions. Vintage Sussex sex sells, it seems!"

Ah, yes, Bough Bottoms' greatest literary export, the late PA, practicing nudist and purveyor of eye-watering smut.

"Say hello to him from me. I've got our new neighbor coming over in a bit. Paperwork to sign off. Beardsley's ballyhoo over Prince Albert's Prince Albert hasn't ended at the grave, you know. His bloody nephew is insisting I stole the thing! You know, I'm not convinced it's genuine, but I'm not letting a Hardacre take it from me."

"What's he like? Shobna says he's a hell of a looker. We need some eye candy in Bough Bottoms!" *Charmer.* Petunia pushed a diamond stud earring into each lobe with military precision. "Is he taking this bloody pig before I have it turned into lardons?"

Tarquin sighed. The pig merrily crunched on the carrot pieces, snapping them like fingers. "He nearly took the Oracle yesterday evening but she didn't want to go. Maybe, like me, she doesn't trust the fellow, handsome though he may be. He's still a Hardacre. If you hadn't been out last night" —*With your bloody hooray friends*—"you would've had the pleasure of meeting him while he wore nothing but a rather small pair of swimming shorts—in our orchard." *So there.*

Petunia's expression changed subtly and she narrowed her eyes, like Tarquin's father did when he was presented with a fat, rare steak. Then she drew in a long, deep breath and said, "Built for action, according to Shobna. She's going to stake out her turf later with a welcome hotpot. Is he the hotpot sort, do you think?"

What would be funnier than encouraging lots of Petunia's annoying friends to run after a gay Hardacre?

Tarquin nodded. "Oh yes, spicy hotpots and big dumplings all the way!"

"I'll give her the nod," his fiancée said. "She can give our Mr. Hardacre a proper village welcome! It's about time she stopped fucking the farmhands and moved on to someone with prospects."

"Our new Mr. Hardacre has a lot of prospects, trust me!"

Tarquin turned away from Petunia to hide his smirk. He crouched down to fuss the Oracle as she pressed her snout into the corner of the trough, polishing off every last crumb of her breakfast.

"You must be the only sentimental farmer in Sussex," Petunia said coldly. "It's a pig, Tarquin, get it butchered or get it gone. I'm going to work."

"Isn't Mummy mean? Isn't she?" he said to the Oracle, not caring if Petunia heard.

"Is Mummy the only one going out to work while Daddy wanders about buying dirty old johnnies like his dad and his grandad before him?" She nudged him with the pointed tip of her shoe. "The pig's on notice. Get Mr. Hunky Hardacre on it, sharpish. And hang the washing out!" She stalked from the room, calling as she went, "And you're not being fobbed off at the village hall. *You* should be the next master of the drag hunt. I'm ready to co-host my first hunt ball, so get *your* balls firm and don't take no for an answer!"

"Strange, she hasn't been interested in my balls for at least twelve months," Tarquin remarked to the pig.

* * * *

Tarquin pottered. He was an arch potterer, and hung out the washing, tidied away the breakfast things and decided on a place to display the Elizabethan dildo. His collection occupied a room under the eaves of the house, and he placed the dildo carefully in an antique velvet-lined box beside Catherine the Great's garter.

Dirty old johnnies indeed.

How dare she?

The doorbell sounded around the house, heralding the arrival of the lawyer and the canary. And they were here to see the squire.

Tarquin headed to the front door. His collection of dogs had got to the door before him, and he fought through the excited pack of retrievers and spaniels — and accidentally cross-bred Retrievers and Spaniels — to admit his guests.

"Morning!" Tarquin held open the door to Christopher, who was managing to look both smart and casual at the same time. *The infuriating bastard.* Jeans and a smart shirt. Tarquin was surprised not to see pinstripes on him, but today those were reserved for the lawyer who was accompanying him. *And with any luck, he'll leave smothered in dog hair.*

"Clothes on this time," Chris announced even as he bent to fuss the dogs, leaving the far-too-sharp lawyer to wonder what *that* must be about. "Mr. *Bow*, this is Mr. Driscoll, Great-Uncle's lawyer. Mr. Driscoll, Mr. Bow."

"Mr. Bow," the lawyer said, holding out his hand. "I was due to make a call on you soon, so it's a pleasure to join Mr. Hardacre to discuss these rather...*personal* matters."

"I've seen your name on letters," Tarquin said, his voice heavy with insinuation. *Many letters, thanks to the late, litigious Beardsley Hardacre.* Tarquin closed the door behind them and led them to the drawing room, the dogs scurrying in their wake. "Yes, well, first things first, my name is Bough, as in *cough*. And second things second — cup of tea?"

"That would be very welcome indeed," Driscoll said and beside him, Chris nodded too. He seemed restless though, peering over Tarquin's shoulder as if he was looking for something.

After a moment he asked, "Where's the Oracle of Delphi?"

"Asleep with her blanky, last time I looked. I'll bring her in, if you like." Tarquin gestured to them to sit on the sofa. "You do know, don't you? Christopher *has* said? She's a pig. Not a statue or some sort of Koh-i-Noor diamond!"

"Oh, I know what she is! She was the apple of her father's eye, as Mr. Bough must know. I have a special letter to be opened in your mutual presence, from the late Mr. Hardacre." That rang alarm bells in Tarquin's head, and from the look of shock that had descended over Chris, he could see that it was more than mutual. He was watching Driscoll closely, clearly waiting for the big reveal. "Once that's been read, we can turn our attention to Miss Delphi's living arrangements. With some tea."

"Right — give me a moment, I'll fetch the tea." Tarquin strode off and banged about in the kitchen. Despite the racket he was making, the Oracle of Delphi didn't wake up from the dog basket she had commandeered in front of the Aga.

What the hell kind of letter is this going to be? If it had anything to do with the overhanging trees or Prince Alberts, then Tarquin would put the damn thing in the nearest shredder.

He emerged from the kitchen a few minutes later bearing a large teapot on a tray and placed it on the coffee table before sitting down in the armchair. "So what's this letter all about?"

"Come on, old thing." Chris tried a smile, but he looked as tense as Tarquin felt. He must have known his great-uncle had been a reprobate as well as anybody, and he must have his own suspicions that there wasn't just a good luck card in that envelope. "Put us out of our suspense."

With incredible care, Driscoll slid his thumbnail into the flap of the envelope and drew it along, unsealing the letter at a painfully slow speed. From within, he removed a single sheet of folded ivory paper, which he unfolded and peered at along the length of his narrow nose. Then he cleared his throat.

Very theatrical.

"My dear Messrs Hardacre and Bow." He paused and said, "He has indicated he wishes me to pronounce your name *Bow*, Mr. Bough, do forgive me."

Chris laughed and sat back in his chair, suddenly looking considerably more relaxed. *Good-looking git.*

Tarquin steepled his fingers. "I am perfectly unsurprised that Beardsley Hardacre should wish to vex me from beyond the grave. Come along, Mr. Driscoll, please."

"If this letter is being read to you by my clock-fixing, bill-fiddling poltroon of a lawyer, Mr. Eamon Driscoll, then I am finally dead. I hope Mr. Driscoll has finally shaved off his moustache and embraced the thin lips that God gave him." He ran his finger over his naked top lip. And it *was* rather thin. "To my great nephew, Christopher, a strutting, arrogant popinjay blessed with good looks if not good brains, I have already bequeathed my ancestral home. To my neighbor, Mr Bow, who never ceased to entertain me with his decision to move from juvenility to middle age, I leave nothing. As he will expect."

Tarquin rolled his eyes.

"Sorry." Chris chuckled. "Not too sure about the me being thick bit, but it's still very Uncle Bea."

"Or perhaps I do," Driscoll went on. "Should Christopher choose to sell the house, then I bequeath my girl, my wonder, my treasure, the Oracle of Delphi, to Mr. Bow. He must keep her in the manner to which she is accustomed, as outlined in the enclosed papers. In these circumstances he will receive a sum of five thousand pounds per month for her care. Should he attempt to sell, slaughter or otherwise play her foul, this sum shall be discontinued and I will haunt his miserable family until the end of days. Should the Oracle of Delphi meet her final breath in the care of Mr. Bow, a sum of one hundred thousand pounds will be paid to Mr. Bow to allow him to bury her in an appropriate manner and mausoleum. Formal mourning should be observed by the village for a period of three months."

"Five grand a month?" Chris sat forward again, no longer amused. "For a pig?"

"She eats a *lot* of apples," Tarquin informed him.

"Should Christopher choose to reside in our ancestral home, my entire estate is his and his alone on one condition. He must also keep the Oracle of Delphi in the manner enclosed herein. Should he fail to do so, he will forfeit his entire inheritance and ownership of my girl will pass to Mr. Bow as outlined above. In that case, my estate will be inherited entirely by my last fancy, whose name is enclosed in a sealed envelope, to be opened only when and if necessary."

As if she had known she was being talked about, Tarquin heard the sound of trotters clicking over the floorboards, and the Oracle suddenly appeared, framed in the doorway. She gave a squeal, as if saying hello.

Tarquin chuckled. "Oh, dear, Christopher! You'll have to try very hard to get into the Oracle's good books, won't you! After all those improvements to your uncle's house, too!"

"Let me see the *enclosed papers*," Chris said urgently, holding out his hand. Driscoll took a small sheaf from the envelope and handed it to him, saying nothing. Tarquin longed to know what the instructions said, as Chris' blue eyes grew wider by the second as he scanned the words. Then he blustered, "*Sing* to her… Take her to the fair?" He looked at Driscoll and said with utter disbelief, "Read her *Madam Fanny's Floral Pomander* by PA bloody Pierce before bed? It's a pig! No sane person could expect this to stand up!"

Tarquin left his chair. With a detour to scratch the Oracle's head, he peered over Chris' shoulder and began to read. "Row her along the river at least twice during the summer months. Walk her on her harness once a day. Take her to visit her surviving children once a year, on their birthdays." Tarquin laughed, then said, "I believe one of her sons resides in a farm just outside Stornoway. You can borrow my horsebox, if you like?"

"Should either of the gentleman wish to contest this will," Driscoll concluded, "I have left a generous fighting fund. And as Driscoll will tell you, it's a wasted battle — he's right, it'd ruin you — so I suggest you learn to enjoy being guardian to the finest pig known to man instead. Yours from the great beyond, Beardsley Rupert Hardacre."

"What if she won't come home with me?" Chris asked desperately. "She doesn't like me!"

"Then I suggest you devote yourself to learning her favorite songs—I believe she has a soft spot for show tunes—and brush up your Madam Fanny," Driscoll commiserated. "I shall give you one month to win her round and bring her home. Otherwise we must look to fulfill Mr. Hardacre's wish and relieve you of your rather generous inheritance!"

"Just a month, eh?" Tarquin returned to his armchair and the Oracle snuffled her way up to him, resting her head on his knee as if hoping for some fuss. Which Tarquin duly gave her.

"And Mr. Bow," Driscoll said, retrieving another of those ominous envelopes, this one already open. "Before he died, Mr. Hardacre left a final request that he wished me to communicate with you. His *fancy* at the time of his death was a source of great joy to him and he hoped to purchase the…erm…the item with the royal connection as a lover's gift, I believe." He looked around as though there might be an unseen audience then leaned forward and whispered, "*The Prince Albert*?"

"You're all so bloody weird," Chris murmured, still reading through the list. "What a place."

Tarquin sighed. "So he may have told *you*, Driscoll, but I think his bidding on the Prince Albert was merely to rile me. You know, it was part of my family's collection, then it disappeared—stolen, we always thought, but we never knew by whom—and my father spent years trying to track it down. Then I got a tip off from an auctioneer, and I *knew* I had to have it." Tarquin smiled at Driscoll, but his gaze drifted to Chris. He looked so handsome, the morning sunshine bathing him in golden light. And there he was, on Tarquin's sofa, and what Tarquin wouldn't do to — *control yourself, you silly man.* "It was a public auction, I was at the auction itself, and I was the highest bidder. And I paid, and I brought it home, and Beardsley then decided that I had somehow stolen it from him. I resent the accusation, quite frankly, and I look forward to laying the odious matter to rest once and for all."

"His friend is still very eager to acquire the item as a memento of their relationship —"

"Yeah, that's normal," Chris muttered bitterly. He lifted his gaze and, quite unexpectedly, his eyes met Tarquin's. And they didn't move away. "Who wouldn't want to remember their OAP boyfriend with a dead prince's cock piercing?"

"That's as maybe, but I've been instructed to make you a confidential offer of fifty thousand pounds for the *item*," Driscoll said. "Considerably more than you paid for it, I believe?"

"Fifty…sorry, you did say *fifty thousand*?" Tarquin still didn't look away from Chris. His blue eyes were filled with sunlight, like a jewel fashioned from sapphire and pearl. "What the devil…?" At last, Tarquin tore his gaze from Chris'. "It's part of my collection now, though. I won't lie, fifty thousand pounds isn't to be sniffed at, but Prince Albert's Prince Albert is the jewel in the crown. Well, a very particular, intimate sort of crown, you understand. And besides, Beardsley insisted I had won the item by unfair means, and even selling it to his mistress now would make me feel as if I'd lost. So no. It's not for sale."

"She is a *very* wealthy lady," the lawyer said carefully. "If you're hoping a refusal will lead to an increased offer, I'd be more than happy to put that to her.

Obviously, I would have to seek some recompense for my time, much as I wish that weren't so."

Tarquin raised his square chin imperiously. "I've said no, Mr. Driscoll. The matter ends there."

"Well said," Chris told him unexpectedly, and the Oracle gave a little snort of approval. "Who needs fifty grand when they can have a prince's penis piercing instead? Good for you!"

Tarquin grinned at Chris, even as a vague inkling dawned on him that Chris was mocking him. "And is this all the business you have with me today, Mr. Driscoll?"

"It is." He slipped the letters back into his pocket. "Don't forget, Mr. Hardacre. One month!"

Chris rose to his feet and said laconically. "I'll mark it on my calendar, don't worry." He gestured with his hand, as though blocking out a headline in thin air. "Start house hunting."

"Oh no," Driscoll said. "I wouldn't expect you to start house hunting in one month. I'd expect you to fully vacate the premises."

Poltroon indeed.

The Oracle reversed from Tarquin, oinking happily, her rump heading for Chris.

"Chris, watch out!" Tarquin warned him. "She's heavy, if she stands on your—"

"Jesus bloody Christ!" Christ let out a howl of pain as her trotter stomped onto his foot. "Get her off! Bloody hell, get her off!"

The Oracle squealed but didn't move, only drumming her trotters instead. Tarquin swallowed his amusement as he reached around the Oracle's middle to pull her away. She squealed in protest, clearly enjoying stamping on her new owner's foot.

"But you're supposed to be making friends with her, Chris!"

"Stupid bloody— I've broken my toes!" *He hasn't, of course.* "How do you make friends with a pig? Is this a set-up? To get the Hardacres out of Bough Bottoms, you've turned the pig against me?"

Tarquin had moved the Oracle aside and she now sat on her haunches, like a well-trained dog responding to *sit.* "Old Spots are independent beasts. I could no more turn her against you than make her like you. You just need to spend time with her. At the moment, you're the stranger who yelled when she accidentally trod on your foot!" Unable to resist a jibe, though, Tarquin added, "Take her out for a row with a copy of *Madam Fanny*— she'd love that!"

Chris glared at him, then warned, "I'm staying put, *Bow*—you won't get rid of me so easily."

"Brush up your show tunes, Mr. Hardacre," Driscoll added helpfully. "Now if you'll excuse me, I shall communicate the matter of the *royal gentleman's jewelry* to the lady concerned. Good day, gentlemen."

"Bye, then!" Tarquin said.

As Driscoll headed for door, the Bough Towers gun-dog pack barked in chorus. Chris followed him, limping so theatrically that it seemed as though he'd suffered an amputation rather than a mildly bruised toe.

"Mabel! Felicity! Giovanni! Bluebell! Chaz! Gladstone! Jasper!" Tarquin shouted. His dogs retreated one by one from their tangle on the doormat, and Tarquin opened the door for his guests. "I'll see you soon, then. Bring a dozen apples, Chris, and that pig will be your friend in no time!"

"Oh, we will!" Chris said brightly, then he narrowed his eyes and leaned very close to Tarquin. So close it made his trousers feel suddenly oddly tight. Then he lowered his voice and said, "Just wait until you hear my show tunes."

"Oh, yes," Tarquin murmured, his chest rising and falling with each difficult breath. "I'm waiting."

His nemesis quirked an eyebrow then strolled out onto the driveway and led the lawyer off down the drive, breaking into a surprisingly rousing rendition of *Oh What a Beautiful Mornin'* as he went. And there at Tarquin's heel, lazily chewing on one of Petunia's Louboutins, the Oracle of Delphi looked on with interest.

Of course he can sing. The annoying bastard.

Chapter Three

Squire Tarquin Bough never felt more at home than when he was under the respectful gaze of Bough Bottoms' residents. Even if he was standing next to a child-sized chalkboard that he'd helped himself to from the playgroup's toys.

The village hall was full of people eager to hear about the drag hunt. Tarquin always enjoyed following the dogs as they raced off after the fake scent. No fox was involved, nothing was killed and everyone had an exciting ride out across the fields. Since Beardsley Hardacre's demise, the hunt had no official master, and who else but Tarquin could replace him?

Certainly not Chris!

Tarquin, elevated on the village hall's stage, gestured with a stick of chalk to his audience of tweed- and padded gilet-clad locals. "Shall we get under way, then?"

There was a polite smattering of applause that ebbed until the only sound was the occasional chink of a spoon on a saucer or the slight munch of dentures on rich tea. What a respectful, pleasant bunch the residents of the Bottoms were, so much nicer than his showy new neighbor. What a peaceful corner of England they had created here, away from the hustle and bustle of the world.

"So, as you know," Tarquin began, "while Mr. Hardacre was in his dotage, I had responsibility for the Cleopatra Cup Drag Hunt while he was nominally the hunt master. I'm sure we're all happy to keep the date of the drag hunt as-is, even if it's not technically in the hunt season, thanks to Beardsley moving it to fall on Cleopatra's birthday—whoever she may be. It's become a village tradition, after all." *Trust Beardsley to move the hunt so he could name it after a mistress.* "Now, I haven't heard any complaints regarding my management of the hunt, and so I am happy—if you are—to continue running the hunt, and perhaps, if you feel it would be right, now that the position of hunt master is vacant, I officially take over that role." Tarquin rocked back and forth on his brogues, roving his confident glance over the Bough Bottoms residents.

None of them will say no.

At the back of the room, a hand went up. A liver-spotted hand whose arm was contained in a wax jacket.

"Am I not right in thinking," asked Mr. Longfellow, who had enjoyed many a glass of brandy with the late Beardsley Hardacre, "that there is a new Hardacre in Bough Bottoms?"

Tarquin chuckled. "There is, yes, but I doubt he'd know a horse's ears from its tail! And he isn't here this afternoon, so I can only assume he's not in the least interested in such country pursuits as ours."

"Did anybody notify him of the meeting?" Longfellow lifted his head and looked pointedly at Tarquin. "Did *you*?"

Tarquin's mouth fell open. "I…that is to say… He was in the midst of a party yesterday, and that was the first *I* knew of a new Hardacre being in residence. I hadn't the opportunity to tell him about the meeting."

Even though I saw him this morning.

"Then it's lucky that *I* did," Longfellow crowed, folding his arms across his chest. "But don't let that throw you off your stroke."

Tarquin tried to smile, but he was fairly sure that it looked more like a grimace to his audience.

And Shobna drastically improved the moment by piping up, "He's coming here? Good-oh!"

Just you wait!

"Well, Mr. Longfellow, you might have invited him but, as I suspected, he hasn't turned up, so in the absence of anyone else as hunt master…?" Tarquin raised an eyebrow. It was a *fait accompli!*

"Have you started without me?" The door flew open and there, standing on the threshold, was Christopher *bloody* Hardacre, looking for two pins as though he'd come to save the day. Every head swiveled to look at him, every mouth curved into a smile and Mr. Longfellow even gave a little welcoming cheer.

Of course he did.

"Just in time for sums!" Chris nodded toward the small chalkboard. "I'll just sit quietly at the back, squire, you won't know I'm here."

"Ah…erm…" The floor seemed to drop from under Tarquin's feet. He couldn't, as a squire, appear rude in front of everyone to the infuriatingly attractive fellow. Protocol had be followed. "Right, time for introductions. If you are yet to meet our new arrival, this is Mr. Christopher Hardacre, great-nephew of the late Beardsley Hardacre, a man whose loss we all felt bitterly, I'm sure." *Cobblers to that.* "There'll be time at the end for you to say your hellos, but if we could keep to the program, please. As I was saying, I'm sure you'd all be happy for me to take over as the master of Boughton Bottoms' drag hunt."

Time at the end. So sit down and shut up.

And Chris went too quietly, Tarquin realized, as his neighbor took a seat at the back of the hall. He crossed his legs, clasped his hands neatly in his lap and said, "Hear hear, squire. What better man could there be to lead the dogs than you?"

Tarquin nodded. "Thank you."

Well, that wasn't too hard.

A scrape of seats against the hall's parquet floor warned Tarquin that someone was on the move — and that someone was Shobna, her voluminous chestnut hair that made her resemble a Red Setter catching the light as she headed for the vacant chair beside Chris.

Shobna patted Chris' knee. "Are you sure you won't take up your uncle's place as Master of the Hunt, Mr. Hardacre?"

"Me?" He pressed his hand to his chest, whispering as though this *was* a classroom. "I couldn't trample all over the squire in his own village."

"Oh, it's only Tarqs!" Shobna brayed with laughter, her hand moving a fraction higher up Chris' leg until it rested on his thigh. *That toned, firm thigh.* Yet still he shook his head. *Perhaps there is a decent Hardacre, after all.*

"Just out of interest," Chris said, loud enough for everyone to hear. "How *does* the new Master of the Hunt get the job? I presume there's a democratic election?"

"Democratic?" one of the older ladies of the village remarked. "We don't engage in modern nonsense like that."

Tarquin wondered what she meant by modern. Had she not heard of the Ancient Greeks?

"We...well, it's a gentleman's agreement, really," Tarquin said.

But if it came to a vote, surely Tarquin would win it hands down. Christopher was an unknown quantity — although Shobna was doing her best to know him.

Another scrape of chair legs on the floor indicated that she had moved closer to Christopher. Whatever they chuntering about now, it really *was* too quiet to hear, but they were definitely deep in conversation about something.

Plotting.

"Come on!" Longfellow called. "I've got sheep to bring down, I can't sit here all afternoon!"

"Sorry, Mr. Longfellow. I'm waiting for our friends at the back there." Tarquin folded his arms. "Shobna, Chris? Care to share your scintillating discussion with us all, or is it too X-rated for public airing?"

And the look Chris gave him in reply could only be described as...well, *saucy*. He tipped his head and widened his eyes, peering up at Tarquin from his seat as though butter wouldn't melt and all the time there was that half-smile, that slight look of amusement that was as annoying as it was— No. It was *just* annoying. Nothing more than that.

Shobna nudged him. "Go on, Chris," she purred.

And slowly, annoyingly, he unfolded his arms and raised his hand into the air.

Dare I just ignore it?

But that lovely square hand.

Tarquin noisily cleared his throat, then nodded toward Chris. "Yes, Mr. Hardcastle?"

"*Hardacre*," he corrected with that same bloody half-smile. "I have a question, Squire Bow."

Just as well I didn't say Hardcock by mistake!

"Right, yes, what?" Tarquin asked, his tone brisk.

"Now, I'm brand new to the Bottoms but I really want to bring something to the village that I hope will be my home." The sound of approval went round, led by the smirking Longfellow. "My great-uncle established the drag hunt sixty years ago. He abhorred blood sports as much as he loved the village and I wondered— if nobody objects, of course— I'd like to be considered for Master of the Hunt. As the next generation of Hardacres in the Bottoms."

"I see." Tarquin pressed his lips together tightly. Then he turned to the chalkboard. On the top left, he scratched out the initials *TMB*, and on the right, *CH*. Then he squatted, his tweed straining uncomfortably across his bottom, as he drew a line down between them, forming two columns.

Tarquin then stood and addressed the audience. "Would a show of hands suffice, do we think? A vote? Now, Ursula, I realize you said you're not fond of democracy, but let's just..." *Because I'll bloody win.* "Chris, would that be all right?"

"Well, I don't actually know anyone here, but I *am* a Hardacre and I believe that counts for something here in the village." He uncrossed his legs then patted his hands on his denim-clad knees. "Let's throw it to the vote. Bow versus Hardacre, as I believe it's been since the Doomsday Book!"

"It was definitely *Boff* in the Doomsday Book, Chris, but I won't get too hung up about it." Tarquin laid the chalk on the top of the board and brushed the white dust from his hands. "Perhaps you'd like to come up here and stand at the front so everyone can see you, eh?"

"I'd love to!" Shobna squeezed Chris' arm as he bounded to his feet and made his way toward the front of the hall. For some reason he ignored the few steps onto the stage and instead put his hand on the edge and vaulted up, earning a ribald cheer from a few of the more game ladies.

Git.

Once he was on the stage he turned slightly from the audience and asked Tarquin in a whisper, "Can I say a few words to them just so I know I'll get one or two votes? We both know you'll win, it won't hurt."

"One or two, eh? As many as that?" Tarquin leaned toward Chris, raising an eyebrow. An extraordinary, spell-binding cologne rose up to meet his nostrils and for a moment Tarquin entirely forgot why he and Chris were on the stage of the village hall. "Erm…right…sorry. Everyone, a few words from Mr. Hardacre."

Tarquin clapped, then folded his hands neatly behind his back.

Chris gave Tarquin a wink, then turned back to the hall and cleared his throat.

"I'm Christopher Hardacre," he told them with a winning grin, "and I like to think I've come home. It certainly feels like it."

How presidential.

"I don't want you to vote for the Hardacre name, nor in memory of my great-uncle, who loved this village although he didn't always show it, nor do I want you to vote for me because I've just signed an agreement to fund the replacement of that battered old bus shelter on the village green with a brand-new one, complete with heating and WiFi. No, I ask only that you vote for me because I love nothing more than a good, fast, hard ride. Thank you, Bottomers!"

That's quite an image — concentrate!

An interested murmur ran through the room. Ursula, apparently now willing to embrace the newfangled concept of democracy, nodded vigorously. The word *bus shelter* was on everyone's lips.

And all Tarquin could see was the bus shelter containing Chris in his swimming shorts, one thumb tucked teasingly just inside the waistband.

Tarquin cleared his throat and clutched his hand in front of him.

"Right, well, that's very nice of you to tart up the bus shelter, Chris, but unless you can charm the pig who is currently rolling about in my shrubs, you won't see it very often, will you?" Tarquin chortled. Then he gestured toward their audience. "So shall we vote? First of all, a show of hands for Chris."

Tarquin didn't bother looking at the audience. Even with the promise of a fancy bus stop, he knew the Bough Bottomsers. And they knew Tarquin Bough.

"Oh my — Thank you!"

What the bloody buggering hell?

Tarquin counted the raised hands. There weren't just one or two, there were…*half the room!* Half the room had voted for Chris.

"Fourteen votes for Chris," Tarquin said, the chalk squeaking as he crouched down to write the number on the board. "And a show of hands for me, Tarquin Bough, who lends his donkey each year for the village nativity play."

The hands went up again. *Fourteen.* Tarquin closed his eyes.

Bugger the bus shelter.

Tarquin blinked at his nemesis. His handsome, charming, bus shelter-upgrading nemesis. "Chris, would you mind counting as well. I see fourteen hands, do you?"

Chris took his time, one finger dancing in the air until he nodded and confirmed, "Fourteen." Then he gave a benevolent smile and asked, "Should I vote for you? Give you a push over the line?"

Tarquin couldn't quite believe what he'd just heard Chris say. But he shook his head. "No, you don't have to do that, Chris. We could —"

"A race!" Shobna shouted from the back of the hall. "The two of you should hop on your horses and have a race!"

Tarquin pointed his chalk at Chris. "But, Shobna, Chris doesn't have a horse!"

"But I do!" Longfellow called. "Oscar, the pride of the shire, the horse Mr. Beardsley Hardacre rode out whenever his diverse social engagements allowed it! Mr. Hardacre, how do you feel about handling a stallion?"

"It wouldn't be the first." Chris grinned. Then he reached out and took Tarquin's elbow in his hand. "What do you say, Tarks? I haven't had a really good race since I captained the Dark Blues against Cambridge!"

"A race…" Tarquin liked the idea of that. "Do you know, it might actually be rather fun! You're on." Tarquin turned to the audience. "Thank you for that suggestion, Shobna. Chris and I will have a race. What a gentlemanly way to resolve our differences — short of dueling pistols. A race it is."

The hum from the gathered crowd and their enthusiastic nods seemed to signal that all was well. Tarquin grabbed the chalkboard rubber. "Right, well, seeing as we're done…"

Shobna jumped to her feet, waving toward Tarquin. "One more thing…"

Oh, hell.

"And what would that be, Shobna?" Tarquin asked.

"Oh, no, this is a question for Chris." She flicked her hair and angled her head as if she was trying to look coy. "Would you like to take over as the village's rowing captain?"

Oh, bloody hell!

"Well…whose noses would I be putting out of joint?" Chris asked carefully, giving just the *slightest* circle of his broad shoulders. "I'm all about making chums. I don't want to upset anyone on the team with ambitions of leadership."

Shobna came up to the front of the hall and folded her arms on the lip of the stage. "No one in the team wants to do it! My dad's retiring to Florida, you see, so he can't be the captain anymore. We're *desperate*, Chris, please!"

She fluttered her eyelashes at him. Tarquin wondered how many other of Petunia's friends would do the same. Maybe even Petunia would too.

"Are you not a rower, squire?" Chris released Tarquin's elbow and let his hand rest on his shoulder instead. "You've got the arms for it."

A shot of electricity zapped Tarquin and he stared in surprise at Chris. *Oh, shit, are the stage lights on the blink again?* But there weren't any loose cables, nothing that could have unleashed that strange tingle.

Tarquin shrugged. "Oh, but my hips got jammed in the boat once. I struggled and it rolled over with me still inside it. Upside down and underwater! Fortunately, I'm a bit of a swimmer, so I managed to get out in the end, but that rather took the shine off rowing for me, I must say."

"Then I'd love to, if the team'll have me," he told Shobna, whose wide eyes were fixed on him. "Let's see if we can bring home some ribbons, eh?"

"Captain Hardacre, I like the sound of that!" Shobna ran the tip of her tongue over her bottom lip. "Let me have your number, Chris, and we can meet up — I mean, I can sort out a meet between you and my dad."

"Deal." Chris grinned. "Now, squire, when shall you and I meet on the field of battle?"

Tarquin looked at his pocket watch. "Why not today? No time like the present!"

The hand on his shoulder squeezed in a show of enthusiasm, then was gone. "And the route? Something easy for an incoming city boy like me to follow?"

"What about from our chapel to Upper Bough's spire?" Longfellow suggested. "The time-honored Bough steeplechase route, as painted by Mr. Constable, I believe! No finer, nor more vigorous ride in Britain!"

"What do you think?" Chris' voice was quieter now, intended just for Tarquin. "Do you like a vigorous ride, squire?"

"I do, but I rarely get the chance." Tarquin held out his hand to shake. "Meet you in an hour, ready for a hard ride?"

"I'm made for them." He took Tarquin's hand and shook it. "May the best man win, squire?"

"I'm sure he will," Tarquin replied. Chris offered him a bright grin then released his hand and turned back to the audience, who raised a cheer for this unexpected battle. Amid the noise, Shobna trotted up onto the stage and clapped her hands together for silence.

"And three cheers for Captain Hardacre! Hip hip, hooray," she announced.

And the village cheered of course, because why wouldn't they cheer for the man who had lived there all of five minutes?

Village life at its finest.

Chapter Four

Tarquin cantered through the lanes, down to the appointed spot for the starting line. Vulcan, his golden palomino, chuntered to himself as Tarquin rode.

"We're going to have a little race, Vulcan. You'll do me proud, I know!"

Chris' efforts were laudable really, especially considering that he wouldn't even be in the village for more than a few months. Even if the Oracle took to him, city slickers like that never stuck it out. They missed the noise and the bustle, the excitement and the lights.

Although Chris was managing to generate rather a lot of excitement himself. Quite a crowd had gathered at the chapel, certainly more people than had been at the meeting earlier. In fact, it even looked as if the local pub's most hardened regulars had come blinking out into the daylight to see the start.

"Afternoon, all." Tarquin tapped the brim of his helmet.

The crowd called a greeting and a few phones were held up to snap photos. The residents always liked a bit of competition, from the annual boat race to pub dominoes, and this was no different. But it was time a Bough led the drag hunt out. The Hardacres had ruled that roost for far too long.

And who'd decided that?

Tarquin trotted Vulcan back and forth. His horse was ready for his run.

Shobna emerged from the crowd and caught Vulcan's reins. Then she dropped her sunglasses down her nose and stared into the horizon, her glossed lips parted.

"Oh, my *God*! Chris is wearing jodhpurs!"

Even Vulcan seemed impressed, if his interested neigh was anything to go by. Tarquin pulled on the reins, keeping Vulcan still. He watched Chris approach, apparently at home on a horse he didn't know, and —

Oh God, those legs.

Even though Tarquin had seen those legs bare, there was something about jodhpurs. The way they clung. The way they made Tarquin want to stroke and grasp every inch of them before slowly teasing them off. *No, yank them off in a frenzy of lust.*

And those boots. Those shiny, shiny boots that fit Chris' legs so perfectly. And he was casually dressed in his shirt, sleeves rolled up, *those arms, oh God, those arms…*

Tarquin looked away, but his head jerked up again, his gaze falling on Chris once more.

Chris tipped his riding hat to Tarquin and patted the chestnut horse that Longfellow had loaned him. He had seen Beardsley on that same horse many a time, but the ancient troublemaker hadn't looked like *this*. Shobna headed for the new arrival, her heels clicking on the road.

"Looking hunky in your jodhpurs, Chris!"

"Almost as good as hunky Tarks!" Chris chuckled.

Hunky Tarks. No one had ever called him *hunky* before. Even if Chris was joking, Tarquin played the words back in his mind on a loop.

Hunky Tarks.

Then he saw Petunia standing in the crowd gazing at— *Oh, not me, of course.* Petunia snapped a photo of Chris and Shobna, then looked at Tarquin and called, "You'd better romp home, Tarquin. Make me proud for once!"

Tarquin gave her a nod of acknowledgment. "I'll do my best, dear. I can do no more."

"Time to start the race, I think!" Shobna grinned up at Chris. "Ready?"

"Chris, join me at the top of the lane, here?" Tarquin indicated with a flick of his riding crop. "Side by side?"

With a tip of his hat to the ladies, Chris trotted his horse alongside Tarquin. He looked down at the crop and asked, "Are you terribly handy with that, squire?"

Tarquin looked deep into Chris' eyes. *Please don't say anything about me offering to spank your arse in my orchard.* "I can be. When the need arises."

"I pinched an apple from your tree on my way down here." He glanced back at the approaching villagers. "But you weren't there to give me what for."

"Is that so?" Tarquin slapped the crop against his boot. "We'll have to see about that, won't we?"

Chris parted his lips but, before he could reply, the audience was upon them. Had he just flirted with another man? No. Chris was a Hardacre, there had to be a sting in it. *Is he laughing at me?*

"Ready, boys?" Shobna took a bright pink piece of chiffon from her pocket and held it up. The villagers watched, and in the air there was a sense of such anticipation that Tarquin could feel it. Sheer excitement. The air positively fizzed with it.

"Petunia will count to three, and I'll drop the scarf!" Shobna giggled.

Tarquin almost rolled his eyes, but smiled at Chris instead. He returned it, widening his blue eyes for a moment.

"One, two," Petunia barked like a sergeant major. "Three!"

Shobna dropped the scarf. "Go!"

Tarquin tapped Vulcan, who went off as if he'd been fired from a gun. Seeing his route ahead was clear, Tarquin looked round quickly for Chris, to ensure they weren't about to collide. It was with effort that Tarquin turned away because Chris in the saddle was a sight to behold, his strong arms tensed on the reins, and a very tempting triangle of chest on show at the neck of his shirt.

But he wasn't going to lose just for the sake of a quick ogle.

Yet as Chris sat forward in the saddle, Tarquin couldn't help but wonder what he must look like from the rear.

By God.

"I didn't know Sussex had such outstanding views!" Chris called over the thundering hooves. "But I'm perfectly happy to be following in your wake!"

"It's a beautiful part of the world!" Tarquin replied. "I can show you some lovely places!"

"I can already see one of them!"

He can't be talking about my arse, surely?

Tarquin glanced at him again. Those blue eyes were full of humor, and he couldn't detect anything spiteful there. Tarquin looked ahead once more, chuckling. He felt Vulcan tense as they came up to a fence and his horse soared over it with ease, landing at a run.

He heard the sound of the pursuing horse's hooves landing safely and saw, in the shimmering distance, the distant church steeple behind a belt of trees. He hadn't felt so free in ages, with the warm sun on his back and the breeze in his face and nothing but nature for miles. And Christopher Hardacre to share it.

Up ahead, Tarquin saw the red tiles and large stone chimneys of Bough Towers. And there, running up against the fence, was his pack of dogs. They ran in a flash of liver and white, golden and ginger fur, their long, feathery coats flying in the breeze. And what a racket they made!

But Tarquin couldn't stop to chastise them. He'd just withhold that evening's Bonio.

"There's my pig!" Chris shouted, and he was right. The Oracle of Delphi was at the center of the pack, snorting along merrily with the hounds. "Hello, pi—"

The greeting was cut off by the unmistakable sound of someone landing on the ground. Hard.

Tarquin slowed Vulcan, then trotted back to see Chris' horse riderless, and a figure sprawled on the ground. He dismounted and left Vulcan to crop the stubby grass.

"Chris...bloody hell, Chris?" Tarquin took off his glove and knelt beside his nemesis, touching his fingertips to Chris' face. He opened his eyes and blinked up at Tarquin, looking rather dazed. But alive, which was the main thing. "Does anything hurt? No broken limbs?"

"Why do I always end up on the floor around you?"

Tarquin patted Chris' shoulder. "I can't help it if you keep falling at my feet! Now, do you need a hand up?"

He nodded, then asked, "Why did you stop? You were winning."

"But you fell off—I couldn't just leave you." Tarquin held out his hand to Chris. Was it usual to leave people lying on the ground where Chris came from? He tried not to read anything into the way Chris twined their fingers together but instead rose to his feet, pulling his opponent up with him.

Tarquin steadied Chris with his other hand, placing it on Chris' arm. He was so close to Chris now, Tarquin felt the heat of Chris' body against his own. And that cologne again.

No, no, no – don't be so stupid, Tarquin!

But there was a gentle smile on Chris' lips. *His full lips.* Without even thinking, Tarquin leaned closer.

Their lips didn't touch. Mostly. Or so Tarquin told himself as the dogs began to bark again, shattering the silence.

And if they *did* touch, it was only by accident. The merest brush of a kiss. That didn't happen.

Tarquin looked away, chuckling awkwardly. "Glad you haven't broken your neck, canary!"

He whistled to Vulcan and clicked his fingers. He heard the creak of leather as Chris hauled himself back into Oscar's saddle, the gentle chink of metal as he took up the reins

"You should get a head start," Chris told him. "It's only fair."

"Nonsense, my dogs were making a racket!" Tarquin swung himself into his saddle and brought Vulcan alongside Chris and his mount. "Let's start again, count of three—together?"

"Just before we do…" Chris leaned across a little in his saddle and crooked one finger, gesturing Tarquin closer.

Tarquin didn't turn away. Holding on to the reins with both hands, Tarquin tipped his head toward Chris. That look of amusement was on Chris' face again.

And this time, there was no denying that their lips touched. And the touch turned into a kiss. Tarquin sighed, pressing his lips to Chris'. He had wanted this for so long, the kiss of a man, and for it to be a man like Chris—a handsome man with a gentle smile and sparkling eyes—almost made Tarquin melt off his saddle and onto the ground.

But he shouldn't be doing this.

Tarquin broke from Chris' lips.

"Please don't tell anyone," he whispered.

"I've been wanting to do that since you leapt into my garden yesterday," Chris admitted, still smiling. "Our secret?"

Tarquin nodded. "Yes. Our secret." He was about to look away when he turned back and said, with a grin, "Our very naughty secret."

"Count us in, squire." He circled his shoulders and lifted the reins again. "Before they send out a search party."

Tarquin shifted in his saddle, his posture upright and perfect. "After three. One…two…three!"

But no matter how perfect his poise, Tarquin's lips still tingled from that kiss. He didn't set off at once, and Chris was now in front of him.

What a view.

It's almost worth losing the race for.

Those shoulders, and the way his back tapered down to his waist, and that arse! *What a spectacular backside!*

Tarquin couldn't remember seeing anything like it. The jodhs were so gloriously tight, unlike Chris' shorts that he'd had on yesterday. The curve of those buttocks was delectable. Tarquin had no intention of overtaking, even though he knew Vulcan wouldn't find it difficult in the least. He was content just to gaze.

So he gazed. He watched the subtle movements of Chris' muscles as he mastered his steed, the slight adjustment here, the little shift there. Half-naked was bloody hot enough, but somehow, jodhpurs had turned up the heat even more. In jodhpurs, Christopher Hardacre was blazing.

Tarquin only noticed the church coming up ahead at the last moment. He'd lost, but he was happy. Why not have a master of the drag hunt as stunning as Christopher Hardacre?

In fact, he was so content after that kiss that he didn't even notice Chris had slowed Oscar to a canter until Vulcan sailed past them. He heard hooves galloping behind him, and Tarquin knew that the victory was his. His nemesis had proved to be anything but.

The crowd of villagers had arrived at the finish line and they cheered as Tarquin raced home in first. He raised his hand, waving to everyone, and smiled over at Petunia, who still didn't look happy.

But I've won, dammit, I'm the master of Bough Bottoms' drag hunt. What more does the bloody woman want?

Shobna trotted forward to meet the returning horsemen, her mobile held in front of her as she approached. Now her smiles were for Tarquin, because he was a winner. He was the Master of the Hunt.

Tarquin puffed out his chest, posing for the cameras, but he beckoned Chris forward. "And Chris, too! What a ride that was!"

"Outridden by the squire!" Chris chuckled, drawing his mount alongside. "But I needed that!"

Tarquin laughed, patting Chris on the back. And left his hand there. *No one'll notice.*

"The victory was yours." Longfellow emerged from the crowd, nodding grudgingly. "A worthy hunt master, Mr. Bough."

And he pronounced it right.

"Thank you, Mr. Longfellow. I was wondering, though…" Tarquin realized he still had his hand on Chris' back, so he gave him another pat before taking his hand away. "Chris, if you ever want to share some of the duties, I'd be more than happy to. You were very keen, and I wouldn't want to restrain you. Not too much, anyway."

"That's very kind." He met Tarquin's gaze. "Maybe I could pop over the fence and we could have a chat about our mutual interests? I've a feeling we could do something really interesting together."

Tarquin nodded. His throat was a little tight. "Yes, we should definitely get together and thrash something out."

Petunia shouldered her way to the front of the crowd, her face now set into a smile. Of course she was happy. She was happy because he had won.

"I believe a little celebration is in order, don't you?" Tarquin said. "A new master of the drag hunt, and a new captain of the rowing team. Everyone, let's go to the pub. The drinks are on me!"

Chapter Five

Tarquin felt like the Pied Piper as he led the villagers into The Floral Pomander. He strode up to the bar and handed the landlord a wad of banknotes. "That should be enough for a round, shouldn't it?"

He glanced round at Chris and said, "First time in the Pomander?"

Chris nodded, peering around the low-ceilinged taproom as though he were a child visiting Disneyland. After a moment he said, "Pomanders seem to be following me at the moment. Bough Bottoms is making the most of its famous son, isn't it?"

"Can you blame us?" Petunia was at Chris' elbow, one hand toying flirtatiously with her pearls. "Not many villagers can boast their very own literary legend, but Bough Bottoms can! Do you know how your Great-Uncle Beardsley came to publish *Madam Fanny's Floral Pomander*?"

Does anybody not know?

Certainly everybody from Upper and Lower Bough could recite the tale.

But Chris shook his head, perhaps out of politeness, and rested his hands on his hips, his gaze set intently on Petunia.

"PA Pierce was incredibly reclusive, so the stories say, and only ever really socialized with the late Mr. Hardacre. But seventy-odd years ago, the late Beardsley wasn't the publishing legend he became, he was just an apprentice who had to cycle into town to get the train to the city to make a pittance," she said, every inch the quintessential Jackanory host. "So the story goes, he and PA had their own steeplechase just like you and my gorgeous future husband, but the rights for the outrageous, *explicit*, *Madam Fanny's Floral Pomander* were the prize. England had never seen a book like it!"

"A book like this would make Lady Chatterley blush and her gardener run for his rosary," Chris said, recalling one of the more famous comments that accompanied the book's scandalous publication all those decades ago. "So Beardsley won and got to publish the book?"

"And made his name!" Petunia put her arm around Tarquin's waist, and he stared at her in surprise. "Bryan's my partner at the auction house and there's nothing he doesn't know about Lady Fanny. He's bound to be here soon. You should talk to him — Beardsley's whole career in publishing was built on Fanny!"

"Did I hear my name?" The loud, confident voice of Bryan Reeve filled the pub as he walked up to them. He passed his hand over his collar-length slicked-back hair, his pinstripes and pink shirt worn louchely. His gaze fell on Chris and he stuck out his hand, his signet ring catching the light. "A new face! Just passing through?"

"Christopher Hardacre." Chris took his hand. No *call me Chris*, Tarquin noted smugly. "I'm *hopefully* staying, but that's rather down to my great-uncle's pig!"

Bryan tipped back his head and guffawed as he shook Chris' hand. "Oh, the Siren of Thingy or whatever it's called? Yes, I've heard all about the pig. Currently plaguing Tarkers and Petunia, poor sods! So you're the new chap at the Grange, then?"

"Our lovely new neighbor." Petunia beamed. "Petunia, Christopher, wonderful to meet you. I'm Mrs. Bough in waiting—such a privilege to carry on the Bough name. It's like being a local celebrity." She leaned forward to kiss Chris' cheek, though he hadn't given any indication that he *should*. "But not a real celebrity, for that, you need to talk to Bryan. He's the resident millionaire!"

"Bryan is the village's answer to Trump," Tarquin told him, who was far from being smarmy Bryan's greatest fan. "But he's not in charge of America—he's an antique book dealer instead."

"Ah, hence your interest in Fanny's Pomander." Chris nodded. "Do you know something shocking? I've never read it. The book that kept my family in the black and I've never even opened a copy."

Bryan rubbed his hands. "I'm just the man for you, then."

I doubt that, Tarquin thought.

Bryan took the purple handkerchief from his breast pocket and wafted it, as if such a display of silk would demonstrate his success as a book dealer, then he tucked it away again. He put his arm around Chris' shoulders. "I can source a first edition, if you're interested? You look like the sort of man who wouldn't mind spending a *lot* of money to have such a thing in your possession, eh? Although I would've thought your uncle would have had some on his shelves."

"I've got a couple of first editions," Chris admitted. "Uncle was rather proud of his big find! Quite the mystery man, wasn't he? One filthy book and nothing else?"

Bryan shook his head, chuckling. "I'm surprised you didn't know about Pierce's other work. His essays on sexual freedom — *The Secret Study*. Still quite shocking even now, to be honest. Advocating open relationships, experimentation, the pursuit of exquisite pleasures. There was talk of him having penned another novel, but none has ever come to light. I don't suppose you've turned anything up in your uncle's house? But then, I doubt he'd have sat on a Pierce manuscript!"

"Afraid not, but I'm looking, believe me! Just a bit desperate to hang around and all that." He chortled, but it sounded hollow to Tarquin. *He just needs a hug.* "You won't believe this, but I have to read the dirty book to my new pig! If I can't win her over, I lose the house, everything!"

Bryan brayed with laughter and slapped Chris' back. "Bloody hell, that's a bit rough for you, eh? Bet you thought you'd won the lottery when you inherited that house, and just think, you could lose it all for a pig!"

Tarquin narrowed his eyes at Bryan. Couldn't he at least try to sound sympathetic? But then again, this was Bryan Reeve. And Bryan Reeve was a pillock.

But Chris didn't answer. He peered closely at Bryan for a long moment before he finally said, "I could! I've got one month to tempt my pig away from the charms of the squire or I'm out on my ear and a mysterious, unnamed *last fancy* gets the lot!"

Bryan raised an eyebrow. "Last fancy? Wasn't his nurse, was it? Heard she was quite a tasty piece."

"Oh come on, Bryan," Tarquin admonished him. "It's not the 1970s, and there *are* ladies present." He nodded toward Petunia, who beamed and kissed Tarquin on the cheek.

Bloody hell.

"I'm as clueless as you are." Chris shrugged, then asked, "Have we met before? Bryan, right?"

"Yes, Bryan. With a *Y*." He raised both eyebrows now and reeled back a little from Chris, studying him. "Erm...no, I don't think we've met before. Or if we have, we must both have been bloody drunk!" Bryan guffawed and slapped Chris' back again.

"Bryan, you'll never guess, Chris is your new worst enemy!" Petunia rested her hand on Bryan's shoulder. "He's just agreed to captain the Bottoms against the Uppers at the annual do!"

Bryan's eyes opened wide and his mouth twisted into a grimace which hastily vanished, and he guffawed again. "You never are? Well, good to meet you, Captain Chris! I'm Captain Bryan, and we *always* win, so you'd better get used to losing, eh? Get ready for a damned good spanking!"

"You *always* win? We'll see about who's doling out my spankings, Mr. Reeve." Chris' eyes suddenly grew wide and he asked keenly, "You don't have a brother, do you? Or a cousin? By the name of Aubrey Reeve?"

Bryan frowned and slowly shook his head. "Nope. Name doesn't ring any bells."

"There's just Bryan," Petunia chimed in. "He's one half of Rudd-Reeve, the *finest* auction house in Sussex, if we say so ourselves! Your uncle sold with us many a time. Nothing from his Pierce collection, alas!"

Something about that seemed to strike Chris as amusing, but he didn't share the joke. Instead he looked at Tarquin and said, "That was a bloody hard ride, squire — you must've worked up quite a sweat! What can I get you to cool you down?"

Tarquin saw naked bodies entwined, a shower raining down on them, a — "A gin and tonic, please. Lots of ice. It's true, I *am* feeling rather warm." Tarquin opened the buttons on his jacket. Why had he even *worn* a jacket? Chris looked so much cooler in his shirt, just enough buttons unfastened to be utterly tantalizing, his sleeves rolled to the elbow.

How have I gone through all these years without ever being kissed like that?

"You look very, very hot." Chris nodded, his expression betraying only friendly concern. "Just looking at you is making me hot too. Let's get a couple of G and Ts in, eh?"

Remembering he still had a fiancée, Tarquin asked her, "Petunia, what will you have?"

"Dry white wine," she said. "And Bryan?"

But before Bryan could answer, Chris had turned back to him, pointing a rather keen finger. "You weren't at Leadbetter, were you? Couple of years above me? *Christopher Hardacre*... I don't ring a single bell?"

Bryan mouthed Chris' name, eyes narrowed. "Nope, still don't recall meeting you before. Leadbetter Academy... No, that wasn't my school, I was at Shillinglaw."

"Must be a distant branch on the Reeve family tree. Same nose, that's what threw me." That seemed to satisfy Chris and he said, "I'm glad though, because I wouldn't row against Aubrey Reeve again if you paid me! Cheating little bugger that he was, he nearly drowned me for his precious gold medal!"

Petunia guffawed and patted Bryan's sharply tailored shoulder. Did Tarquin detect a flinch? "We all play fair here, Chris. Let's get those drinks and settle in!"

Chapter Six

Tarquin couldn't sleep. He should've done, after drinking several pints and whiskey chasers at *The Floral Pomander*, but every time he closed his eyes, he saw Chris, and he felt their kiss again, and his body was stirred to such a pitch that sleep was impossible.

What was he going to do?

A squire couldn't be gay. He'd accepted Petunia's proposal of marriage to hide the fact, and although he'd tried to make her happy in the bedroom, within a year of their engagement, that side of things had fizzled out. According to her, a go-getting career woman had no time for sex. And Tarquin had never thought about getting his jollies elsewhere. He'd never been unfaithful. It was a point of honor with him.

But what had he done? Kissed a man. And not just any man—a Hardacre. His neighbor. Not someone he could easily avoid, but hadn't Chris promised him something more?

Whatever would he do?

But that kiss. He hadn't felt so happy in years.

And yet, and yet…squires don't kiss city boys. It's not the done thing.

From outside he heard the sound of movement, no doubt the Oracle wandering out through the doggie door as she did when the call of nature disturbed her rest. How ridiculous to think that Chris' future in the village rested on a pig. How very Beardsley Hardacre.

Would Driscoll even know the pig hadn't taken to Chris? What if, when Driscoll came to check, Tarquin *just happened* to be at Hardacre Grange, and the pig would appear content? What if — ?

Tarquin froze. In the house he heard a very human-sounding footstep.

Please not a thief, not someone after my collection!

He'd hidden the Prince Albert well, though. No thief would ever find it.

But somebody was definitely downstairs, he was sure of it.

Did he need to unlock the gun cabinet?

Tarquin slipped out of bed and crept out of the room, treading lightly so as not to wake Petunia. He paused on the landing, trying to listen for sounds downstairs, but heard nothing more than the drumming of his heartbeat in his ears.

Then he heard the gentle trot of the Oracle's feet on the flags and — *singing*?

Someone was downstairs singing to the Oracle of Delphi, regaling her with a soft rendition of *Over the Rainbow*, and it could only be one man.

Chris. In *his* house. Trying to win over his late uncle's pig.

Tarquin took each step of the staircase as softly as he could, keeping his back to the wall. He stopped on the last bend in the stairs and sat there on the step, not wanting to head downstairs and interrupt the delightful communing of man with pig.

Had Chris crawled through the doggie door? At the thought of it, Tarquin's heart skipped, picturing that gorgeous bottom in those skintight jodhpurs once more. Was it too much to imagine that he might still be wearing them?

Tarquin could have a look, at least, couldn't he? Chris wouldn't necessarily spot him. Tarquin continued his silent journey, and was finally on the ground floor of the house. He heard a curt yap from one of the dogs, who would have known their master was awake, but they went back to sleep.

They weren't much good as guard dogs, that was for sure.

Tarquin followed the singing. It was coming from the back of the house. The kitchen door was slightly ajar and Tarquin paused, realizing the singing was coming from inside. What a beautiful voice Chris had. Tarquin could've listened to him for hours. He peered around the doorframe, just enough to see, but not be seen in turn.

Moonlight spilled over the floor and there, his jodhpur-clad legs stretched before him, those gleaming leather boots crossed at the ankle, was Christopher Hardacre. The Oracle was sleeping on the tiles beside him, her eyes closed and her gentle snoring somehow the sweetest accompaniment Tarquin could imagine to Chris' soft song. Surely nobody could resist a silken-voiced canary like him, even a Gloucester Old Spot? Chris' future in the village depended on it, after all.

Chris had found a way to the Oracle's heart, it seemed. A pig who could be won over with show tunes — who would have thought it? But as Chris' rendition went on, a tear rolled down Tarquin's face. *That song...* He'd never really cared for it much before, but there was something unexpectedly fragile in Chris' timbre that spoke to the longing within Tarquin. He wiped his pajama sleeve across his face and sniffed.

As the song ended, only the sounds of the night surrounded them, inside and out. Then he heard Chris' quiet voice as he told his sleeping audience, "You don't have to like me. Just...put up with me. Please."

Tarquin decided to emerge from his hiding place. He gave Chris warning by deliberately stepping on a creaky floorboard, then slid around the edge of the door.

"Evening," he said quietly. "She enjoyed your singing, then."

For a moment Chris didn't say anything at all, but watched Tarquin with wide eyes, as though caught cheating by a teacher. He looked like he was expecting trouble. When none was forthcoming he said, "That's a big cat flap you've got in the door."

Tarquin stayed where he was, leaning back against the wall. What on earth would Chris make of his silk paisley pajamas? "It's for the dogs! And pigs. And...next-door neighbors."

"Is Ms. Rudd asleep?" How innocent it sounded. Perhaps it was.

"Yeah, sleeping the sleep of the hardworking, go-getting auctioneer."

He nodded. "Sorry for breaking into your house. Crawling in, really, no jemmy required."

"It's all right. No harm done. The Oracle's happy, at least."

Chris stroked his hand over the pig's head and said, "She seems to be. A month isn't very long. I've got to deploy all of my charms if I'm going to tempt her back!"

"No, a month isn't very long at all. It's almost as if old Beardsley was set on you losing the house." Tarquin twisted one of the buttons on his pajamas. Should he really have said that to the man's nephew? "Did you ever meet him?"

"Once, when he came to take me out after speech day when I won every sporting trophy going — made a hash of my exams in the process, not that school cared. Nor did he." Chris shrugged his broad shoulders and went on. "Winning trophies mattered to a man like him more than exam results. You must know how competitive he was? You lived next door to the old bugger!"

He only met his great -uncle once?

Tarquin nodded. "Oh, yes, I know all about how competitive he was. Why would he fight me for Prince Albert's Prince Albert? He didn't want it, not really. He only wanted it because *I* did. He did all sorts of things to grind my gears — blocked our shared lane with a bollard, 'accidentally' tipped a lorry-load of muck into my front garden, grew leylandii so tall it felt like I was living in constant twilight, claimed my fence was six feet too far over into his land and sent me a bill for half a million quid…that sort of caper. The only thing we did agree on was the Oracle — she's a very special pig. But he beat me in the auction at the market for her when I said I wanted to buy her! He was an absolute pain in the arse to live next door to."

Too honest?

"You've just described every member of the Hardacre family," Chris told him with a grin. "We have a family motto, *absolutum dominium*, and nothing but that is acceptable. The first and only time I won a silver medal on sports day my father turned his back on me and it wasn't even my fault, it was Aubrey *cheating* Reeve. I never took home anything but gold after that."

Tarquin left his spot by the wall and sat cross-legged on the floor next to the sleeping pig. "I'm sorry. I don't mean to sound disrespectful to your late uncle— I..." Tarquin stroked the Oracle's side and her trotter twitched in her sleep. "But what you've said about your father—I can't say it surprises me. Knowing Beardsley."

"We're high achievers. Got the car, got the career, got the chance to retire before I'm forty? *Absolutum dominium.*" He quirked his eyebrow. "Can't get the pig to like me though. A rare Hardacre failure."

"Your uncle spoiled her, but she's not a bad pig at heart. Thinks she's a dog, actually." Tarquin chuckled softly. "Just spend time with her. That's all. If you have time? Are you still working in the city, then, or is that it for you now? Retired and all that?"

Chris sighed and ran his hands over his face, as though he was suddenly exhausted. Then he smiled and told Tarquin, "That's about the size of it. Dad's very proud, of course. He didn't retire until he was thirty-seven, so I beat him. Which means he gets to say he brought me up well. Or at least sent me to a school that walloped me into suitable shape."

"Bravo you!" Tarquin patted Chris' arm, but hastily withdrew his hand. "Sorry. Didn't mean to be overfamiliar."

"You're very good at kissi—" Chris began, silenced by the sound of Petunia's voice from upstairs.

"Turn the bloody telly down, you've got cows to wrangle first thing! Get to bed!"

Tarquin winced and pointed at the ceiling. "Sorry. I'm so sorry. I best be off. You can stay if you like, though, with the Oracle. Just make sure Petunia doesn't see you."

Then there were footsteps crossing the landing above and the sound of the fragrant Almost-Mrs. Bough descending the stairs, no doubt with one of her most particular heads of steam. Chris was on his feet in an instant and he looked around, a man cornered where he really shouldn't be. With a last wave to Tarquin, he darted behind the curtains and disappeared, at precisely the moment Petunia strode into the room in a cloud of ivory silk and face cream.

"Who were you talking to?"

Tarquin glanced about, just as the Oracle grunted in her sleep. As if there was nothing at all strange in the idea of a man getting out of bed to pay a visit to a porcine resident in the middle of the night. Tarquin stroked the Oracle and flashed a grin at his fiancée. "Erm…the pig."

A lie. To Petunia.

A frisson of forbidden delight ran through Tarquin as Petunia looked around the empty room. Her arrival seemed to have disturbed the Oracle, and she lifted her head and looked directly at the curtain behind which Chris had concealed himself.

"What's going on, Tarquin?" Petunia asked carefully, readying herself to begin his interrogation. "You're up to something."

And so are you, with horrid Bryan.

"I had an exciting day. I couldn't sleep." That wasn't a lie, at least. "And the Oracle won't be here for much longer. I'll miss the old girl."

The old girl who was now rising to her trotters and strolling toward the curtain, her ears twitching merrily as she went in search of her chanteur. For a moment Petunia looked set to follow her, then she tutted and thrust one finger toward her husband.

"It's time Tarquins were in bed," she informed him. "Put the pig in the boot room and then upstairs. I'll see you in the morning. I want to talk about your so-called *win*. Sweet dreams."

"For the first time in months, you've demanded I go to bed!" Tarquin snorted. "Although not *with* you. Of course not."

And Tarquin wouldn't have wanted to even if she'd asked. But what did she mean by his *so-called win*? She hadn't seen Chris throw the race, had she? At least she hadn't seen the kiss.

"Sleep tight," she said, slamming the door as she left with enough force to rattle the windows.

Tarquin stayed where he was on the cold flags of the kitchen floor, rubbing his temples. Then he got to his feet and teased back a corner of the curtain where Chris was hiding.

"She's gone, but you ought to go."

Chris' reply wasn't quite what Tarquin had been expecting. He looped his arms around Tarquin's neck and pulled him back behind the curtain, kissing him with a heat that he didn't think Petunia was *capable* of, let alone had ever felt for him. Once he'd overcome his surprise, Tarquin held Chris at the waist and pressed him against the cool glass of the window as he kissed him return. A tremor went through him. He wanted this so much, but he couldn't go behind Petunia's back. Even so, he couldn't stop. Didn't want to stop. Chris' body and Chris' kisses were spectacular, and were Tarquin's to enjoy.

"Bed!" Petunia bellowed from above and Chris laughed softly, resting his forehead against Tarquin's. How his blue eyes sparkled, and those strong arms loose around his neck…it felt like being tipsy!

"I really" — Chris paused to flutter another stolen kiss to Tarquin's lips — "fancy you."

Tarquin held Chris' face, touching the tip of his nose to Chris'. "Are — are you sure? Because bloody hell, I really fancy you!" He kissed Chris' lips, then whispered, "I want you, Chris. Carnally."

Carnally? Did I really need to specify?

"Carnally," Chris repeated with a grin. Then he flicked his gaze up to the ceiling. "I suppose I'd better take my jodhpurs and go. Sweet dreams, squire."

"May I say, before you head off… You have a fantastic arse." Tarquin drew one hand down from Chris' face and ghosted it across Chris' bottom. At the last moment, his hand became unsteady and Chris must have felt a distinct wobble in Tarquin's caress. "Does things to me, that rear of yours!"

"You should hold on to that thought," he said. "Because I'm hoping you'd like to see a lot more of this rear of mine."

"Darling, we mustn't," Tarquin said, but he was embracing Chris again. *Why can't I let go?* With Herculean effort, Tarquin dropped his arms down to his sides. "Sorry, Chris. I need to stop pawing at you."

"We shouldn't." Chris nodded, agreeing even though his arms were still around Tarquin's neck. "But shall we anyway?"

"I really want to," Tarquin murmured. "And you're a terrible tease!"

"Tarquin!" Petunia thundered. "Get these lights out!"

Tarquin rolled his eyes. "You remember where the doggie door is, don't you? If she hears me faffing about with the back door, I'll be for it."

"Goodnight, Squire Bough." Chris finally withdrew his strong arms, stroking one fingertip over Tarquin's cheek as he did. "Sleep tight."

Tarquin took Chris' finger and kissed its tip. "And you, too. Dream lovely dreams about me, Chris?"

"Lovely and probably fairly saucy too." He winked, then stepped out from behind the curtain to scratch the Oracle behind her ears. With one last wave of his elegant hand, he slipped from the room, leaving Tarquin alone.

Chapter Seven

Maybe Petunia would forget. Maybe Petunia would have left the house by the time Tarquin had come in from milking the cows. Maybe he would wake up and discover that the past three years of his relationship had all been a horrible dream and he was free and single, loud and proud.

But no.

Tarquin paused on the gravel driveway to fuss Jasper and Mabel, his wellingtons still claggy with mud and cowpats from the dairy. Not that the dogs seemed to mind. "Has Mummy gone out? Is the coast clear for Daddy?"

The dogs blinked up at him, then, at the sound of clanking metal from next door, they swiveled their heads to stare at the trees that bordered the lane. *What on Earth is Chris up to?* Tarquin wondered, as he listened to the roar of a car engine that split the morning.

The Aston, probably.

Tarquin went up to the fence and peered through the trees. Someone was loading the Aston Martin onto a tow truck. Had it broken down? But something didn't seem quite right, and Tarquin lurked, wondering what was going on.

There was Chris, jeans instead of jodhpurs today, a mug clutched in one hand. In the other was a clipboard and his attention was fixed on it, his expression almost stricken. The sleek silver car was safe on the truck now and a man slipped from the driving seat, calling, "If I had a car like this, I'd never sell it!"

In that moment Chris' expression changed to his usual look of bonhomie and he lifted his head. "I need a new toy, someone else can enjoy this one. Just a signature here, right?"

The driver nodded. "Then she's off to her new home in Dubai!"

Dubai?

That desert city of shiny skyscrapers was a world away from Bough Bottoms. Tarquin couldn't understand why Chris was selling the car. It wasn't as if he didn't have the space to park as many cars as he wanted to on his land, and he certainly wasn't short of money. Tarquin wondered what was on that clipboard Chris was holding. Fascinated, he still lurked, his green waxed jacket and tweed flat cap offering him, he hoped, an excellent disguise among the foliage.

He saw Chris' hand move as he signed the paper on the clipboard, then he handed it back to the man. The driver tore off a sheet and passed it to Chris, whose smile by now looked as though it hurt.

"Bye, old girl," Chris told the car.

"Pleasure doing business with you," the driver said. Tarquin watched him get back into the cab and start the engine. All the time Chris kept his eyes on the Aston, rubbing the back of his neck as it was driven away and finally, out of his driveway and into the road.

Only then did Chris spit, "Bloody hell!" Then he turned and went back into the house.

Tarquin waited there a moment, processing what he'd just seen. If Chris hadn't wanted to sell his car, why had he?

But it wasn't any of Tarquin's business, and now he kicked the mud off his boots against the fence. With every ounce of effort he possessed, Tarquin forced himself not to go over to Chris' house to kiss him and make him happy again.

"Tarquin!" Petunia bellowed from somewhere inside the house. "Are you coming in?"

"It's a lovely day. I'm quite happy outside," Tarquin shouted in reply. He was the squire after all — he wasn't going to be yelled at in his own home. Yet. All he had to do was avoid Petunia until she left for the auction house, then maybe — No. He couldn't see Chris. He *shouldn't*.

"I saw what happened yesterday." Petunia appeared at the corner of the house, a pillar box in her red trouser suit and scarlet lipstick. "I saw what you and Mr. Hardacre did."

How the hell did she see that?

A prickle of fear shot up Tarquin's spine. But he decided to play the innocent.

"Saw what?"

"When I was parking, I had to go down that bloody cul-de-sac behind the church and do a nine-point turn and I saw you through the trees. He threw the race."

Phew.

Tarquin felt pleased. At least she hadn't seen — *oh, bugger.*

"He didn't throw the race! Don't be silly."

"He pulled up." She thrust her finger at him, the red talon on the tip just inches from his face. "A Bough taking charity from a Hardacre! Couldn't you win it on your own? Do you need him to let you win? What sort of a man are you?"

The sort of man who likes to admire another man's bottom in the saddle.

"He *didn't* pull up. He was on an unfamiliar horse, on an unfamiliar route. All he did was see that slope and the approaching gate, and sensibly slowed down. But I know that route like the back of my hand, and Vulcan does too — we kept on going and overtook!"

There. Sounds plausible.

"He pulled up. I saw him pull up." She shook her head. "And what if he tells people he pulled up? We'll be the laughingstock of Upper *and* Lower Bough! Damage limitation, Tarquin. I think we should invite him for supper, maybe Shobna too if he doesn't have a plus-one? We need to be sure he's not going to show us up."

"He won't show us up!" Exasperated, Tarquin shoved his hands into his jacket pockets. "He's not like his uncle, he's actually a nice sort of bloke. I'm sure he'd love to come round for supper, but really, we can't invite the poor fellow then grill him!"

She rolled her eyes and gave a huff of utter exasperation. "Sound him out on girlfriends then get him invited. Friday. I'll do something nice. Maybe pork, in honor of our unwanted houseguest!"

"No you bloody won't!" Tarquin's voice came out higher in pitch than he'd meant it to. "You know I've gone off sausages since the Oracle's been living here. I won't sit there eating a pork chop in front of that creature!"

Petunia shrugged and said, "You've had a letter. From a solicitor."

"I *have*?" Tarquin scratched his head. "Oh, I suppose you could tell from the return address on the envelope?"

She reached into the pocket of her jacket and held up the letter. The *opened* letter. "Five thousand a month for the care of a pig? A hundred thousand if it meets with a natural death in your custody? Come on, Tarquin, catch up."

Tarquin blinked, amazed at her brazenness. "That's my post. You have no right to open my post."

"I didn't notice the name on it," she said. It was a lie, of course. She held out the envelope. "Mum opens all of Dad's post. Men need women to keep them on track, every girl knows that. Here's your precious letter."

Tarquin snatched it from her. "Yes, there's money involved regarding the pig. A lot. We need to look after her."

"If she dies, Tarquin, we get one hundred thousand pounds. If she dies." She raised her eyebrows, waiting.

"Of course she'll die eventually. She's not getting any younger. None of us are!" Tarquin scanned the letter. Satisfied that it contained no nasty surprises, he shoved it into his pocket. "But when she finally goes trotters-up, that one hundred thousand will have to go to building a mausoleum and ensuring the whole village is in mourning for an age. It's not to blow on handbags and a fortnight in the Seychelles."

"What if she were to" — she lowered her voice — "meet with an accident?"

Tarquin pictured the pig running alongside the dogs, and heard again Chris' beautiful voice as he sang to her. "No. Absolutely not. I'm not murdering a pig. No way."

"I never said murder, *you* said murder!" She pressed her hand to her breast, as though shocked at the very idea of it. The diamond engagement ring she had chosen and presented Tarquin with caught the sunlight, blinding him for a moment. "What's that line in the letter about an increased offer for the Prince Albert? Who's making offers? How much?"

"The mad bastard's last mistress, whoever she may be." Tarquin shook his head. "It's not for sale. I don't care how much they offer me, that little piece of tilly-tadger jewelry finishes off the Bough Collection of Regal and Notable Sensual Artefacts. I'm not selling!"

"We can talk about it tonight," Petunia informed him. Then she turned her cheek, ready for a kiss. "I'll see you later. Hoping to shift a job lot of nasty Victorian lace today, so we might have something to celebrate when I get home."

Tarquin didn't want to kiss Petunia. He felt like an almighty imposter, but he gave her a peck on the cheek just to be done with it.

"I'll get the champagne on ice," he said, his words dripping with irony. With a tut she turned, straightening the Alice band in her red hair as she hurried away to wield her gavel once more.

I need a bloody good ride.

Chapter Eight

Tarquin went indoors and changed into his jodhpurs and boots. It was a warm day, so he opted for a waistcoat over his shirt instead of a jacket. He headed out to the stable block and from the path, he saw his dog pack on the veranda, sleeping in a heap with the Oracle of Delphi. The sight made him happy.

He tucked his riding crop under his arm as he pulled on his leather gloves, crossing the stable yard in easy strides.

The very thought of Chris Hardacre so close sent a frisson through his blood, but it shouldn't. It couldn't. He was the squire, the farmer, a pillar of village life, and he was to become Mr. Petunia Rudd and embark on a life of respectable domestic bliss. He couldn't think of his neighbor's legs in those skintight jodhpurs, nor his sculpted arms and wide shoulders, or the strong torso that tapered into a trim waist. That wasn't any way for a Bough to look at a Hardacre.

A ride would get it out of his system once and for all.

Catherine Curzon and Eleanor Harkstead

Tarquin slid his crop into his boot and went into the tack room. He paused a moment to inhale the pleasing, masculine scent of leather and saddle soap. And straight into his mind came the image of Chris on horseback, that bottom tensing in the saddle as he rode.

And straight into Tarquin's jodhpurs came an erection.

"Oh, bloody hell."

"Hello, squire."

I'm imagining things. That can't be Chris.

But it was. Tarquin turned to see a vision in a dark blue shirt, ample chest showing as the garment was scarcely buttoned.

Tarquin tried to casually drape his hand in front of his jodhpurs, but there really was no disguising his erection.

"I wasn't expecting you! Good morning — how nice to see you."

And your jodhpurs. How nice to see all of that.

"I thought I'd come over and ask if you fancied a ride?" Chris leaned on the doorframe, one shoulder casually resting there. Then his gaze dropped momentarily but very deliberately to Tarquin's groin. "Can I tempt you?"

"You can and you do," Tarquin replied, almost breathless with longing. "I really need a ride. A good, hard ride, and if that was with you, then..."

Tarquin tried to readjust himself inside his jodhpurs, but he had a feeling the move hadn't been quite as discreet as he'd hoped.

Chris stepped farther into the room, closing the door softly behind him as he did. There was no hiding the evidence of *his* desire in those skintight jodhpurs and nor did he try to. Instead he took a few paces toward Tarquin, closing the gap between them.

Tarquin breathed raggedly as he reached out to lay his hand on Chris' waist. "You handsome, devilish bastard—I want you more than I've ever wanted anyone."

Chris studied Tarquin's face, then put the palms of his hands on his chest, resting them on the stiff fabric of his waistcoat. A very soft gasp escaped Chris' parted lips as he caressed Tarquin's chest with a sensuous touch.

"I can do devilish," Chris promised. He pressed his mouth to Tarquin's ear and drew one hand down his body until he cupped Tarquin's erection in his palm. "Can you?"

Tarquin pushed his hips forward against Chris' hand. "I—I'm willing to give it a jolly good go."

Is this actually happening? Maybe it's a dream and Petunia's snoring will wake me up before—

Chris' teeth nibbled at Tarquin's ear and he whispered, "Let's give it a jolly good go together?"

And—*oh, God*—he dropped to his knees.

We shouldn't be doing this.

But no one would find out. Would they?

Tarquin combed his fingers through Chris' hair. "We're well on our way to devilish, that's for sure."

Chris looked up at him, that gentle smile on his lips once more. He held Tarquin's gaze as, with a nimble movement of his fingers, he unbuttoned the squire's jodhpurs and slowly, carefully, teased down the zip.

A delicious shudder went through Tarquin. "I feel like I'm dreaming."

"So do I," Chris purred, edging Tarquin's boxers lower and releasing his erection. He dipped his head and kissed the very tip, caressing with his lips. Then he drew his tongue down Tarquin's length, and all the time that bright gaze was fixed on him.

Tarquin leaned back against the wall, sighing. "Oh, you *are* a tempting devil!"

And the answering smile was positively, wonderfully wicked. He stroked his tongue along Tarquin's erection again in one sinuous movement then asked, "Do I have your permission, squire?"

"Erm..." Tarquin's mouth hung open. "Erm...my permission? I haven't said *what are you up to on the floor there, Mr. Hardacre? So...*" *Maybe this is how they do things in the city?* Eager not to look like a country bumpkin, Tarquin squared his shoulders and said, "Yes, Chris, you most certainly have my permission." And stroked his gloved fingertip down Chris' cheek.

Chris' eyes fluttered closed and he gave a groan that could only be pure, heated desire. Then he looked up at Tarquin again and parted his lips into an *O*. With another soft moan he took the tip of Tarquin's erection in his mouth and swirled his tongue over it.

"You are...my God...you're exquisite!" Tarquin moaned as he ruffled Chris' hair, making him look as tousled as if he'd been for a romp in the hay. *Now there's a pleasing thought.* Tarquin's hips jerked forward and he moaned again, then apologized. "Sorry. Bad form."

But Chris didn't seem to think so. Instead he clearly realized it was a hint and in one glorious, smooth movement, he took the rest of Tarquin's erection into his mouth, his lips tight around him.

"Good bloody God, man!" Tarquin's knees nearly buckled and he grabbed for purchase on the first thing he could find—a metal ring on the wall where animals had once been tethered. The chain it was on clanked against the brickwork as Tarquin held tight, pleasure shooting into every part of his body. "Christopher Hardacre...oh, you ruddy marvelous chap!"

This was so forbidden, so utterly wrong, that it made the whole thing blaze even hotter. And Chris was clearly rather skilled in how to make a man happy, his tongue laving over Tarquin's body as his mouth moved back and forth.

And it had been so long since Tarquin had been pleasured, so long since he'd been with a man— Tarquin tightened his grip on the metal ring. "Chris, you're so naughty... I can't hold back."

But the look in those blue eyes suggested that wasn't a problem. As for the low growl of desire...that definitely sounded like encouragement.

Tarquin tipped back his head and, gripping Chris' mop of hair, gave himself over to the bliss that burst through him. His hips rocked forward against Chris and Tarquin panted as he flopped over, holding on to him.

"You are a very talented man indeed," Tarquin said. With exquisite slowness, Chris released Tarquin from his lips, licking his softening cock gently as he did so.

That tongue.

Tarquin leaned back against the wall. "Kiss me, Mr. Hardacre."

Mr. Hardacre.

Chris rose to his feet and put his hands on the wall on either side of Tarquin's shoulders. Then he leaned closer and kissed him. Not a prim, careful, sensible kiss, but a real kiss. A kiss that seemed to go to the very core of them.

Tarquin was lost inside it and held Chris to him as closely as he could. Chris was still erect and Tarquin pressed his hips against him, enjoying the knowledge that *he* had aroused this wonderful man. Even when the kiss ended they didn't move, their lips still brushing, their bodies held together.

"Do I have the squire's permission," Chris murmured, stealing another soft kiss, "to do something about my predicament?"

"Yes, you do. I'll help if you like?" Tarquin teased the tab on Chris' zip. "If I'm honest, I'd love to get my hands on you. And I still haven't punished you for eating my plum!"

"That ripe, juicy plum," he breathed, brushing kisses along Tarquin's jaw. "A cocky city boy like me, helping himself to your orchard? You should *definitely* punish me for that. You don't have to ask."

Well, that makes a welcome change.

"Are you sure?" Tarquin worked down Chris' zip as slowly as he could bear.

"You're the squire," Chris said. "You're the boss."

Tarquin blinked. *I am?*

He puffed out his chest and with a solid yank pulled down Chris' zip in one movement.

And discovered that Chris was wearing nothing under his jodhpurs at all.

"Is that for me?" Tarquin asked, eyebrow raised as Chris' perky erection appeared.

"Who else?" Chris purred.

"*All* of it?" Tarquin ran his gloved finger along the underside of Chris' cock.

"All of *me.*"

"Every gorgeous inch? Lucky old squire!" Tarquin grinned, then closed his hand around Chris' erection. He began to stroke. "Tell me how you like it."

"I like it however you want to do it," was his reply. "How else *would* I like it?"

Tarquin stroked more firmly, the thrill of holding an erection—and such a large and nicely shaped one, too—sending zaps of pleasure through him. With his other hand, he tugged down Chris' jodhpurs to the top of his thighs, then grasped his buttock. It was just as Tarquin had hoped. Better, maybe, because even through his glove—*oh, God, why am I still wearing my gloves?*—he could feel the heat of Chris' skin. "There… Your squire approves, Captain."

"I hoped you'd like a bit of spirit." He caught Tarquin's earlobe between his teeth again, his voice husky as he said, "Those gloves…"

Tarquin groaned, the sensuality and naughtiness of their encounter a heavenly intoxication. And feeling that naughtiness in every fiber of his being, he released Chris' buttock long enough to swing back his hand and give him a firm tap on his bottom. The answering gasp of pleasure was hotter even than the summer sun promised to be, and he felt Chris' hips jerk toward him in response.

I am the squire.

And Chris clearly loves it.

"I'll do that again," Tarquin said huskily, and this time his spank was just that little bit harder. And so was the thrust of those hips in reply. Tarquin shifted his feet, then remembered the riding crop in his boot. He pulled it out and stroked it up Chris' leg, from his knee to his bared thigh. Tarquin's heart raced. A spank with a hand was one thing, but should he really go about wielding a riding crop?

Should one ask?

Are there rules to this?

"How do you want me?" The question was a whisper, hoarse with desire.

"I want you hard," Tarquin said. He would ask. It was only polite, after all. "And…with my riding crop across your arse."

That seemed to be the right answer, because Chris' next kiss would've knocked Tarquin off his feet if he hadn't been quite so…*anchored*. Tarquin kissed him back just as passionately, delighting in Chris' soft, full lips, the scent of cologne strengthening on Chris' warm skin. Tarquin pressed the crop against Chris' buttock, testing him to see if it was what he really wanted.

"Every time I pass your orchard, I steal something," Chris teased him. "Are you going to let me get away with it?"

"No, I'm going to spank you." Tarquin was fairly sure he had the hang of it now. He released Chris' erection, then kissed his neck. "Hold that metal ring. Your squire wants to see this arse of yours properly. And get your shirt off."

Chris took the slightest step back and for a moment Tarquin wondered if he had somehow overstepped the mark. Only when Chris put his fingers on the first fastened button did he realize that, far from resisting, his companion was peacocking instead.

Tarquin pressed the riding crop more tightly against Chris' buttock. He ran his tongue across his bottom lip. "Yes, very good, strip for your squire."

The shirt had hardly been fastened when his visitor arrived, but now, with teasing slowness, the last buttons surrendered. Chris paused for just a second then rolled his shoulders and peeled the sleeves down his arms and off, letting it pool on the tack room floor.

No piece of fabric more erotic than that shirt had ever landed on the floor of the tack room. Tarquin took in a breath as he gazed at the sight before him. He'd seen

Chris' torso bared before, but there were no demure swimming shorts now, only the lewd, unfastened jodhpurs with that hard, ready cock emerging from them.

"You're a bloody handsome fellow, but you know that, don't you, captain?"

"I'm far too modest to say," he replied, though his grin said it all. Then he asked, "So you want me to hold on tight?"

"Yes, hold that metal ring tight." Tarquin kissed Chris' shoulder, then added, "If you don't mind."

"I don't mind anything for my squire," Chris told him in that low voice, his smile utterly beguiling. He reached up and took hold of the metal ring, then, with a glance over his shoulder at Tarquin, stepped back and put his arms at full stretch, his back arched just enough for it not to be an accident. "Is this how you want me?"

"Yes," Tarquin said. *Yes* was all he could say, because this was just what he wanted, those arms so toned, and the muscles of Chris' back tensing, all the way down to that wonderful rear. He cracked the air with the riding crop. "Ready, old bean?"

"Ready." And in case there was any doubt, he gave a wiggle of that glorious, tempting arse. "Give it your best shot."

Tarquin took a deep breath, then swung the riding crop against Chris' buttocks, a tap more than a spank. Chris glanced over his shoulder again, one eyebrow raised.

"Is there a butterfly in here, squire? I think I felt a flutter."

Tarquin quirked an eyebrow. "Harder, captain?"

"Harder, squire," was the reply, and there was that smile again, filled with the promise of what might follow. "Or is that the best you've got?"

Tarquin kissed Chris' shoulder. "I won't hurt you, I promise." Then he drew back his arm and this time gave Chris a good, hard *thwack*. And there was no jokey comment but instead his whole body seemed to buck at the switch of the crop, and the cry of pleasure Chris gave sent a fizz of excitement through Tarquin's body. A glow of perspiration had settled on the muscular planes of Chris' back and he tossed his head, planting his feet on the floor again, readying himself.

Tarquin stroked Chris' reddening skin. They were both enjoying it, Tarquin knew.

"And again, I think..." Tarquin drew back his arm, pausing just a moment so that Chris could halt him if he wanted to. Instead he nodded, tensing his buttocks in one more bit of peacockery for his squire.

And with a *swish* that cut the air, and a groan from Tarquin, down came the riding crop again across Chris' buttocks. He gave another cry of pleasure, every muscle snapping taut, his back arching into a smooth curve like a classical marble. Tarquin had never seen anything quite like it, had never even dared to dream of it. Yet here it was, an extraordinary sight indeed in his tack room.

"I think that's enough for now." Tarquin kissed his glove then stroked Chris' behind. Emboldened by Chris' clear reveling in his spanking, Tarquin rested his chin on Chris' shoulder and kissed his neck. "Your erection needs attending to. Allow me."

Still stroking Chris' buttocks, Tarquin ran the tip of his riding crop along the underside of Chris' cock, his lips pressed to Chris' neck. He could feel the racing pulse beneath his salty skin. It was racing for him. For Tarquin Bough. For the squire.

Tarquin threw the riding crop aside and pulled his glove off with his teeth. Then he took Chris' erection in his hand and stroked him, whispering through his kisses, "My lovely, handsome captain."

Chris' lips met his with a fierce hunger and Tarquin felt his hips thrust once, sensing the effort it must be taking for him to hold back. Nobody had ever *really* done as Tarquin had told them before — it was just part of being Tarquin — but that had changed here in this tack room, with its scent of leather and saddle soap. That had changed as soon as Christopher Hardacre gripped onto that metal ring and didn't let go.

Realizing that Chris was restraining his climax, Tarquin intuited that he might be required to give Chris permission for that too. He broke from the kiss for long enough to sigh, "Come for me, captain…" then crushed his lips to Chris' once more. He felt the force with which Chris' cock thrust against his hand, sensed the need in his body as he finally surrendered to his orgasm.

Tarquin slipped his hand around Chris' waist, holding him up, and he kissed his sweat-sheened face. "Would you like to lie down on that blanket there, sweetheart?"

Through his gasping breaths he managed to grin. "I think I need to!"

Still with one arm around Chris, Tarquin grabbed a horse blanket from a nearby shelf with his free hand. He shook it out and laid it on the floor, then dropped to his knees, bringing Chris with him.

"Well, that was unexpected," Tarquin said.

"I couldn't believe my luck," Chris admitted mischievously, snuggling against him. "First day here and I meet a gorgeous man who's offering to smack my arse? I had an idea as soon as you appeared but... My sixth sense didn't fail me!"

"Well, you *had* threatened to nick my apples, so a spank seemed in order!" Tarquin chuckled and propped himself up on one arm. "Do you know, I've got Catherine the Great's riding crop in my collection, and apparently that's seen more than a few backsides, but I'd never actually tried spanking before. It was rather fun, wasn't it?"

Chris lay back on the blanket, one arm pillowed behind his head. He peered up at Tarquin, his eyes dreamy as he asked, "Are you teasing me, squire?"

Tarquin dipped his head to kiss Chris' biceps, then smiled at him. "Teasing you? What about?"

"You've never done this before?" Chris shifted and pulled his jodhpurs up over his hips, leaving them unfastened. Then he stretched, like a cat settling before a warm hearth. "Honestly?"

"I haven't, no! I've thought about it, but it's never really come up before—if you'll pardon the pun." Tarquin combed his fingers through Chris' tousled, sweaty hair. "I'm glad, though—that was bloody good fun!"

Chris looked so decadent there on the rug, sated and happy and glowing, those jodhpur-clad legs stretched before him. Tarquin had been the one to do this, to turn this sculpted, vibrant man into the sleepy, satisfied figure who now reclined on the floor beside him.

Am I having an affair?

No, it's not an affair. We're not in bed together. We're still wearing clothes. More or less.

And we haven't...consummated.

"I could happily stay here all day." Chris closed his eyes and gave a long sigh of contentment. "Getting to grips with the squire next door."

"That'd certainly be fun, but you'd have to help me feed the sheep and milk the cows this evening!" Tarquin blew a puff of air at one of Chris' tousled locks, which quivered before flopping down on his forehead. He opened his eyes and met Tarquin's gaze, then slipped one arm around his neck and pulled him into a gentle kiss.

"I might be a city boy canary," Chris told him, "but I'm sure I could milk a cow if the situation demanded it."

"I have a feeling you probably could!" A filthy chortle escaped Tarquin and he buried his face against Chris' bare shoulder. Then he whispered, "How do you look so gorgeous, Chris? You're so...toned. Your figure is just perfect."

"Rowing and riding keep me looking halfway presentable." Chris' arm was still around him and Tarquin felt the soft brush of his fingertips, sketching out shapes on his crisp shirt sleeve. "And the odd glass of something naughty. And the occasional cropping."

"You're full of surprises, Hardacre." Tarquin stroked Chris' chest, fascinated by the manly hair Chris sported. *Just the right amount too.* "A beautiful singing voice, a fondness for a spanking. Gosh, I do hope you stay in Bough Bottoms! You're a marvelous sort of chap to have around the place."

"It's very, very different to London." Chris chuckled and opened his eyes. They danced with merriment, but did Tarquin see the barest hint of a shadow? *The chap's left his old life behind, he's bound to need a moment or two.* "I feel like I'm sort of...decompressing? Coming up to the surface for a big breath of fresh air." He drew Tarquin to him for another kiss. "I want to stay, so put a word in for me with Miss Piggy?"

"I most certainly will," Tarquin said softly. As he gazed into Chris' large blue eyes, something changed within Tarquin. Something he couldn't have put a name to—he could only explain that it was as if he'd put on someone else's spectacles. Everything was sharper, somehow, more defined.

Am I having an affair?

Because if Chris stayed, Tarquin would be living permanently next door to the very handsome man who he couldn't stop kissing. This wasn't going to be a one-off, Tarquin finally realized. It would be torture to want Chris as much as he did and avoid another encounter like this.

It feels like an affair.

Tarquin ruffled Chris' hair, then, just as his lips were hovering above Chris' face, he heard a furious squeal from the stable yard. Tarquin glanced up.

"That's the Oracle!" he said under his breath, as if that wasn't obvious.

Chris nodded, still dreamy. "Is she telling me to sling my city-slicking hook?"

"I don't know! I hope not—it'd be very rude of her after that delightful serenade you gave her last night."

The Oracle squealed again and her trotters clipped across the yard, back and forth. Fear lanced through Tarquin.

"I think... I think someone might be out there. You know pigs can be fearsome guard dogs? Guard pigs? Quick, get dressed!"

It seemed to take Chris a moment or two to clear his head enough to understand exactly what Tarquin had just said, but once he did, he sat bolt upright and reached for his shirt.

Someone was outside, Tarquin was sure of it, and if someone was outside then it was only a matter of time before they made their way to the stable yard and found this far-from-innocent scene.

Thank God I didn't get undressed.

Chris leaped to his feet, fastening buttons and zips with an astonishing speed. He nodded toward the door and asked, "Are you expecting anyone?"

Tarquin shook his head as he gathered up the blanket and shoved it onto the shelf. "No one!"

But soon enough, the identity of their visitor was revealed.

"Knock, knock!" Bryan shouted. "Anyone in?"

At least it's not Petunia.

"You've caught us slacking," Chris called in reply, by now as decent as he ever was. He didn't seem too fond of fastening his shirt buttons, which Tarquin wasn't about to complain about. Tousled seemed to suit him.

The Oracle squealed again as Bryan opened the door and appeared with the pig. "Can you sort out this bloody pig? I'm having a barbecue after the boat race — feel free to donate her!"

Tarquin folded his arms. "I should really barbecue *you* — what are you doing wandering around my yard?"

"Just…saying hello." Bryan didn't sound convincing, and even the pig seemed to notice as she grunted in what sounded like exasperation. From the corner of his eye Tarquin saw Chris stoop to pick up the discarded riding crop, all innocence as he approached and held it out.

"Don't forget your whip, squire."

"Thanks, Chris." Tarquin took it from Chris, then looked down as the Oracle nudged something with her trotter. *My bloody glove!* Tarquin picked it up from the floor. "Did you want to have a word, Bryan?"

Bryan didn't appear to hear. He was staring instead at Chris. And Chris, a playful smile on his lips, was staring back at Bryan.

"Hello," Chris said, his voice filled with mischief. "Let me guess, it's just hit you that Bough Bottoms are going to row you into oblivion this year!"

Bryan flared his nostrils. "No, I'm merely sizing up the enemy. Prepare to lose, Captain Hardacre!" Then the schoolboy tone vanished. "Just thought I'd pop by in case anything had turned up in the house—any of your uncle's old books or his authors' manuscripts that you want to sell."

"But that's in *my* house," Chris observed, his innocence doing a marvelous job of shining a spotlight on Bryan's unctuous snooping. "I can see this is the sort of village where nobody locks their doors. If you did that in London, you'd wake up with no house! I *have* found a treasure trove of bits and bobs, actually, right back to the earliest days of Hardacre Books, when Great-Uncle Beardsley was struggling to get it off the ground." He dropped his voice. "And a few bits about Pierce too. Nothing important, just the odd handwritten letter and…what was it, now? Oh yes, the original signed contract for *Madam Fanny's Floral Pomander.*"

Bryan's eyes had been growing larger and larger. "You—you found all that? Do you have any idea—? If you want me to find a buyer, you need only say. Sorry—I popped over as I didn't get an answer at your house and thought maybe you'd asked Tarkers for some sugar."

Tarquin pressed his lips tightly together as he restrained his urge to laugh.

Some sugar!

"I came over to get some riding tips from the Master of the Hunt," Chris told him, stepping out into the sunlight. "I can't sell any of it yet, Bryan, even if I wanted to, which in the case of the Hardacre Books stuff, I don't. If I don't have the Oracle of Delphi living under my roof one month from today, I forfeit everything. The house — all my improvements to it included — the contents, the Hardacre Books archive, it all goes to my great-uncle's *last fancy*, as he put it. Whoever she is, she's probably telling the pig I'm a real villain behind my back! It's in her best interests, after all."

Bryan curled his lip. "Last fancy, eh? Not much fun for you — all it would take is for Porker here to take a dislike to you, or go wandering out and get run down in the road, and…lucky old *fancy!*"

"I'm going to win her over no matter what it takes." Chris grinned. "We Hardacres have our hidden charms, you know."

At Chris' words, an expression warred over Bryan's features, somewhere between surprise and chronic indigestion.

"It's true, I didn't get on with Beardsley one bit, and I never thought I could be friends with a Hardacre, but Chris and I seem to be knocking along fine!" Tarquin patted Chris' shoulder, making sure not to linger. "Aren't we, old bean?"

"Rubbing along," he agreed. "So you can look me up in a month, Bryan, and we can have a pint and go through whatever stuff I might have taking up space. Anything Pierce's off the table though. By rights it'd be the squire who got first refusal on that, the guy used to live in his house, after all!"

Bryan nodded. "He did indeed, so they say. But there's no evidence, is there, other than gossip, of course. And who'd believe gossip!"

"There's many a grain of truth in gossip, I'd say!" Tarquin grinned, but he really didn't like Bryan's rudeness to Chris. "I wouldn't be surprised if old Pierce at least visited the Bough Collection. Right up his street!"

"Well, I'm *hoping* our squire might give me a personal tour when he's got a moment." Chris patted Tarquin's back, sending a shiver through him. "I'm a bit of a wide-eyed innocent, so I'm looking forward to being thoroughly schooled."

"I'm sure you'd find it educational," Tarquin replied.

"Wouldn't mind a tour of it myself!" Bryan remarked, but he backed away as the Oracle approached him, oinking at him with interest. Chris, however, bent down and patted his knee, as though summoning one of the resident dogs.

"Can I take her for a walk on the harness?" he asked, rubbing his fingers together to tempt her closer. "Do you think she might let me?"

The Oracle turned to Chris and gave him a spirited grunt.

"Worth a go!" Tarquin said. "It's in the house. I'm not quite sure how she got out to the stable yard, unless she's sprouted opposable thumbs and opened the gate, but she might've jumped over the fence. Maybe she came to see you?"

Then got distracted because Bryan was poking about.

"Well, I'll leave you be. But, Chris?" Bryan drew one of his silk-embossed business cards from his pocket and braved the pig in order to slip the card into the pocket of Chris' shirt. "Call me, okay?"

"I will, Bryan Reeve of Shillinglaw." He patted his pocket. "But not until my month is up."

"Bye, then!" Bryan swaggered away over the yard, and once he'd vanished around the corner, Tarquin rolled his eyes.

"He's so smarmy, isn't he? I don't know how Petunia can bear to work with him!"

"No Reeve is getting his hands on anything of mine," Chris admitted. "If he's related to the guy I knew at Leadbetter, I wouldn't trust him as far as I could throw him. I'd trust this little Miss Piggy though, look how cute she is!"

The Oracle had been sniffing the ground, as if memorizing Bryan's scent for future reference. Now she looked up at Chris, one ear flopped back, wrinkling her snout at him. He cocked his head to one side, matching her gaze.

"Fancy a walk and a song?" Chris asked the pig. "Uncle Tarkers too, unless he's got farming to get on with."

"Other than sorting out the cows and sheep later, I haven't got much on today," Tarquin said. *Other than some very tedious paperwork.* "If we head over to the house, I'll grab the harness and you can have a go at putting her into it!"

"Go on then, I'm in the mood for a challenge!"

As Tarquin led the way, he shoved his hands into the pockets of his jodhpurs, to avoid raising the issue of holding hands. It was cowardly of him, he knew, but he couldn't quite bring himself to mention it. "This way, over here. See the — well, that's funny, I'm sure I shut the gate earlier. But I came out of the side door when I was geared up for my ride, so I wouldn't have noticed if it was still open. Oh, blast it!"

The gate between the garden and the stables was open wide, and had to have been the route taken by the Oracle.

"No harm done, thank God she didn't head for the road." He stooped again, scratching the Oracle's ears. "There's a lot riding on this old girl!"

"Just a bit! I'll make that gate more secure, Chris. Don't worry!" Tarquin gave him a wink, then headed through the backdoor, where the Oracle's harness hung on the back of a kitchen chair. He reappeared, holding the harness aloft. "Here we are! Fancy having a go?"

"How tough can it be?" Chris held out his hand. "Let's get her safely fastened in! Anything I need to know before I start?"

"Erm...you need to know she's very strong, but I'm sure a strapping chap like you should manage!" Tarquin passed him the harness. Their hands touched and Tarquin sighed. "Sorry. And the other thing to know is, *that's* the front. It was tailor-made for her, so it fits her perfectly."

Chris knelt down before the Oracle, clutching the harness in his fists. What followed seemed to Tarquin something close to watching a man try to put a harness on a large, water-filled balloon. The pig was never keen on the device and now, faced with an amateur, she slipped free time and again. Only when she managed to elicit a groan of frustration from Chris did she seem to grow tired of the sport and allow the harness to be put around her. Then she trotted into a shaft of sunlight and settled down to snooze.

The Captain and the Squire

Tarquin clapped softly. "Well, you got there in the end, although it doesn't look like she's in the mood for a walk!"

The Oracle shifted in her sleep and the harness slid down on the yard, slipping from her plump form. Chris winced and shook his head, a man defeated.

"The pig has spoken," he sighed.

Tarquin patted Chris' arm in consolation. "Nonsense! You just need to make it tighter next time."

Chris smiled and nodded. Then he rose to his feet and said, "You've probably seen enough of me for one day, after all! Thank you for the most wonderful time, squire."

"Thank you, too!" Tarquin held out his hand to shake and Chris took it. Was that what men did after an enjoyable spanking session? It seemed the gentlemanly thing to do.

Chapter Nine

Tarquin had been down into the cellar to choose the wine for dinner and emerged garlanded with cobwebs. Chris wouldn't have thought much of the squire like this, with a layer of dust on his jumper. But Chris shouldn't think of the squire at all, because Tarquin was engaged, and even if he really liked Chris, and kept thinking about him, but had been deliberately avoiding him for the past couple of days —

"Found a very nice claret, if that'll go with dinner, Petunia?" Tarquin held out the bottle toward Petunia, who was cooking at the stove.

"It should," she called over the strains of Classic FM. "My beef Wellington is looking typically amazing! No soggy bottoms here, Mr. Hollywood!"

Bottoms. Oh, Chris. Chris and your lovely bottom and your lovely erection and your lovely kisses and your lovely chest and your lovely arms and your lovely hands.

The bottle!

"Oh, bloody hell!" Tarquin's experience as a fielder in Bough Bottoms' cricket team came into its own at that moment as he managed to catch the bottle of claret an inch before it hit the stone flags of the floor. "Whoops, clumsy old Tarks!"

She rolled her eyes, then twirled and asked, "How do I look? Summery? I want to look like I might be off to the Proms." Before Tarquin had a chance to answer, Petunia peered intently at the bottle he had saved. "Oh, not that one, Tarquin, we're not our parents at Christmas!"

"But I had to go into the far reaches of the cellar for this!" Crestfallen, Tarquin slowly turned the bottle, admiring its vintage label. "Do you want me to go back down there and get another? There's spiders down there."

"*There's spiders down there,*" Petunia mimicked. "Go and get something less...*boring*. And tell me I look adorable in my dress! If we're not going to Henley this year because of your boring old farm, I'm wearing it tonight instead!"

"You look very nice." Tarquin crossed the room and puckered his lips to give her a peck on her cheek, his stomach churning with guilt. "Sorry about Henley. I'll make it up to you."

"Well, you know how to do that." She puffed her fingers through her hair and cocked her hip so her full skirt with its pattern of pink roses flared toward him. "Three little words?"

"Erm... the Oracle of — oh, no, that's four words." Tarquin stared at her blankly. "Chilled pinot grigio?"

Petunia smiled and shook her head. She did it to be coquettish but instead it just made Tarquin think that he was sailing very close to a telling off. That meant he had given The Wrong Answer. She tapped one finger to his chest and tutted. "No. What three little words would I love to hear from my fiancé on this gorgeous summer night?"

Oh hell.

Tarquin took her finger, as if grabbing a woman's finger was somehow romantic, and stuttered, "I…I love you?"

Petunia frowned, then her expression grew dark and she snatched her finger back. "Centre Court tickets! For God's sake, Tarquin, you promised! For the gents' final!" She turned back to the Aga and stamped her foot. "I *love* you? That's not going to get me into Wimblers, is it?"

Tarquin blinked at her, deflated.

Silly me, of course she doesn't care if I love her or not.

"Centre Court? I don't know — I could try to get some. Erm…let me go and get another bottle."

"Don't try," she spat as he retreated. "Do!"

Tarquin shuffled back to the cellar. Perhaps he could stay down there and never come out again. *That'd be nice.* No Petunia hassling him about Henley and Wimbledon, no delicious temptations from Chris.

He turned the light on at the top of the stairs, his head bowed. And as he reached the last step, he noticed something he hadn't before.

Footsteps in the dust.

Not his own. They were smaller than his. Someone else had been down here. And there was nothing there — apart from the wine, a fuse box and the gas meter. Tarquin handled those. So why had Petunia come down here?

Tarquin followed the footprints and found that they went in a circuit of the room, up against the walls.

What the hell had she been doing?

Unless…perhaps it hadn't been Petunia at all. Perhaps it had been an intruder. But the cellar had been locked – even though the key hung on a board in the pantry. It was hardly the most secure set-up.

Tarquin picked up two bottles of pinot noir and headed up to the kitchen again. "Tuney? Have you been in the cellar?"

"God, no, never!" She didn't look up, intent as she was on stabbing the blade of a sharp knife into a large camembert at the kitchen table. "I thought we might start with a Pimms and eat out on the lawn. Don't you think?"

"Outside? But wouldn't it be nice to use the dining room?" Tarquin rummaged for the bottle opener in the drawer, instantly annoyed by the plethora of elastic bands and corks he had to fight through first. "Be nice to show off the Stubbs painting to our guests now it's been cleaned!"

"I know." She nodded. "So pop out and make up the table, nothing like eating out as the sun goes down!"

"But –" Tarquin swallowed. *Anything for a quiet life. And I've been a very bad man.* "Right. Outside it is, then. Tablecloth and umbrella?"

Her reply was another roll of her eyes and another stab of the knife. It was up to him, then. Of course it was, how else could Petunia find something to pull him up on?

Tarquin gathered up the cutlery and the tablecloth and headed outside to begin the task of laying the table. He heard drilling coming from somewhere on the evening breeze, and that same breeze caught the tablecloth, which billowed out like a sail. And that set off the dogs, who right at that moment had rounded the corner of the house with the Oracle in pursuit.

"Shush, you pack of noisy sods!"

"Is that Christopher drilling?" Petunia was at the door, her knife in one hand and the boxed camembert in the other. "He's due in twenty minutes. Why is he drilling? What time did you tell him, Tarquin?"

"Time?" Tarquin paused, mid-wrestle with the tablecloth. "Why would I be telling Chris the time? Doesn't the man own a watch?"

"Did you tell him seven for seven-thirty?" she asked, but it was more like an accusation than a question. "You didn't tell him to *arrive* at half past, did you? Oh, Tarquin, why would you tell him that?"

The cold truth dawned on Tarquin like a bucket of icy water over his head.

"Oh, bloody hell, I forgot!" Tarquin threw the tablecloth onto one of the chairs and ran his hand through his hair. "Clean left my mind!"

Because, to be fair, Tarquin's mind had been occupied with rather a lot, the memories of the tack room dominating his every waking thought.

The dogs and the pig retreated.

"You—" She stared, her eyes wide with fury. *Oh God. The dam's breaking.* Then the dam burst and Petunia bellowed, "Well you'd better get over there, get him by the nose and march him over here because I'm baking a camembert, my beef Wellington's in and the Eton Mess is chilling. I wonder why I put up with you sometimes, you're useless! A complete waste of bloody space!"

"Fine. I'll go and see Chris, then."

Because at least he doesn't think I'm a waste of space.

And as Tarquin turned and stormed off toward the fence dividing his garden from Chris', he wondered how the heck he'd ended up engaged to Petunia. In fact, he wondered why she had insisted they get married when he was fairly sure she didn't like him very much at all.

Tarquin was careful this time to avoid any nails as he clambered over the fence and landed on Chris' lawn. He strode across his neighbor's garden, up to the house, and on the steps of the veranda he found himself looking through the French windows at an extraordinary sight.

It deserved to be in a calendar.

Chris was kneeling like Narcissus, but rather than gaze at his inestimable beauty, he was hammering at the parquet floor. His torso was bare, his arm flexing with each hammer blow. A quantity of his dark blond hair had fallen into his face, and Tarquin wanted nothing more than to kiss it back. He was sheened with a patina of sweat, and Tarquin's lips parted as he remembered the taste of Chris' skin.

Tarquin pressed his hands to the window, gazing, his body thrilling as the hammer fell.

Those perfect muscles. Like a thoroughbred stallion.

With one last strike of the hammer, Chris rose up to his knees and blew out a long breath of exertion, fluttering the fallen locks of hair against his forehead. His chest glistened with perspiration, and Tarquin was catapulted back into the tack room all over again. Chris drew the back of his hand across his brow then, as if driven by some mysterious sixth sense, his bright gaze traveled across to the French windows. And he smiled.

Tarquin gave him a small wave. "Can I have a word?"

"Come on in," Chris called, standing to greet him. There in his belt loop Tarquin couldn't help but notice a bunched red shirt. It was such a careless gesture, underscoring what a free spirit Chris was, that it set Tarquin's heart pounding all over again.

Tarquin trembled as he opened the French window. He stepped into the room, placing his brogues carefully as he was very aware that he was walking on Chris' hard work. "I... Umm... I forgot to mention something the other day."

"Hey, don't worry about it." Chris settled one hand on his hip, where his jeans sat just low enough to be irresistible. There was a sweet aroma in the air, the smell of something tasty in the oven. "We both had a good time, didn't we? You're engaged, I'm not about to try and wreck your life. You don't need to say anything."

"Oh." Tarquin shoved his hands into the pockets of his corduroy trousers. "*That*... Actually...I was here to say that I meant to invite you to dinner the other day, only I forgot because..."

Tarquin gazed into Chris' eyes, mesmerized. "I didn't know what to do. Afterward. After Bryan came stamping in, I thought, *We can't hold hands, people will know. And they mustn't know.* I'm sorry. I keep thinking about what happened in the tack room, and it was the most wonderful time I've ever had. I keep thinking of you, and..."

Tarquin's gaze drifted down from Chris' eyes, as if the rest of the man's body was exerting a hypnotizing pull. That soft, dark hair on Chris' chest, and those toned planes, and the arms. *Oh, those arms, pulling against the metal ring.*

"And...?" He took a few steps toward Tarquin, until there was nothing but an arm's length between them. "It doesn't have to be a one-off, squire. A guy like me needs keeping in line, and I need a strong guy like you to do it."

"I want you." Tarquin dared himself to touch Chris' cheek, stroking Chris' nascent stubble. "I want more than a few snatched moments in a tack room. But my God, Chris…we'd be having an affair."

And he pictured Petunia. Furious Petunia who even now would be stabbing at that innocent camembert, cursing her fiancé's name.

"We would." Chris closed his eyes and turned his head just enough to kiss Tarquin's fingertips. "I'd be all yours."

Tarquin took in a breath, then said, "I don't think she loves me. And I don't know what I can offer you."

"You sound like you need to have some fun." He put his hand on Tarquin's hip. "Let that squire out a little more, Tarkers. Enjoy being you."

"He'd like that!" Tarquin grinned. "He would, and so would I! Would you…would mind terribly giving me another kiss?"

"Are you asking, squire?" Chris teased his lips against Tarquin's, smiling softly as he drew away a little, denying him his kiss. "Or telling?"

"Let me rephrase that." Tarquin's voice sounded, even to him, deeper now, richer in tone. "Captain, kiss me."

Tarquin felt Chris' smile as they kissed, then he parted his lips and sank against Tarquin, looping those wonderful arms around his neck. It was the most fierce kiss Tarquin had ever felt, and the fire ignited all over again.

Tarquin combed his hands through Chris' hair, reveling in its thickness, and pressed his hips against Chris' thigh, showing him he was hard again.

"I bloody want you," Tarquin murmured against Chris' mouth, then kissed him again, more passionately than before. More passionately than he'd ever kissed anybody, maybe, this forbidden embrace filling him with a tingling electricity. But he had an invitation to deliver. The last thing they wanted was Petunia knocking at that French window, her stabbed camembert clutched in her hand.

"Have me." Chris roamed his lips over Tarquin's jaw. "Take me."

Tarquin groaned with frustrated lust. "After dinner, perhaps? Please, you will come to dinner?"

"Dinner's now?" The surprise in Chris' voice was understandable, but if he refused, Petunia would be roasting Tarquin alongside her famed beef Wellington. "You want me to come to dinner tonight?"

"Will you?" The squire melted away, replaced by *good ol' Tarkers* instead. "We were going to have claret, but Petunia insisted she didn't want it, and she stuck a knife in the camembert, and I scared the dogs with a tablecloth, and there's footprints in the cellar, and she'll kill me if you don't come."

"'Course I'll come for you. I'm all done with hammering for the night."

Thank God he said yes.

And the fruits of Chris' labors — though Tarquin hadn't expected his Canary Wharf captain to be doing the work himself — were obvious. Gone were the dusty, threadbare furnishings that Hardacre had refused to replace despite his wealth, and in their place was comfort, vivid throws and deep cushions, the faded paintings on the walls replaced with vibrant scenes that Tarquin recognized as the Georgian paintings of Bough Bottoms that had once been hidden by a patina of dust.

The antique furniture that was so much a part of the place was still here, but it was polished and bright, loved once more instead of just tolerated because it was worth money. All the many generations of Hardacres who had lived and loved in Hardacre Grange would surely be looking down and smiling, because for the first time in more decades than Tarquin knew, the place was alive again. Not a moldering den of malice owned by a curiously hedonistic Scrooge, but a place that was filled with joy. The house suited the man who now lived here, just as the dark, forbidding interior he had swept away had suited his late uncle. It was still the Grange, but it was Christopher Hardacre's Grange.

"Can you spare me ten minutes to have a shower and throw some clean clothes on?" Chris kissed Tarquin's cheek. "I've got something for you too. I was going to bring it over tomorrow and ask if we were still mates."

Chris. In the shower.

"Oh—sorry. Mind wandered off there. Yes, do hop in the shower. I won't watch, promise!" Tarquin said. "Erm…a present? Well, that's very kind."

"If you want to watch, come and watch." He kissed Tarquin's nose. "You can see the house on the way, let me know what you think. I hope you don't hate it, I've put my heart and soul into this place—I didn't realize I might not get to keep it!"

"I'd very much like to watch. And I am impressed, you've put so much work into this house." Tarquin held Chris' hand. "Don't worry about the Oracle, she'll come round, I know she will. I just hope she doesn't wreck your lovely floor with her trotters!"

"I'm not just a pretty canary in pinstripes, I like getting up a bit of a sweat." But all this time, the hammering and drilling…that had been Chris? Surely not. Although apparently so. "Besides, it's been a challenging year, I wanted something to take my mind off the markets. I can't take credit for the garden but…yeah. It's not quite finished but it's getting there. Best of all, I get to say, *I did all of this.*"

And *all of this* was quite something. And it was exactly what Tarquin would've expected from him — color and comfort and light.

"You should be very proud of what you've done here — you've transformed it into a lovely home." Tarquin grinned, then assumed the tones of the squire. "I hope you've installed a bally decent shower! I want to see my captain damp and handsome."

"You're going to see your captain absolutely *soaking*," Chris told him as they climbed the staircase. Generations of rather less handsome Hardacres glowered down from canvas at the two men and Tarquin realized with a frisson that they must be heading for the bedroom.

The captain's bedroom.

At the top of the stairs a door stood open and Chris led Tarquin through it into what felt like the promised land.

And the biggest bed in Bough Bottoms.

The room carried the exotic scent of Chris' cologne and birdsong poured through the open window, filling it with cheer. From that same window Tarquin could see all the way down to the river at the bottom of the garden and he pictured Chris in bed, propped against the pillows in the morning sun, his skin dappled with the rays of light. He pictured something else too, two masculine figures entwined atop the covers, illuminated by moonbeams.

"What a charming room!" Tarquin remarked, as he tugged at the hem of his jumper.

"I'd love you to join me but I guess I need to be quick if Ms. Rudd's waiting." Chris kicked off his trainers to reveal his bare feet, long toes sinking into the rug. Tarquin raised an eyebrow and unfastened the top button of Chris' jeans as Chris put his arms around Tarquin's neck. "And I'll be spending all day tomorrow *very* hard at it, if you can spare any of your Saturday to lend me a helping hand?"

Tarquin offered a helping hand right there and then by opening another button on Chris' jeans. "I could always say I need to have a look around and recommend any modifications you might need to make for the Oracle?"

"I like it." Chris stroked Tarquin's cheek. "Who could argue with *that*?"

"No one!" Tarquin winked. "Now, into the shower, captain, chop-chop!"

Beneath Chris' jeans were the most crisp, white boxers that Tarquin had seen this side of a commercial and he remembered again that calendar-worthy vision downstairs. And tomorrow...such promise.

"I don't suppose you ever saw the old bathroom." Chris laughed, leading him to a closed door that he pushed open onto a gleaming vision of white, blue and chrome. "But believe me, this is better."

"I was spared your uncle's bathroom!" Tarquin remarked. "This is extraordinary. And must've cost you a packet! Just keep singing to the pig, Chris, and all shall be well, I'm certain of it."

Chris laughed again, but Tarquin was reminded of his sadness at saying goodbye to his car last week. The day of the tack room, in fact. The day on which everything had changed. Perhaps he was just all done with city show though. He had Beardsley's ancient Land Rover to bowl about in, after all. It was better than nothing.

"If I'd known about this *one month from moving in* clause before, I might have held off on the home improvements. I was here for a few weeks on and off, sleeping in a sleeping bag, beans on toast for every meal, just me and my DIY. And all the time you were next door." He walked past the claw-footed bath to the shower and reached in past the screen to press a button. A moment later, jets of water seemed to be shooting from everywhere, filling Tarquin with a whole raft of fresh *new* thoughts. "I suppose if they chuck me out, I could fight it, but that'll cost another fortune." Chris turned back to Tarquin, one thumb hooked beneath the waistband of his shorts. "Permission to drop 'em, squire?"

Tarquin was grinning so broadly, he feared his face might jam forever in a huge smile. "Permission *definitely* granted!"

"You look gorgeous tonight," Chris told him as he finally kicked his last scrap of clothing aside. "But I bet you know that."

Tarquin had to force himself to speak. His gaze roamed Chris' body. He couldn't decide to what to gawp at first. "I do? I'm just...dressing for Friday night dinner really! Sorry — well, this is the first time seeing you without a stitch on, and can I just say... Good Lord, Chris, you're a strapping chap!"

"A strapping, sweaty chap, I'm afraid." He stepped into the shower. "What's the dress code for guests?"

"I don't suppose you wear corduroy trousers?" Tarquin ran his hand back through his hair. *I'm dressed like a bloody geography teacher on a field trip.* "Smart casual. Throw on a shirt. Just make sure it's seen an iron recently!"

"Well, I actually ironed one ready for my gift mission tomorrow, so I'm good to go." He closed his eyes and tipped his head back beneath the water, letting it run over him. "God, that feels good after today."

Tarquin glanced at the bathroom's fittings, wondering if he really should be doing this. But hadn't he paid to watch videos of handsome men showering, then hastily closed the browser when Petunia appeared? This was the real thing. And a man who wanted him, and seemed to be enjoying the fact that Tarquin was there.

"Lots of soap, captain!" Tarquin demanded, in the voice of the squire. "Get yourself into a lather, man!"

Because you're getting me into one.

Chris shook his head to clear the water droplets from his lashes, then opened his eyes. With his gaze dancing over Tarquin, he took a bottle from the shelf and opened the lid, squeezing a dollop of the liquid it contained into his palm. The aroma was a heady spice, the same scent that Tarquin had tasted on his skin, and now he watched as Chris ran his assured hands across his chest, trailing decadent bubbles over the contours. This was better than any video and it was just for him.

"That's excellent, captain! Impressive work!" Tarquin moved closer and took the large bath towel from the rail. It was so soft, and Tarquin held it to his cheek as he watched.

Nobody had ever done anything like this for him. It didn't seem quite real. Yet it *was* real, because there was another botanical scent as Chris squeezed a pool of shampoo into his palm. He turned as he reached up and shampooed his hair, all the better to show off the rippling muscles in his back.

The finest man I ever saw.

Tarquin said in an undertone, "And don't forget the buttocks, my dear fellow!"

And of course he did as he was told, throwing Tarquin a heated look over his shoulder. Then he brought both hands round to his buttocks, massaging the shower gel into a lather. Tarquin pretended it was *his* hands massaging those buttocks, and he imagined himself there, naked with Chris as the warm water cascaded over them.

All of Tarquin's Christmases had come at once.

"Firm strokes, that's it!"

And he watched Chris's hands move with increased vigor, sweeping and caressing, swirling bubbles across his firm buttocks.

"Do I have your permission to touch myself, squire?" His voice was a low whisper. "Please?"

"Yes, captain, you do. And make as much of a spectacle of yourself as you wish!"

The world seemed to have fallen away now, leaving nothing but Hardacre Grange and this gleaming bathroom, one man so respectably clothed, the other so lewdly naked. There was no Petunia, no dinner waiting, no Pimms and no camembert—there was just Tarquin and Chris and, as they now both knew, their *affair*. Chris turned back toward Tarquin, his erection standing out shamelessly between them then. With his elegant hand still garlanded with rich suds, Chris wrapped his fingers around himself.

"You know…you know when I said I had no wish to see your tilly-tadger?" Tarquin's gaze was now fixed on it, a wonderful specimen of manhood in Chris' square hand. "Did you know I was lying?"

"When you used the word *Grecian*, I knew you were lying." He reached up behind his head and wrapped the fingers of his free hand around the chrome shower fitting, the muscles in his arm and torso tightening with the gesture. Any more words were lost in a soft moan of pleasure as he made a spectacle of himself, just as Tarquin had asked him to.

"Brazen and lewd and marvelous—captain, you make your squire very happy indeed." Tarquin loosened his belt, his roomy corduroy trousers straining somewhat as Chris performed just for him. The water cascaded down over his body and his hand moved fast and hard, his lips parting to release another moan as every moment Tarquin's sensible cords grew tighter still.

"Don't hold back—let go when you need to, captain." Tarquin could have skipped with glee, but he took a steadying breath before he said, "You have my permission to come."

"Thank you, squire," Chris gasped.

As Tarquin watched, his muscles tightened just a little more, the change almost imperceptible were Tarquin not studying him *quite* so intently. A second later Chris' orgasm seized him and his whole body buckled forward, anchored only by his hand on the gleaming chrome fitting.

"By God, you're a glorious sight!"

Tarquin risked the enthusiastic jets of water to reach into the shower and turn it off, then he draped the bath towel around Chris' shoulders. "Let me help up, you dear old thing."

"Was that a nice pre-dinner treat, darling?" Chris asked, kissing Tarquin's cheek and taking the corner of the towel in one hand. "If you're going to help me with the house tomorrow, we might *both* need a shower."

"It was a lovely treat and I'm sure we'll work up quite a sweat tomorrow, hammering away!" Tarquin amused himself toying with Chris' wet hair, which only made the tightness of his cords worse. "I have a slight trouser-related issue to deal with. Erm…"

"*Erm*?" he teased, innocently. "Maybe I can help with that?"

Tarquin wondered if Chris would see that he was blushing. "I'd be very grateful. Not to mention *very* happy!"

"Maybe you could dry my hair? Multitasking at its finest." Chris put the towel in Tarquin's hand then dropped to his knees. He unbuttoned the sensible cords and slid the zip down, gazing up at him all the time.

"You have lovely hair," Tarquin told him as he began to rub Chris' hair. "It reminds me of a field of wheat. You know how the wind stirs it and—sorry, I…I do sound like a right twit sometimes."

"Don't ever say that about yourself. There's nothing twittish about showing some sensitivity." Chris eased Tarquin's boxers down, freeing his erection. "And there's nothing wrong with being sexy in cords either. Do we need to be quick?"

"Sadly, yes." Tarquin had slowed in his hair drying, but sped up now, vigorously rubbing. "But to be honest, that shower performance of yours was so arousing, I don't think it'll take very long!"

And as Chris' full lips closed around his erection, he was *sure* it wouldn't. How could he resist that nimble tongue, the warm caress of that gorgeous mouth?

Ripples of bliss went through Tarquin almost at once and as he moaned and sank his hands into Chris' hair, the towel tumbled to the floor. His hips moved against Chris, and Tarquin gave himself over to his unslaked desires, sighing Chris' name ever louder as his pleasure built. In the late summer evening the squire and the captain had become Tarquin and Chris once more, sharing their secret.

Tarquin's orgasm was so powerful, something so out of place for a man who wore *a nice jumper* to dinner, yet that somehow amplified its strength. This was forbidden and exciting, and Tarquin laughed softly, his legs as unsteady as if he was drunk. Chris laughed too as he rocked back on his knees. He kissed Tarquin's cock and told him, "That felt like you enjoyed it."

"I did – I really, really did." Tarquin offered Chris his hand. Only when they were standing toe to toe again did he allow himself to remember Petunia and her Pimms. They couldn't tarry any longer. "Best get that shirt on, Chris. Oh, and perhaps some trousers as well, although I wouldn't complain!"

And watching Christopher Hardacre dress was unexpectedly hot in itself, because his nudity had been for Tarquin alone. Surely no man ever had a more appreciative audience and bit by bit that wonderful body was concealed beneath fresh clothes and a pink shirt that *must* meet Petunia's ironing standards. And of course, he didn't pay too much heed to the buttons. Just enough to be respectable, few enough to be Chris.

Tarquin kissed him fondly. "Don't bother with a comb – I like your hair like that. As if you've just got out of bed."

"I'm going to save my gift for tomorrow," Chris decided. "Just for us."

Chapter Ten

Tarquin was surprised not to get a pasting from Petunia when he finally arrived with Chris at a quarter to eight. She and Shobna were already sitting at the table outside, the dogs and the pig wisely keeping their distance. But Chris was the special guest, of course, and Petunia was nothing but charming as soon as Chris appeared.

She and Shobna had already had a good go at the Pimm's, which seemed to have put his fiancée on the path of bonhomie rather than fury, and Chris' appearance was clearly the cherry atop that for all present.

And his pink shirt was, by coincidence, the same shade as Petunia's pink dress.

Tarquin poured the wine for everyone and with the butchered camembert in pride of place, garlanded by bread baked in Petunia's mother's Aga in Little Plumley, dinner could finally begin.

Shobna moved her chair closer to Chris'. Her gold halterneck dress and dangling earrings meant she was in Seductress Mode, and Tarquin smiled to himself. *Poor old thing won't get very far there!*

"So you were drilling," Petunia said. "I like a man who's good with his hands."

"I like to think I'm fairly handy," Chris replied. "And that house *really* needed some attention. It's honest sweat for a guy like me, who sold his soul to the stock exchange."

"Retiring to the countryside—lucky you!" Shobna said. "We're very friendly round here, aren't we, Tarkers?"

Tarquin nodded. "Oh, very friendly indeed."

"And there was me worried about the stern squire next door." Chris chuckled. "So what do you farm, Tarks? Great-Uncle B said you had battery hens and unhappy cows crammed into windowless milking sheds, but I'm guessing that wasn't quite true!"

Tarquin spluttered. "Good God, that man!" He shook his head. "No, I have a small herd of Jerseys, a flock of sheep and some cereal crops as well. There's a few chickens here and there, and Vulcan, who you've met. The dogs, and a temporary pig! I farm in a very small way. I've sadly lost both my parents, so I inherited the farm, and other…well…my mother came from a well-to-do family, so…"

Tarquin hated talking about money. He was comfortably off, but that really was no one's business but his. And had someone said he could have his parents back in the land of the living as a swap for the wealth he'd inherited, he would have said *yes* in a heartbeat.

"I'm sorry about your folks," Chris told him gently. "Mine split up when I was at school but…I never saw that much of them anyway. Beardsley was a habitual fibber, he told me that he'd built his fortune on a lie, so Lord knows what he meant by that."

"Fraud, I expect," Petunia said, picking up a fresh chunk of bread. "We see it all the time in the antique trade. Publishing is probably no different!"

"It was so sad when your mum died, Tarks," Shobna said. "She was so lovely, then your dad went off to Japan, and…" Shobna pressed her lips together. Tarquin knew she had to be suppressing a grin, and he didn't blame her. His father's sudden death hadn't been a tragedy so much as high farce.

"Yeah, well, it's what he would've wanted!" Tarquin started to laugh. What the hell would Chris think? Whatever he thought, he didn't ask, perhaps wondering whether he *should*.

"He certainly died doing what he loved," Petunia agreed, dipping her bread into the camembert. "And I'm sure your mum had something to say when she met him at the pearly gates!"

Chris picked up his glass and looked around the table. Then he said, "Go on, what?"

Shobna finally gave up holding back her giggles and held herself as her body rocked with mirth. Tarquin sipped his wine to compose himself, but started to laugh halfway through and nearly snorted wine out of his nose. He dabbed his lips with a napkin before speaking.

"Well…he went to Japan on holiday," Tarquin told Chris, "and he attended a fertility festival, and during the parade, there was a small earthquake. Nothing the good people of Japan would worry about, however. But, oh dear, one of the floats wobbled over and my father was crushed under… Under…" Tarquin guffawed, then reined it in long enough to say, "A giant phallus!"

"A gi—" He grinned and narrowed his eyes. "What's this? Laugh at the city boy?"

"No!" Petunia put her hand on Chris' bare forearm and left it there. "It's true! What a Bough way to meet his maker!"

"I miss the old sod, and I wish he hadn't gone so early, but...it seems appropriate." Tarquin grinned. "He always said he hoped his death wouldn't be boring, and it certainly wasn't!"

"I've never heard anything like it." Chris chuckled, his gaze lingering on Tarquin. "So is your dad the man behind the collection?"

"Sort of." Tarquin sat back happily in his chair, more than a little squire uppermost in him at that moment. "I didn't even know about it until my twenty-second birthday. Dad took me upstairs to this room that I thought was some boring office where he did farm business, and there it was! It used to be a ragbag collection, all started off when a Bough in a ruff was a Groom of the Stool and was given some rather intriguing artifacts by a royal. Grandad added to it, but it was Dad who organized it and grew it, and I'm carrying on the family tradition. I could open a museum!"

"I'd like to see that!" And as Chris spoke, Tarquin felt his lover's foot brush his own. "I bet he'd be proud of you, squire."

Tarquin wasn't sure what his father would make of what Tarquin had been up to, but then, the man *had* been killed under an enormous cock, so Tarquin told himself that his father might not have thought too badly of him.

"I hope so," Tarquin said. "I can show you around the collection later, if you've time?"

"I'll make time." Chris grinned. And Petunia patted his arm, meeting Shobna's eye with a smile.

"In between waving your hammer about?" Shobna indulged in a fruity giggle.

"And wielding your screwdriver?" Petunia giggled too. She squeezed Chris' arm and asked Shobna, "Beef time, Shobs?"

Shobna leaned forward and squeezed Chris' other arm. "Oh, yes! It's *definitely* beef time. Do you need a hand dishing up?"

"Come and help me." She nodded, and though Chris' smile remained in place, it looked a little fixed now. Perhaps he was as choosy about who pawed him as Petunia would be.

As Petunia and Shobna headed off to the kitchen, Tarquin picked up the bottle of wine and offered it to Chris.

"Top up?" Then, once he was sure the women wouldn't be able to see, he mouthed, *Sorry.*

Chris nodded. "I'm fine really, it's just... Petunia's got a hell of a grip on her, hasn't she?"

"I wouldn't know," Tarquin said, as he poured some more wine into Chris' glass.

Chris picked it up and lowered his voice to ask, "A toast to the squire?"

"And to the captain," Tarquin whispered, and tapped his glass against Chris'. "To us."

"To us." Their glasses clinked. "Am I going to have to let Shobna down gently?"

"I'm afraid so. I think she likes you!" Tarquin bit his lip. "How awkward!"

Chris shrugged. "Should I gay it up a bit?"

"Could do. See if she takes a hint." Tarquin frowned as he glanced toward the house. "Maybe Petunia will take a hint too."

"Sorry." He chanced a quick squeeze of Tarquin's hand. "She's not my type!"

"And who might be? A certain squire, perhaps?" Tarquin returned the squeeze, then drew his hand away.

"This gorgeous guy who lives next door," he said. "He has the most magnificent cock I've ever seen. I get hard just looking at him."

Tarquin pressed his finger to his lips. "Are you hard even now? This very moment?"

"Desperately."

"If I come and sit next to you, it'll look odd, won't it?" Tarquin looked back at the house again. "Darling, I'm so sorry. Unless I stick my leg out under the table and use my foot, I'm not quite sure what I can do."

"Come to my place tomorrow," Chris urged. "I need my squire."

Did anyone need Tarquin, other than the animals he cared for on the farm? Petunia didn't, he was certain of it. *But Chris?* Tarquin gazed across the table at him and those blue eyes, which were so much like the sea, drew Tarquin in until he was helpless and happy in their clear depths.

"Then I will, captain. I need you, too."

"How do you want me when you arrive?"

"Dressed just as you are now, with not another button fastened or unfastened." Tarquin tapped his foot against Chris'. "And barefoot. Your feet are gorgeous."

Chris passed the tip of his tongue over his lower lip. "I'll be waiting for you, darling. Shoes off."

"Good."

He glanced toward the house as Shobna and Petunia emerged, each carrying two steaming plates of food. In a louder voice, Chris asked, "Where's the Oracle tonight?"

"She's hanging out with the dogs, I think," Tarquin said. "Once we've moved on to pudding, we could give her a whistle—she likes strawberries! Thing is..." Tarquin watched the plates advancing. "I do feel rather awkward eating meat in front of her."

"Not that bloody pig again!" Petunia scoffed. "Chris, when your thirty days are up I know a great butcher. I bet you like a tasty sausage, don't you?"

How right you are.

Shobna shivered. "It's enough to make you veggie! But I don't think I'd like a pig living in my house. Does she make a terrible mess?"

"Awful!" Petunia grimaced. "And those dogs are as bad!"

"You can't live in the countryside and turn your nose up at animals," Tarquin told her. He winced as he heard the squire in his tone. So he laughed gently, *silly old Tarks* once again. "You *are* engaged to a farmer, Tuney!"

"A squire," Chris added helpfully. "A man of the land!"

"Yes..." Tarquin winced again as he glanced at Petunia. Was she about to bite his head off? But instead she smiled and took her seat in front of her plate. Then she picked up her cutlery and turned to look at Chris again.

"Tarquin isn't my idea of a squire." She gave a hoot of mirth. "I think of a squire being all...I don't know...*sexy*. Striding about in his jodhpurs, cracking his whip? It's Jilly Cooper's fault!"

Just call me Bough, Tarquin Bough — Petunia's unsexy fiancé.

Under the table, Tarquin stroked his brogue against Chris' foot. "So what do I do instead, Tuney?"

"You're a pushover," she informed him. "I mean, look at the pig — any normal farmer would've had her on a full English, but not you, not Tarquin! Obviously the five thousand a month sweetens the pill but… I suppose I'd expect a squire to be a little harder."

"I bet Squire Tarquin can be hard when he needs to be," Chris said. "And I'm glad you gave the Oracle a billet rather than a bullet!"

Tarquin speared a potato on his fork and wagged it at Petunia. "I might not've seen eye-to-eye with Beardsley Hardacre, but he loved the Oracle, and he treated her like a pet. *She* was the one who raised the alarm when Beardsley died by squeezing under the fence and running circles around our lawn. And she's not mine — I've been babysitting until her new owner came to take her." Tarquin nodded toward Chris. "And here he is!"

"Ohh," Chris murmured thoughtfully. "I feel ashamed to admit that I've only just realized *why* the Oracle took against me on sight. She's lost her best friend — her dad, really — and I've come in and started installing hot tubs and hammering and drilling and — I haven't once asked her how she's feeling! Instead I turned her home into a building site!"

"You weren't to know." Tarquin offered him a smile. "She just needs to spend time with you. She's anyone's for piggy pellets and an apple!"

As if on cue, the sound of barking dogs and a squealing pig could be heard, mingled with the roar of a powerful car engine in the driveway. Petunia looked up, annoyance on her face when she said, "Go and see who that is, Tarquin? Of all the times to drop in — chase them away if you can!"

"All right, I'll go." Tarquin sighed as he pushed back his chair. Then he paused. "How did they get round the front? I secured the gate."

"Lucky she didn't wander into the road," Petunia called, earning a keen nod of agreement from Shobna that turned into a grimace when the pig squealed again. "Or we'd be a hundred grand richer and Chris'd be homeless!"

Tarquin jogged round to the front of the house, and there before him was Bryan.

Bryan bloody Reeve.

"Caught you in the middle of dinner?" he sneered.

Tarquin wondered what he meant, until he realized he was brandishing his speared potato on his fork.

"As a matter of fact, yes."

The dogs and the pig dutifully gathered round Tarquin. Bryan turned and pressed his car's remote, causing the Porsche to lock with an electronic blip, then he grinned, showing his luminous white teeth.

"I haven't eaten and I've been thwacking it on the squash court for the last few hours — got to keep trim for the ladies — how about I pull up a plate and join you?"

"Erm…" Tarquin wasn't particularly hungry, and he knew it was easier to tolerate Bryan until he inevitably shoved off of his own accord than try to be shot of him at once. "Erm…yes, why not? Although no talking shop with Petunia!"

He took the potato from his fork and lobbed it at the Oracle, who squealed with glee as she munched it.

"Would I do such a thing?" With that he strode off, waking around the side of the house with a cry of, "The party can finally start!"

Behind his back, Tarquin mimed prodding Bryan with his fork. But at least Tarquin could bring the animals with him into the garden. *That'd* annoy Petunia.

"Look what the dogs and pig dragged in!" Tarquin said, trying to sound jolly as he secured the gate.

And of course, Bryan was already making himself at home. He kissed the ladies on the cheek and shook Chris' hand. They were both wearing pink shirts, Tarquin noted. Of course, Chris was a far more attractive proposition in his.

The dogs trotted up to the table and Tarquin carefully steered them away to the edge of the veranda.

But the Oracle?

"Chris, would you like the Oracle to come and sit beside you?" Tarquin knew Petunia wouldn't have allowed him to have the pig at the table, but she seemed to like Chris.

"If she'd like to," he agreed, and Petunia smiled through thin, set lips. *Tough.*

"I'll get you some supper, Bryan." Petunia pushed back her chair and stood. "Come and see how big a portion you can manage."

"Tuney, can you bring a carrot for the Oracle?" Tarquin shepherded the pig toward Chris. Bryan trotted after Petunia as she headed for the house, already clutching a glass of wine. "Look, Orry, it's Uncle Chris. You remember Uncle Chris?"

Remember his lovely singing, but please don't remember the harness.

The pig blinked up at *Uncle Chris*, her snout wrinkling as she sniffed.

"Hello, cousin." Chris left his chair and knelt on the grass, his hands resting atop his knees. Shobna looked at them, a very wistful smile on her lips. "Sorry about all that upheaval to your house—I didn't know about you then or I would've asked if you minded. And sorry you lost your dad. He was a bit of an old bugger, but I bet you miss him, don't you?"

The Oracle snuffled her snout over Chris' hands, grunting as if she was replying to him.

"Give her a song, Chris." Tarquin stood beside the Oracle, stroking her back.

"I don't think Shobna wants to hear my impression of a strangled cat." He looked up at her. "Would you mind? I need to convince her I'm all right!"

Politely amused, Shobna raised one perfect eyebrow. "Singing to a pig? Well, it's not what I'm used to at dinner parties, but…go on, why not?"

"Do you like Cole Porter, Orry?" Chris asked. He lifted his fingers and gently stroked her snout, launching into a dreamy rendition of *In the Still of the Night*, the melody as soft and smooth as butter. Shobna half-closed her eyes, swinging her foot in time to the music. Tarquin did his best not to melt into a puddle.

And the Oracle's stream of grunts slowed as she laid the side of her face against Chris' knee.

"She does that when she's happy," Tarquin told him. Chris smiled up at him and as the song went on even Bryan and Petunia seemed to realize that this was a time for peace, tiptoeing as they made their way back to the table.

"All right, I'll admit it, that's really cute," Shobna said.

"She's a sweet thing," Chris sighed. "And she lost her best friend, but she found another in the squire."

Tarquin wished that he and Chris were alone because at that moment, as Chris looked at him with those spectacular blue eyes, Tarquin could've kissed him.

"She has a new friend now, though," Tarquin said.

"It's a pig," Petunia announced. She shook her head. "Obviously Christopher makes it all look very cute but…it's not a dog, it's a pig. Bryan, Shobna, come on, would you want it in your house?"

Bryan brayed with laughter. "Of course not! I wouldn't want its snout all over my papers. Must make a mess, and the smell, by God! And can you imagine me trying to a get a pig into the ol' Porsche? Not a chance."

Shobna shook her head. "If I had a pig that Chris was willing to come round and sing to, then I wouldn't mind if she made a mess!"

"I'll sing for you, Shobna, but I only do songs from the shows," Chris said. "Go on, I'll take a request."

"A request?" Shobna clapped. "I do like *Grease*, but do you know any Bollywood?"

He frowned and rolled his eyes heavenward, deep in thought. The Oracle blinked dreamily up at Chris too, apparently waiting for the verdict.

"How does *Badtameez Dil* suit you?" he asked after a few moments. "I drove to Edinburgh with a Bollywood fanatic last year and picked a few tunes up!"

"Oh, go on, Chris, do it!" Shobna raised her glass. "You're a man of many surprises, aren't you?"

"But I'm not going to do the dancing." He laughed. "I've seen the film, I don't have his moves!"

"You've seen it?" Shobna looked amazed. "*No one* in Bough Bottoms watches Bollywood! You should *try* doing the dancing — go on!"

"With a beef Wellington in his stomach and a pig on his lap?" Bryan scoffed as he carved into his generous serving of dinner. "I'd like to see you try, Chris!"

"Oh my God, let's have a dance-off!" Petunia announced excitedly. "We can play the vid on YouTube and the boys can give it their best shot! Winner gets the biggest bowl of Eton Mess?"

A look of wariness crossed Bryan's face, then he set down his cutlery. "I'm game!"

Tarquin shook his head. "I'm a *terrible* dancer."

"Me versus Bryan then." Chris bent his head to kiss the Oracle's head. "Wish me luck, Orry."

The pig snorted and lifted her head, eyeing Chris.

Is she smiling? Tarquin wondered.

"Dance-off it is, then!" Shobna shifted in her chair, evidently in her element. Still kneeling on the grass, Chris took out his phone and soon he and Bryan were studying the video, a riot of bling and celebration and some *very* spirited dancing. They might not have a pyramid of champagne glasses or a glitter cannon here in Bough Bottoms, but what they did have were the two captains of the opposing rowing teams, about to continue centuries of competition in a Bollywood dance-off.

Bryan flung aside his pinstriped jacket, letting it fall louchely over a chair. He slicked back his hair and popped his collar forward.

"Ready to lose, Chris?"

Tarquin tried not to roll his eyes.

"Oh, confident! Petunia, you're in charge of the phone." Chris rose to his feet. "Let's get this dance-off started!"

Petunia clapped and swept her finger across the screen, cueing the video back to the beginning. Then she said, "Shobna, count the brave boys in!"

"One…two…three — dance!"

The music filled the summer night and Bryan and Chris went into battle, one laughing but one, Tarquin noted, taking it very seriously indeed. From the look on Bryan's face anyone would've thought his very life depended on winning the impromptu contest. He seemed to be doing his best, but placed a large emphasis on wiggling his bottom and grabbing his crotch, like an end-of-the-pier Michael Jackson impersonator.

"Watch out, Chris, I'm going to do a spin!" Bryan declared.

"Spin! Spin!" Petunia whooped, clapping her hands. "Woooh!"

Bryan held out his arms and spun round on one foot. It wasn't too unimpressive, as spins went, but he lunged into another dance move at the end and caught Chris across the cheek with his fingers.

With a grin, Bryan said, "Ooops, sorry, Chris!"

But Chris, unfazed, caught Bryan's fingertips and pulled him into his arms as though they were on Come Dancing, making a partner of his competitor. *Or a supporting artist.*

"He's making you his backing dancer," Petunia howled, clapping her hands as the two men spun on the lawn. "God, Shobs, *look* at them go!"

Shobna danced in her seat, clicking her fingers. "They've got the moves!"

Tarquin clapped along, awkward and devoid of rhythm. So he stopped, and wished that he could dance with Chris like that.

Bryan tried to lead, but he wasn't as nimble on his feet as Chris and had to rely on some rather unusual arm movements as if he was swimming on dry land. And Chris was clearly no stranger to Bollywood dancing, which Tarquin wasn't entirely surprised by. He moved with a nimble elegance that Bryan entirely lacked and unlike his opponent, he looked as if he was having the time of his life.

Tarquin called, "Come along, Bryan, shake it, old bean!"

Bryan glared at Tarquin, as if he'd rather shake *him*, then something glorious happened. Just as Bryan appeared to be on the cusp of another spin, the Oracle entered the fray. She shot off from under Tarquin's caresses at speed and ran at Bryan's legs, sending him flying.

"Bryan!" Petunia exclaimed. "Are you all right?"

"I would be if it wasn't for that bloody pig!" Bryan was trying to pull himself up while the Oracle snuffled and snorted at him. Tarquin knew he should've gone to help the man up but he couldn't move because he was doubled over with mirth. And Shobna returned to her wine.

As the song ended Chris collapsed on the grass on his back, his arms flung out to either side. He was laughing too, and even Petunia cracked a smile. Bryan, however, was corralled by the Oracle, who had penned him like a sheepdog.

"Let me just—" Tarquin intervened. With a whistle and a snap of his fingers, he led the Oracle away, and Bryan pulled himself to his feet, glaring at Chris.

"He's got that bloody thing trained," Bryan said.

From his bed of grass Chris called, "Who won? Let the Oracle decide!"

The pig headed back to the impromptu dance area and looked from Bryan, who glared at her as he brushed himself down, to Chris. Who she trotted up to, then circled with an excited squeal.

"Fetch the Eton Mess, Tarks," Chris instructed. "To the victor and his niece, the spoils!"

Tarquin hurried into the kitchen and returned bearing the pudding, straight from the fridge. He plucked one of the strawberries from it, and the Oracle tried to sniff his hand.

"Sit," Tarquin said, and she did so, her gaze never leaving the strawberry. "Chris, would you like to do the honors?"

"I'd love to!" He sat up on the grass and held out his palm, meeting Tarquin's gaze. "It's a juicy one!"

"A big juicy one." Tarquin grinned as he placed the strawberry on Chris' hand. The Oracle's allegiance had shifted now and she stared at Chris. He leaned forward, holding out the strawberry to her.

"Come on, Miss Hardacre," he cooed. "Get your pud."

She sniffed at the strawberry, then the juicy fruit vanished. The Oracle got to her trotters again and nudged Chris' hand, as if she expected to find an endless supply of fruit.

"Another, squire?" Chris smiled up at Tarquin. "She's got a taste for them"

"Oh, go on." Tarquin passed Chris another. "See…you'll win her round, don't you worry."

"Christopher, that's revolting." Petunia grimaced as the pig happily snuffled her second strawberry from his palm. "Fresh strawberries for a pig! I'll serve the *humans*."

Tarquin decided not to engage with Petunia's grumbling. "Look at how happy the Oracle is!" He took a third strawberry and put the pudding down on the table. Petunia dug in, serving up delicate helpings for all.

"This is awfully rich," she said, as though apologizing. "I shouldn't really, not until I'm married! And Tarquin eats like an elephant if I let him, I have to keep such a strict eye on him."

Tarquin caught Chris' glance. "I've got a big trunk!"

"Tarquin," Petunia warned. "Don't be vulgar."

"I met the rest of the rowing team yesterday," Chris told Bryan. "We had our first training session and you lot've got yourselves a race!"

Bryan was still polishing off his beef Wellington and had to swallow his large mouthful before replying. "Fighting talk, eh, Hardacre? May as well give it your best shot, but you can rest assured, you might win the dance contest, but you won't win the rowing!"

"How many years is it that you've taken the trophy?" Chris returned to his seat and took a drink of wine.

After a pause, Bryan said, "Haven't done too badly."

Shobna spluttered with laughter. "My dad wouldn't agree! He says he could beat your team with his eyes shut!"

"You'll have to stream to him in Florida," Petunia told her friend. "Oh my God, I literally said stream. A boat race. Stream!"

Shobna and Bryan hooted with amusement, Bryan's laugh easily the louder of the two.

What must daily life be like in their office?

Tarquin hoped he'd never find out. He'd seen them both behind the lectern in their saleroom and while Bryan went with smooth, oily ingratiation, Petunia was the sergeant major, berating her cornered buyers into bidding on whatever she decided they should buy. He'd almost bid himself a few times, feeling rather like a man facing the hanging judge. Why he'd made a snap decision to take up fishing when Petunia had begun the bidding on antique fishing rods which had seen better days, Tarquin couldn't say.

Well, perhaps he could. *Anything for a quiet life.* The rods now moldered in the cellar with the claret.

"So has it been a shock coming to the rural Bottoms after the city?" Petunia asked Chris. "Why on earth *did* Beardsley leave everything to you?"

"No idea," Chris admitted. "But I love it here already. I've got a river at the bottom of my garden instead of the Thames fifteen stories below. The air's clean, the people say hello and the beer's cheap. It's heaven! And it'll be *perfect* once we bring that Bough race trophy home!"

Bryan shook his head. "Keep on dreaming, Chris! That trophy is mine!"

"Ours, surely?" Tarquin came back to the table, leaving the Oracle to enjoy her strawberry. "No *I* in team and all that!"

"Come on, you're saying that in the company of a city boy like Chris!" Bryan playfully nudged Chris in the ribs. "Bet you've walked over a lot of people to make your moolah, eh?"

"Let's not talk business over dinner." Chris seemed happy, but there was a warning edge in his tone. "It's bad form."

And even Bryan seemed to heed it. "Fair enough. Although…" He shone Chris an ingratiating smile that curdled Tarquin's stomach. "Those Hardacre documents you mentioned… I'll gladly give them a look-over with my expert eye, if you like?"

"That's very kind, but they're at the London office as we speak, in the capable hands of the Hardacre archivist." Amusement danced over Chris' face, and Bryan's expression darkened. "I thought the publishing house was the safest place for them. They're part of Hardacre history and my father's the boss over there so…keep it in the family and all that. Besides, I've heard the squire's collection is far more interesting than mine!"

"The squire?" Bryan raised an eyebrow. "Who's that?"

"Our host. Mr. Bough himself!"

Bryan slapped his thigh, guffawing. "Bloody hell, that's hilarious! The squire!"

Tarquin ignored him and told Chris, "I'm happy to show you the collection, if you're curious?"

"I'd love to. Pierce wrote his book here and my great-uncle made his name publishing it. It's part of my family history too." He put down his spoon. "I'd like to see what might've inspired PA Pierce's dirty book! You know, I found a couple of mentions of a sequel by Pierce in Bea's notes, but I guess that came to nothing. A shame, think of what it might be worth if I'd found *that*!"

"Well, why not pop upstairs with me and I can show you all sorts of saucy things!" Tarquin pushed back his chair. "Follow me!"

And there might have been just a hint of the squire in that lighthearted command.

"Yes, sir," Chris told him smartly. "Show me the way!"

Chapter Eleven

Tarquin felt rather proud of the old place as he led Chris into the hallway, where the large wooden staircase curved its way up to the first floor. "Your house is a bit older than Bough Towers, but this has always been a farmhouse, so they say. It's all stone and wood, and when the craze for covering everything in columns came along, my family resisted and the house remained more or less as you see it now. You'll notice they weren't big on family portraits and that sort of thing, but we've got lots of paintings of animals!"

As Tarquin led Chris up the stairs, he showed him the paintings — the cows and sheep, the dogs and chickens, rendered in oils. When Petunia had first visited, she had treated these heirlooms like a house clearance, pricing up the pieces as they went, but Chris had no such comments. Instead he seemed genuinely interested in the rich history of the Boughs and their age-old feud with their neighbors, the Hardacres, which went all the way back to that first Groom of the Stool. It had been the first time a Bough had bettered a

Hardacre, and from that moment, the families had been thorns in each other's sides.

Until now.

"My family love a portrait." Chris chuckled as he followed Tarquin through the house. "Wearing as much bling as they could pile on. I've got a fantastic Hogarth of my great granddad a few times back, *Mr Hardacre of the City*. Brilliant!"

"I'd love to see that!" Tarquin grinned as he swept aside a heavy damask curtain. "Up this way to the attics."

The ancient stairs creaked under their feet, and Tarquin hummed to himself, excited that he was going to show Chris his treasures. And he was so aware of Chris behind him, more aware than he had been of anyone for a long time. This was how a summer evening was supposed to be spent.

At the top of the stairs, Tarquin reached for Chris' hand and kissed it. "I really hope you'll love this."

Chris touched his fingertips to Tarquin's face and told him, "I know I will."

Tarquin reached down inside his jumper and pulled out the key that he wore around his neck on a cord. He unlocked the ordinary-looking door and it swung open with a creak. The room inside was dark until he felt for the light switch and the space before them was illuminated.

Tarquin stood aside to let Chris see. It looked like a room in an old museum, with wood-framed display cases and artifacts under domes. Still other objects waited for them inside polished wooden boxes.

"Where would you like to start?"

"Why don't you give me the guided tour?" Chris slipped his arm around Tarquin's waist. "I can't wait to see what you're hiding in your respectable attic!"

"A lot of saucy stuff, I promise!" Tarquin kissed Chris' cheek, then took him to the first case, where a slender riding crop lay on a velvet cushion. "Now, see the wood…what do you think those figures are that are carved into it?"

"Tell me," he requested, his arm still around Tarquin's waist as he leaned forward to look more closely. Was it Tarquin's imagination, or did he hear Chris' breath become just a little faster at the sight of the ornate crop?

Tarquin brushed his lips against Chris' ear. "They're Cossacks. This once belonged to Catherine the Great, and it is said it wasn't only used on her horses. I'm sure you know what that means, don't you?"

"My God, if that crop could talk and I could understand Russian!" He put his hand on the case, shielding the slight glare of the lights. "How did you get this? Tell me about this Groom of the Stool of yours!"

"Well, take your mind back to the reign of James I, or James VI if you're Scottish—and you will meet Hugh de Bough. A landowning sort in a small way in Sussex, King James takes a shine to him, and Hugh becomes the Groom of the Stool. Which, as jobs go, isn't all that delightful, but earns you the ear of the king as well as his rear! And earns you…ahhh…where is it?"

Tarquin took Chris to another case. "So here we have a handwritten copy of a Shakespeare sonnet. Or some people *think* it's a Shakespeare. Bryan would give his eyeteeth and his firstborn for it, I would expect. But if you look at the first letter of each line, look what it spells out... GEORGEVILLIERS. The first Duke of Buckingham — George Villiers — and allegedly the lover of the Scottish chap. Whoever wrote it had a thing for George's finely sculpted arms! And I don't mean his family crest."

"My God..." Chris' voice was a whisper. Then he shot Tarquin a smile. "I'm led to believe my arms aren't too shabby. I wonder if I could get a sonnet out of them? And it was a Hardacre who got knocked out of the stool job, am I right? And my family took it personally for about four hundred years!"

"Yes, sorry about that!" Tarquin kissed Chris' cheek again. "And after Hugh de Bough got that job, other de Boughs — and eventually just good ol' Boughs — got roles at court. And that's how many of the items which form the basis of the collection came into our hands. Sorry, I sound like a curator...that's how they got here. My grandad put them in their cases, and my father organized them and started to add to the collection."

"I didn't know that the monarchs of Europe were such a saucy bunch," he admitted. "What's your personal favorite? And which ones have you used?"

"*Used*?" Tarquin chuckled. "Oh, no, I've never used any of them. I've never felt naughty enough. But...but now..."

He drew his fingertip down Chris' cheek to his lips. "Would you like to try something from the collection?"

"Which brings us back to your personal favorite," Chris told him. "But I know what collectors can be like. I don't want to bring you out in a nervous sweat by touching — I don't know — a priceless butt plug that once belonged to Julius Caesar!"

"Well, funnily enough..." Tarquin raised an eyebrow. "My father brought an artifact that for a long time people had thought was a bottle stopper. But…" Tarquin opened a wooden case, revealing a smooth amber cone with a gold top. "Some people thought it was a child's dummy, but it's far too large. So *other* people surmised that it was, in fact, a butt plug. And there's a name engraved on the gold, too."

"Show me?"

Tarquin took two pairs of white gloves from a drawer. He passed a pair to Chris then put on his own. "Gloves on!"

With meticulous care, Tarquin lifted the antique from its case and laid it on Chris' gloved hands. "It belonged to William Beckford. Fond of the finer things in life. And bottoms, too, apparently! See his name engraved in it?"

"And how much would you pay for something like this?" Chris held it up, studying the smoothly turned surface. "It's a work of art."

"Thousands," Tarquin said. "But it depends who's bidding. If only one collector of sensual artifacts turns up, and everyone else thinks it's an elaborate bottle stopper, then it could be picked up for a couple of hundred. It didn't cost Dad very much at all, and he was very proud of it!"

"I'm not sure, all things considered, that I'd put a second-hand butt plug to the test, even one that *wasn't* worth a fair bit of cash," Chris admitted with a soft laugh. He turned it over in his hands, peering at the ornate inscription. "Catherine the Great's crop though… I know we *can't*, but you can't blame a fellow for dreaming!"

Tarquin's mind was filled at once with memories of the tack room. "Do you…you mean, you'd happily be spanked with Catherine the Great's crop? Gosh. Well, maybe we could give it a gentle swish?"

Chris looked at him, his blue eyes wide with anticipation. "Could we? I mean, is that allowed?"

"The previous owner is no longer with us, thanks to the intercession of a whopping great phallus. And the current owner is me." Tarquin pointed to his chest. "So...erm...I suppose the answer is yes!"

"With that in mind, show me the rest of the collection," Chris urged with unbridled enthusiasm, handing the intimate artifact back to Tarquin. "I don't know what those other Hardacres were *thinking* for all these years! Falling back on a life of roguery, gambling and sex when they could've left the first two behind and called round next door for the other!"

"I think your uncle rather envied this collection. Hence all that business about the PA!" Tarquin closed the lid on the butt plug. "Speaking of which, would you like to see it?"

"I was at a pretty low ebb before you hopped my fence." He kissed Tarquin's cheek. "How the hell did I bump into a man like you?"

A low ebb, Tarquin reflected, remembering the fond farewell to that gleaming sports car, not to mention the curious fact that a supposed Canary Wharf high-flier could spare weeks to hide away in the middle of Sussex and bury himself in DIY. He wouldn't ask. At least not yet.

"As it's such an important piece..." Tarquin crossed the room to a rather dingy painting, which at first sight looked like nothing but a gloomy sylvan scene. On closer inspection, though, well-endowed satyrs frolicked with nymphs — and other satyrs.

Tarquin hinged it open to reveal a safe hidden behind it. He unlocked it, then withdrew a rectangular jewelry box.

"It was part of the collection for many years, but was lost. As soon as it came up at auction, I knew exactly what it was, and I had to get it back. Would you like to open it?"

It was another secret shared between them and he didn't focus on the box that Chris was opening with such care, but on his lover. *My lover.* How wonderful it sounded, even though it shouldn't.

My lover, Christopher Hardacre.

"So this is the cause of all the trouble at t'mill," Chris murmured. "Makes me wince just thinking about it!"

"I can't say I'd want one either, but apparently it feels very nice for one's..." Tarquin gazed at Chris, his words gone. *Good Lord, the man's beautiful.* With effort, he finished his sentence, "One's lover."

"Kiss me," he begged, suddenly breathless, "squire."

"If my captain wishes me to kiss him." Tarquin rested his forehead against Chris', then brought their lips together. A kiss in a room full of the saucy ephemera of the ages—it seemed more than appropriate.

"Tarquin!" He heard Petunia's voice from outside. "Tarquin! We're having coffee and Chris must be bored witless, come down!"

Tarquin broke from the kiss and said in quiet, squirely tones, "We'll continue this tomorrow."

"And if you happen to be at the bottom of the garden at nine o'clock, you might see us rowing past," Chris told him. "I'll be at home from ten. And I'll be waiting."

Chapter Twelve

Tarquin wished he hadn't had coffee after dinner. He could never sleep if he drank the stuff, but maybe that wasn't the only reason he couldn't sleep. Because tomorrow, he'd see Chris. And when they should be doing the DIY, they'd be doing something quite different instead.

Petunia was sound asleep, which made Tarquin's inability to drop off all the more annoying.

He pictured the sheep, gamboling in the front garden, and as he did, they began to turn into clouds, white cumulonimbi drifting by, creeping through the house.

Tarquin woke as suddenly as if he'd been shaken awake.

Someone's in the house.

He could hear them downstairs. It wasn't a dog or a pig. He'd heard a human footstep, he was certain of it.

Would Chris have come back to see the Oracle?

Tarquin slid carefully out of bed, but nothing would wake Petunia, especially not now as she began to snore.

He silently crossed the bedroom, but just as he peered around the door, onto the landing, he heard a foot on the stairs.

And no singing.

Chris would be singing. He'd be with the pig. He wouldn't risk coming upstairs, not with Petunia there.

Creak.

Another step on the stairs. And again. Someone was coming upstairs.

Tarquin gripped the doorjamb, trying his best to see in the dim light. He could almost make out a human shape down below.

The squire wouldn't suffer this. He'd whip out his riding crop and chase away the burglar!

Perhaps summoning the squire hadn't been a brilliant idea, as Tarquin opened the door, as if allowing his brave, gruff alter ego to zoom off in pursuit of the trespasser. The door whined on its hinge, and whoever was on the stairs froze.

Then when Tarquin heard their footsteps again, it was in retreat. They crept down the stairs, then the footsteps tapped across the floorboards of the hallway, and finally the stone flags of the kitchen.

Tarquin stood for a while—it could have been seconds, but in the dark it seemed like a hundred years. Then he went downstairs.

Someone had definitely been in the house. Tarquin had gone up to bed after Petunia, and he knew the cupboard under the stairs had been closed. Now, however, the door was ajar, as if someone had been nosing inside. He went into the kitchen and counted the slumbering shapes of the dogs, who had once again proved that they were useless guard dogs. They were all there, and so was—

No. What Tarquin had assumed to be the Oracle was in fact a heaped blanket. The pig wasn't there.

Maybe she's in a different room?

But the doggy door was swinging. *She hasn't been taken, has she? No, how could someone pignap the Oracle?*

Tarquin was out in the garden in seconds, so fast he barely remembered opening the back door. "Orry!" he called. "Orry!"

Tarquin strained to hear—was that an engine? No, no, it was Petunia's snoring. But he strained again and heard…

The click of the Oracle's trotters over the veranda.

The security light had turned on, and there she was, calmly heading back toward the house, with something in her mouth.

Food dropped under the table during dinner, perhaps? But as she trotted toward Tarquin, he realized that it was a scrap of fabric. Tarquin crouched and she butted her snout against his knee. He took the fabric from her mouth and noticed that it was a piece of denim.

"So," Tarquin whispered, "my enemy wears jeans."

Which didn't really narrow it down, but it was a start.

Chapter Thirteen

At nine o'clock, Tarquin just happened to be at the bottom of his garden, standing on the jetty that stuck out into the river. Cup of tea in one hand, slice of toast loaded with strawberry jam in the other, he awaited what he knew would be a treat. The first he knew of the approaching boat was the barking of his dogs as they ran along the lawn, the Oracle in their midst, signaling the arrival of the Bough Bottom Blues.

Shobna sat at the bow, her megaphone held in her lap, but this time the long-suffering coxswain didn't have to gee her boys along, because they were rowing not like a boys' club, but like a team. Perhaps Chris was right and Bryan *wouldn't* walk away with another victory this year, because it didn't look as though the team had it quite so easy under this new captain. The new captain, he thought with a smile, had done some whipping into shape of his own.

And Tarquin's eyes were only for Chris, because how on earth could he have looked at anyone else when presented with the vision of his lover in the boat, an oar in each hand and his gaze turned to Tarquin?

"Morning, neighbor!" Tarquin said, and raised his cup. Then, deciding he shouldn't appear partisan, he added, "Morning, Shobna! Morning, crew!"

Had Bough Bottoms ever seen the like of it before? Chris, in a tight vest, his glorious biceps displayed to their full advantage as he pulled on the oars. And his legs, each muscle defined under the lightly tan skin.

Tarquin set his jaw — the squire wouldn't stare open-mouthed like a brainless twit, and neither would Tarquin.

Maybe they'll row back this way?

A man can dream.

"Morning, squire!" Chris called as they passed. "Nice day for it!"

"Splendid morning!" Tarquin replied. "Keep your end up, chaps!"

It would do no harm to linger on a beautiful Saturday morning, would it? Petunia wouldn't have cause to complain — she'd set off early to flog a consignment of Art Deco teapots and Tarquin had greeted the dawn out on the tractor, putting in the hours of work so he could enjoy hours of fun later. No, he'd earned the right to stand on his jetty beneath the morning sun, his dogs and pig at his heels, and gaze at the river.

And the returning boat, just fifteen minutes later.

"Squire!" Chris shouted to him. "Ready for some dedicated drilling?"

"I most certainly am!"

What a sight Chris was, perspiration emphasizing his muscles. And he would be in Tarquin's arms very soon, enjoying exercise of a different sort.

"I'll see you soon!" The boat sped past, taking its captain along with it. "Don't be late!"

Tarquin waved until the ripples in the river from the passing boat had vanished. Now all he had to do was occupy himself until ten o'clock, when Chris would answer the door dressed just as he had been last night, the tempting buttons unfastened and those gorgeous feet of his bare. What a time they were going to have on this day of forbidden freedom.

Just before ten o'clock—because the squire would be punctual, of course—Tarquin knocked at Chris' door in his finest tweeds, with a bundle under his arm. Tarquin could have been bringing dust blankets or painting overalls, but he grinned as he pictured the bundle's contents in action. He and Chris would both enjoy it, he was sure.

His heart pounded with excitement as he waited, or rather didn't, because Chris was at the door with admirable speed. And he was every inch the city canary in his pink shirt and carelessly just-so tousled hair, holding a white china mug from which a curl of coffee-scented steam arose. He looked Tarquin up and down and smiled, then said, "How do, squire?"

"Very well indeed!" Tarquin stepped inside the house. His brain processed the differences in the place since Chris had overhauled it, but his focus remained on Chris. And what lay under those clothes. "Quite a vigorous way to start the day, captain—are you sure you've got enough energy for what we're going to be up to today?"

"I'm not some bumpkin who spends his Saturday lolling in the haystack," Chris told him as he closed the door. "I've had time to knock the team into shape *and* help myself to the best from your orchard while you were having a good old plow up in t'top field. I bet you were thinking about me all the time, weren't you?"

"Of course I was! I was thinking about how hard I'd spank you for wearing that tight vest in public. And how much you'd enjoy it!" Tarquin closed his square hand around Chris' biceps and squeezed. "It really got my dander up!"

"So you liked seeing me in a boat full of strapping men," he teased. "A city boy like me, waltzing in here and taking over the rowing team? You must be furious."

"I bloody well am!" Tarquin pressed his lips to Chris', bestowing a brief but passionate kiss. "So furious, I'm going to tie you in the silken cords that once belonged to de Sade himself!"

He heard Chris' breath catch at the very idea of it, but he marshaled his braying city boy quickly to reply, "That's what I call a bit of country hospitality!"

"Too bloody right." The sound of Chris' hitched breath sent desire prickling through Tarquin. "Where does a city canary like you enjoy a good spanking then, if not in the squire's tack room?"

"Take your pick, squire." Chris took a far too casual sip of coffee. "Where's your tweed leading you?"

"You showed me your bedroom yesterday — we'll go there." Tarquin grasped Chris' buttock. "Seems like a good place for a walloping."

"Coffee first?" Chris teased, even as his breath leaped with desire again. "Or shall we get straight down to business?"

"I want you in that bedroom," Tarquin purred. "Now."

Chris put the mug down on the hall table beside a vase of bright sunflowers and seized Tarquin's hand.

His feet — bare just as requested — padded on the woven rug as he turned, leading his squire through the house. Tarquin was left with the intoxicating view of Chris' broad back and firm buttocks, and drifted after him on a cloud of anticipated lust.

They climbed the stairs together, heading to the promised land without a thought to the rest of the world. How free it felt to be so able to explore, to discover the shores of this hidden part of himself that he had thought locked away forever. The squire wasn't a character Tarquin donned, but just another thread in the tapestry that he had allowed respectability to dull.

They crossed the threshold into the bedroom as one, their fingers entwined. A ray of sunlight fell across the bedcover, picking out the colors in the cushions and throw in its path, and a new thrill ran through Tarquin at the sight of it. They would have all day to enjoy this enormous bed together.

"Do you think I'm overdressed, captain?" Tarquin indicated his tweed three-piece. His pocket watch glinted on its chain across his stomach. Who but the squire would wear such an outfit, including a silk tie, on a sunny day like this? "Or do you like your squire a little buttoned up?"

"You're splendidly overdressed for a Saturday," Chris told him mischievously. "But I can't imagine a squire like you *ever* lets his standards down, do you? Not like me, barefoot and half unbuttoned."

"Good Lord, no, I wouldn't go scruffing about the place dressed like that. Heaven forbid!" Tarquin dropped the bundle of silk cords onto a chair and brushed his hands together. "You're insolently scruffy, you utter tyke, and it'll only mean more spanks for you!"

Chris took hold of Tarquin's lapels and pressed their noses together. Then he kissed him, fleeting and cheeky.

Tarquin tried not to laugh as he said, "Oh, you'd chance a kiss, would you? Did you have permission?"

"I think you like a little bit of naughtiness from your handsome captain, don't you?" Chris asked, his gaze sparkling. "Do tell me if I'm mistaken, squire."

Tarquin raised an eyebrow. "You're handsome, are you? You flatter yourself that I'd noticed?" He grinned. "And yes, you are very naughty, and I do like it."

"I think you noticed." Chris nibbled Tarquin's earlobe lightly, nuzzling against his jaw. "Why don't you show me how a squire spends his Saturdays?"

"Well, I can show you how he spends it with a handsome city canary type who needs disciplining." Tarquin grabbed the collar of Chris' shirt and dragged him close. "First, a kiss."

This time when their lips met there was no teasing peck, but a deep, sloppy kiss, filled with heat and need. It was the sort of kiss that Tarquin hadn't really imagined outside of films, and everyone knew that films weren't real but...but this was. It was the squire and his captain, his city boy, bathed in the warmth of summer, with de Sade's silken restraints just waiting for them.

Tarquin smoothed his hands over Chris—through that thick hair which inspired poetic flights, across his back and finally over the vee of chest that showed thanks to his barely fastened shirt. He could feel Chris was hard against him, and Tarquin pressed his erection against Chris' thigh, a promise for later.

"I saw you down by the river," Chris said, breathless. "Were you hard for me then?"

Tarquin unfastened one of Chris' few buttons. "Oh, yes. I would've grabbed you out of the boat and had my way with you if there hadn't been an audience."

"You must've been terribly frustrated." He ghosted his lips across Tarquin's face. "All pent-up and raring to go?"

"I bloody was. Then you made me wait an hour — an *hour!* — to see you alone. But then, having the chance to ogle you at your oars, pulling on those two solid lengths of wood." Tarquin opened another button and stroked Chris' revealed chest. "You knew what you were doing. I was impressed."

"You've got me now." He smiled. "I'm all yours."

"Shirt off, not that you were wearing it as such in the first place." Tarquin swept the fabric from Chris' shoulders and let it fall. Then he crushed his mouth to Chris', unfastening Chris' jeans by touch. He felt so strong, so wanted, and it was intoxicating. There was something intoxicating too in the rasp of his tweed against Chris' naked skin, and the realization that underneath those jeans, his lover was naked.

Tarquin had the jeans undone in moments, and without slipping them off Chris' hips, slid his hand inside to stroke Chris' erection. "You're so very big, captain, aren't you? Proud, peacocking sort of chap, with the appendage to match!"

"It's the pride of the city," Chris crowed. "But it's *your* cock I've been dreaming of, squire. Making a million doesn't come close to *that*."

"If you receive your discipline to my satisfaction, then you may just get to see it." Although Tarquin knew very well that Chris would already be able to see its outline through his trousers. A moment later Chris closed his hand over Tarquin's erection, cupping it in his palm.

"Oh, I know I'll get to see it." He stroked softly and licked his lips. "You can't resist me."

Tarquin closed his eyes, savoring the moment. "You know, I could really take my time, but I'm not sure either of us wants to wait too long."

"I want my squire," Chris told him in a low voice. "Hard and hot and very, *very* big."

He wants me. Tarquin nearly melted into a puddle of happiness, but the squire was made of sterner stuff.

"Then that's what you'll get. But not without a thorough rasping first. Trousers off and on the bed, captain!"

What utter joy he felt as he heard Chris' jeans hit the floor in response to the command. Then, with a last kiss, his lover strolled over to the bed and draped himself among the cushions, a very saucy smile on his face.

"Good chap." Tarquin brought the cords over to the bed and began to tie the end of one of them to an upright at the bed's head. "Stroke yourself, captain. I'm going to make sure these are tied firmly. I don't want you breaking your bonds."

Almost lazily, Chris reached down and took his own erection in his hand. His gaze never left Tarquin as he began to stroke, but he parted his full lips to allow the softest gasp of pleasure to escape.

"Yes, yes...that's it, captain, I want you to stay hard for me until I'm ready to spank you."

Tarquin gave the cord a tug and, satisfied that it was firm, leaned down to Chris to kiss him before breaking away to tie another cord to the upright at the other side of the headboard. He couldn't help but notice that

Chris' lips chased his, hoping for the kiss that he was denied, and still his hand jerked, just as Tarquin had commanded.

Tarquin anchored the cord then, with one knee braced against the bed, wrapped the loose end around his hand and pulled. "Mmm…that holds fast. Should stop you from wriggling about too much!"

"You'd like a little bit of wriggling, I bet?" Chris winked. "Just enough to get you even harder."

"You've got an arse made for wriggling—amongst other things." Tarquin lay down on the bed next to Chris, his head propped up on his hand. "Now, are you going to be comfortable kneeling?"

Chris stroked his free hand down Tarquin's cheek. "Very comfortable and very happy."

Tarquin ruffled Chris' hair. "Excellent. So kneel, captain. Arms outstretched and bottom ready."

And of course his captain kneeled, taking hold of one cord in each fist to steady himself as he waited for the squire to bind him. It seemed almost unreal, so perfect was the tableau. As Tarquin tied each wrist, he brushed his lips against Chris' arms, which were now beautifully defined as he strained against the cords.

"Tight but not too tight, captain?" Tarquin tapped his bottom. That earned him another of the little gasps and Chris glanced back at him over one sculpted shoulder. He gave a tempting wiggle of his bottom.

"How do I look, squire? You can tell me, I won't let it go to my head."

"You look exquisite. Debauched and *exquisite*." Tarquin got off the bed and sat in an armchair by the window. He crossed his legs and leaned back, admiring the view. "You'll have to wait, captain. If you're going to look gorgeous, then you'll have to give a fellow like me time to take in the sight."

"You absolute bastard!" Chris laughed. "I love it!"

Tarquin had no idea what he was doing, merely going on instinct. And it seemed to work. "Of course you do. Now, captain — tense those buttocks for me."

And as Chris obeyed, Tarquin was reminded of the shower again, of those assured hands lathering decadent soap bubbles over the buttocks that were currently tensing. Just for him.

"And are those buttocks ready to be spanked, captain?"

"They're very ready." He looked over his shoulder at Tarquin again, eyebrows raised. "Are you ready to spank them, squire? I'm a demanding sort of fellow!"

Tarquin left his seat and stood beside the bed, arms folded. "You are, you naughty thing! Now, what would you like to be spanked with? I'm afraid, in my haste to come over and give you a good seeing to, I left my riding crop in the tack room. Will my hand suffice, captain, or is there something else you'd like me to use instead?"

"Use your hand," Chris purred. "Skin on skin."

"Good. I'll work up a sweat doing this, so it's time for the jacket to come off." Tarquin shrugged it off and carefully hung it over a blanket box. He leisurely unfastened his cufflinks and laid them on the bedside table where Chris could see them, then rolled up his shirt sleeves to his elbows. As he climbed onto the mattress behind Chris, he asked, "How's that erection of yours? No coming until I give you permission, remember."

"I'm not just a pretty face," he teased. "I have amazing self-control. Do your worst, squire, let's have some fun."

Tarquin took a deep breath and brought back his arm. He held it there for a moment, committing everything about this to memory, then he swung his arm forward and with a grunt, slapped his palm across both buttocks. Chris gave a cry of pleasure, jolting forward as the spank landed. He arched his back and begged, "Give me another."

Tarquin rubbed Chris' buttock before slapping it again, a little harder this time. The sound was more like a groan and Chris tensed his shoulders then shifted backward almost imperceptibly, presenting that too-tempting bottom again.

"Very good." Tarquin reached around to Chris' erection and gave him a couple of firm rubs. "And still hard. Excellent."

He cracked his knuckles, preparing for another spank, and delivered it with aplomb.

"Yes!" Chris shouted, arching his back to show off that glorious physique. "Bloody hell, squire, you're a talented man!" He turned his head. "Kiss me."

Tarquin kissed him sloppily and pressed his chest to Chris' back, hoping he would enjoy the rasp of the tweed against his skin. He stroked Chris' stomach, then teased his erection. It never got dull, feeling that warm length in his hand. How could he ever have tried to convince himself he was straight when this…this was perfect?

Chris moaned into their kiss, pushing his tongue against Tarquin's and sending a dart of heat through his blood to his groin. He pushed back again, his toned nakedness pressed to that respectable tweed. Against

Chris' lips, Tarquin sighed, "Do you want my cock, captain? Do you want your squire to fuck you?"

"Hard," he begged, breathless. "Fuck me. I need your cock, please."

Oh bloody hell, I've still got my trousers on!

But Tarquin was wearing nothing underneath them. He unbuttoned himself and let his erection press against Chris' leg.

A shiver of pleasure ran through Chris as he breathed, "Are you going to make me wait?"

Tarquin whispered against Chris' neck, "In a sense. I'm going to ask you where your johnnies are."

"Top drawer to my left." He nodded toward the bedside table. "Everything we need for hours of fun."

Lightheaded, Tarquin went to the bedside table. Chris was quite right — there were enough supplies for a three-day orgy in there. Not that Tarquin had ever attended one.

He prepared himself, then got back onto the bed and ran his hand over and between Chris' buttocks. "You look delicious, you know that? I have a mind to fuck you tied up, like this. What do you say, captain?"

"I say yes," he declared with a toss of his dark blond mane. "As hard as you like, squire!"

Tarquin gasped. No one had ever said that to him before, and his cock twitched in anticipation.

"I intend to!" he replied, and pressed the tip of his erection to Chris' buttocks. As soon as he entered him, Tarquin held Chris tight around his waist with one arm, and with his free hand took Chris' erection. He clung on, wanting nothing more than to be as close as he could to this man, to feel every sensation as their bodies joined. And as they finally became one, Chris gave the most intensely erotic moan of pleasure he had ever heard. It was low and breathless and his back arched again, his body pressing back toward Tarquin.

"Fuck me," he whispered. "I need you."

Tarquin pressed his lips to Chris' neck, and after a couple of gentle thrusts, Tarquin thrust harder, with swift, firm bucks of his hips. He groaned through his kisses, his body tingling with a depth of sensation he'd never known before.

We need each other, Tarquin realized, and he brushed his lips against Chris' ear. "I need you too, Chris. I mean, captain…"

"You're so good at this." Chris strained against his bonds, every muscle taut, every contour defined. "Don't stop— Spank me again—"

Tarquin had never known lust or passion like it. Even as he went on thrusting, he did his best to reach between them and slapped Chris' buttock. Then he paused and said, "Consider yourself disciplined, captain," before going on.

Chris thrust against him, his head thrown back in a transport of pleasure. He sighed Tarquin's name, pulling against the bonds again when he said, "I want to touch you—"

Tarquin stroked his way down Chris' arm to his wrist. "You want me to untie you?" he panted.

"I— Maybe just one?" Chris said. "I just need to touch you."

"I would very much like you to touch me," Tarquin murmured against Chris' neck. He toyed with the knot, teasing Chris a little longer, then unknotted it with one pull. Tarquin stroked Chris' wrist. "Not sore, I hope?"

He shook his head and reached back, tangling his fingers in Tarquin's hair. "You bloody gorgeous thing."

"Darling Chris, you wonderful man." Tarquin roamed his hands across Chris' body, tweaking his nipples before grasping his erection, his strokes matching his thrusts. "I need you, old thing! I really do."

"My man," Chris said, his voice strained with exertion. He was right on the edge, Tarquin knew, ready to topple into ecstasy.

Holding their bodies as close together as he could, each thrust measured and deep, Tarquin whispered, "You have my permission to come."

Chris' head tipped back against Tarquin's shoulder and their lips met again, hungry and fierce. Tarquin felt a ripple run through his lover's body then Chris finally surrendered, fountaining over Tarquin's hand. Chris' bliss seemed to pass into Tarquin and he trembled in every limb as, with one final thrust, his climax coursed through him. He kissed Chris' shoulders as their orgasms shuddered out.

"Tarks…" Chris sighed, stroking Tarquin's hair. "Bloody hell."

"I can't quite believe…that really was us, wasn't it?" Tarquin said with a chuckle. "I'm not having a really saucy dream, am I? Good Lord, that was incredible!"

"Definitely us," was the cheery reply. "And you're definitely wearing tweed. And I'm definitely not."

Tarquin nibbled Chris' earlobe, then said, "Lie down, darling—you must be exhausted. I need to strip out of these things."

Chris sank onto the covers. "Unknot me, Tarks."

Tarquin untied the last bond and kissed Chris' wrist. Gazing at the delicious sight of his naked, debauched and very happy lover, Tarquin stripped off the rest of his clothes. He let them fall wherever gravity decided, then gladly slumped down on the bed beside Chris and hugged him.

"You're all warm and lovely," Tarquin said. Chris gave a happy murmur and snuggled into Tarquin's arms.

"And very, very happy," he said. "With you."

Tarquin was quiet for a moment, his thoughts gathering themselves together once more. He glanced over at one of the silk cords and chuckled. "I think the shade of old de Sade would be very impressed. I know it's naughty to use museum pieces like that, but why not have some fun with them? It's what they're for, after all! And they held up bloody well."

"Precision French engineering," Chris teased. "Built for strapping chaps like us, obviously."

"*Obviously*." Avoiding Chris' gaze, Tarquin danced his fingertips across his chest. "You know, I felt so terribly aroused seeing you bound like that. I've never seen anything quite like it. Ready—*wanting* to be debauched. And trusting. It was very intense, darling, but such wonderful fun."

"I knew I could trust you," Chris told him, tightening his arm around Tarquin's waist. "I don't know why, I just… You're bloody lovely, Tarks, and I don't know how often you hear that."

"Erm…not all that often, I must admit." Tarquin stroked his fingertips down Chris' spine. "I really like it when you say it, though!"

"You're lovely," he said. "And sexy. Very sexy, actually. My sexy, hot man."

"Something else I don't hear very often!" Tarquin said, flustered. "Oh, I'm so glad I found you, Chris. You're wonderful fun!"

"So you really *haven't* let your inner squire out before? Then we need to enjoy getting to know him…and I get to enjoy getting to know Tarquin at the same time."

Tarquin curled a length of Chris' hair around his finger, charmed by the different shades of gold as they caught the summer light. "He's there inside me somewhere, the squire. All the time. But I have to be *good old Tarquin* to the world and, well, I can't begin to tell you how pleasant it is to let the squire out on the rampage!"

"Any time you want to, I'll be here." Chris ran his hand down Tarquin's back. "This is home for me now, if the lady of Delphi agrees to move in!"

"I'm sure we can convince her." Tarquin kissed Chris' forehead then said, "Can I pop into your bathroom for a moment? Loathe as I am to leave you."

"Help yourself. I've got a treat for you when you get back — that little gift I was going to drop round!"

Tarquin slipped from the bed, whistling on his way to the bathroom to freshen up. He didn't normally stride about naked with such confidence, but today was different. Today, the squire had shown Tarquin how to take charge, and how to have a bloody good time doing so.

He heard Chris moving around the bedroom again, no doubt bearing the gift he had teased. Tarquin wasn't sure what it was, but he knew he wanted it. He wanted to enjoy his gift with his lover on this perfect sunny Saturday.

Tarquin headed back to the bed. He was more than aware of Chris' appreciative gaze, which felt like a warm caress against Tarquin's body. "Is that… My word, it is, isn't it? Pudding!"

"It's a scrumped-fruit-crumble!" Chris held up two bowls. "With decadent ice cream, of course!"

"I should expect nothing else than scrumped apples and decadent ice cream." Tarquin took one of the bowls as he got back into the bed. He gave a long-suffering squire-like sigh. "I suppose I'll have to spank you again?"

"What can I say?" He blinked, all innocence. "I love to rile my squire!"

"You like to get his dander up, eh?" Tarquin said, in the most squirely tones he could manage. He snuggled into the bed against Chris, then took a mouthful of the crumble. It was the most extraordinary pudding — the crumble was crunchy and sugary, and the fruit so tart, and as for the ice cream — "But you also seem to be using some very impressive cookery skills to win over the squire too. How did a city canary like you learn to cook like that?"

"Honestly?" Chris kissed Tarquin's shoulder. "When I was at uni I didn't want kebabs and pot noodle every night, so I broke out the cookbooks and started with boiled eggs!"

"Sensible fellow!" Tarquin had another mouthful, and half-closed his eyes in delight as he savored it. "You'll make someone a wonderful husband!"

"Nobody would be daft enough to have me, no matter how tasty my crumble is." Chris gave a gentle laugh and let his head rest on Tarquin's shoulder for a moment. "I have to keep the Oracle of Delphi on side. If I lose this place, I don't even have a car to sleep in anymore!"

"So you've spent — " But Tarquin stopped himself. If Chris had hired a contractor to overhaul the grange, then it would've cost a packet. But he'd done all the work himself. Not that paint and fixtures and fittings were cheap, but surely it wasn't all that much for someone who'd made a mint in the city and was retiring in their thirties. Then again, Tarquin had witnessed him selling his car. Something, somewhere, had gone wrong for Chris. "Far be it for me to intrude, but...I thought you were in the pink. Are you...are you in difficulties? Shares plummeted or suchlike?"

"Oh, you know how it is!" He gave a careless wave of his spoon. "Got involved in a charitable scheme, found out said scheme is looting indigenous treasures across Asia and laundering them for cash... I had a choice, Tarks. Say nothing and get rich or blow the whistle and lose my investment. Unfortunately, tanking *that* fund would unsettle others and cost me a packet. I actually called Beardsley for advice—nobody played the markets like he could—and he *advised* I should count the cash and forget the peasants. I blew the whistle that night. I'm not quite broke, but the days of Astons are done. Having this place to work on was...well, I was shell-shocked. I got here and just started ripping down wallpaper, tearing up floorboards... Sweating, I guess. And it kept me occupied until the clouds lifted, if that makes sense? It's gone down badly with the family too, not exactly *absolutum dominium*. The city's pretty unkind to a chap with a conscience and no cash to splash!"

"Good Lord, I had no idea! That's...well, you're a capital fellow, blowing the whistle like that. Even at such personal cost." Tarquin kissed the top of Chris' head. "You did the right thing, and not enough people do these days."

"I was never very good at playing the markets, but I was good enough." He took another spoonful of crumble. "And I had a reputation for having a bit of a conscience, which I imagine made me an easy mark. The bastards at the top got away scot-free, but I hope they slip up one day. The fund's frozen, they can't get their hands on the cash, but until they're caught, neither can anyone else. I've written that money off — they're probably in Rio by now mocking stupid old Hardacre who thought he was helping preserve, not funding bloody raiding parties! What matters most is that the treasures they stole are being found and returned to their rightful places — that's more important than an idiot's money. You would've liked one of them. Little tiny soapstone fellow with an enormous hard-on three times his size! Belonged to a Nepalese Shah, supposedly. They're still looking for that one though!"

"Well, thank goodness some of the damage can be undone!" Tarquin put his empty bowl on the bedside table and slipped his arm around Chris. "If I can help at all, you just say. And I don't just mean with the pig-wrangling."

"My biggest regret is that I *was* planning early retirement. I wanted to find somewhere in this neck of the woods and — don't laugh — I sort of fancied a little smallholding, a world away from London. Just me and some animals who might need a place to live out their days being spoiled rotten." He reached out to put his own empty bowl safely aside. "There is *something* you can do, actually. Keep the kisses, snuggles and amazing sex coming?"

"I'd be more than happy to." Tarquin kissed a dab of ice cream from Chris' cheek, then held him close. "And I can help you with the smallholding, wherever you end up living. But let's hope it's here — I like the idea of having a handsome next-door neighbor who has a taste for being spanked."

"I was never very good at being a city boy, but I did it because it's what Hardacres do," he admitted. "The only thing that Great-Uncle Beardsley and I had in common was that we couldn't stand to see an animal in need. I bet you didn't know that about Beardsley, did you? He was happy to publicize the boozing and mistresses and greed, not so much the charity side of things."

Tarquin shook his head. "I had no idea! Other than the Oracle, he didn't seem much interested in animals."

"The one time we met, he decided to take me to see *Guys and Dolls* in town for my ninth birthday — thought I needed to develop a love of show tunes to match his." Chris smiled. "Halfway to London we saw a little tabby cat in the gutter, she'd obviously been hit by a car. Well, we both said together, *pull over*! And we took the cat into the Daimler and off to the vet but…oh, she was in a dreadful mess, her leg was broken. We never saw the show because we sat nursing the moggy instead and eventually Uncle B took me back to school and the now three-legged cat came to live here, where I believe she had a long and happy life. She was called Cleopatra, do you remember her?"

"Cleo?" Tarquin blinked. "Cleo as in the Cleopatra Cup Drag Hunt? I thought Beardsley had named the hunt after a girlfriend — not a cat! But goodness me, yes, I do remember the three-legged cat. She used to come over to Bough Towers. I had no idea she was Beardsley's! She lived to a grand old age. And to think she was here partly through your doing!"

"She was! And after our little excursion, Uncle B and I used to exchange letters, so maybe…" Chris shrugged. "Perhaps that's why he remembered me in his will? He hated most people, but maybe he grudgingly respected my giving up *Guys and Dolls* for that little kitty."

"Did he give you updates on Cleo?" Tarquin kissed Chris. "Do you know, you could be right — and it's why he wanted you to have the Oracle. Because he thought he could trust you with his pride and joy."

"He used to tell me all about Cleo's progress and the various cows and donkeys and what have you that he'd lodged with sanctuaries and willing adoptive homes around the country," Chris recalled, snuggling against Tarquin. "But he never mentioned the Oracle. I wonder if he wanted *that* to be a surprise once his will was read!"

"It bloody well was!" Tarquin chuckled. "My opinion of that curmudgeonly old sod is changing, I must say. I had no idea about all this work he was doing with animals!"

"Mr. Driscoll's still unpicking it all. Beardsley was on this charity board and that charity board, all over the world. Not bad for a chap who proudly hated his fellow man." He grinned. "When — *if* — I get this inheritance sorted out, I'm going to do what I can for those same animals. Not exactly the squire's city slicker, but I hope he won't mind!"

"*Charity boards*!" Tarquin stared at Chris, amazed. "Well, he certainly kept those to himself. My goodness, and to think I dismissed him as a rude hedonist! Which he unquestionably was, but the charities... I never knew."

Chris smiled and told him, "I think, though, he'd prefer to be remembered as a rude hedonist, you know. Far more *him*."

"You can say that again." A thought occurred to Tarquin. "Hmmm... Beardsley was the one who insisted on the village having a drag hunt instead of a fox hunt. I assumed he'd done it to annoy everyone, but now I think I can see why he did it."

"I can't wait to see you in your hunting pinks tomorrow for the Cleo Cup, which you now know was named after a legless cat!" He widened his eyes. "Don't let on though, let's keep everyone guessing!"

"I do cut rather a dash in my pinks, even if I do say so myself! As do you, I'm sure," Tarquin said. "But don't worry, I won't say a word about Cleo. We'll let everyone go on assuming she was some glamourpuss who your uncle couldn't resist."

"Perfect." Chris lifted his head and kissed Tarquin. "I'm so glad I met you, darling. And I'm so glad you wanted to help with my DIY."

Chapter Fourteen

Vulcan was in an energetic mood as Tarquin waited to start the Cleopatra Cup Drag Hunt. The lane was crowded with horses and dogs, and people who'd come to see the hunt off. As Master of the Hunt, Tarquin was playing a very public role, a complete contrast to the very private role he had played the day before.

And it wasn't easy to concentrate on the hunt when memories of his and Chris' sordid day of not doing DIY came to mind. It was a wonder he could keep awake, but far from exhausting him, all that sweaty fun had invigorated him. He was the squire and, as Tarquin sipped his drink, observing the dogs and the horses, he felt as squirey as he ever had.

"You could *try* to smile. Look at Bryan, he's sparkling," Petunia told him in a hiss as she steered her horse closer. How perpetually grumpy she had been these last six months, Tarquin thought, and how often he had been in the firing line. "I'm surprised you didn't insist on bringing that bloody dirty pig along."

"Her legs are too short to reach the stirrups," Tarquin replied. "Look at you, eh, sort-of-but-not-quite the mistress of the hunt!"

"But soon," she said. It sounded more like a threat than a promise. "Oh, look at Christopher, back on board Longfellow's Arabian!"

Tarquin tightened his grip on Vulcan's reins. *Chris, oh, Chris, lovely Chris.* He was an extraordinary sight, his figure shown off to perfection by his pinks, and those firm legs against the horse's flanks...

"He's very erect in the saddle," Tarquin remarked with a terse smile. "An impressive ride."

"Morning, squire!" Chris called, raising his hat to reveal a glimpse of that tousled dark blond hair. "Lovely morning for a good, hard gallop?"

"The very best!" Tarquin nodded. "Looking forward to it, captain?"

Bryan rode up alongside Chris and replied, "Yes, I bloody well am." He looked Chris up and down, his lip curled. "Sorry to do this to you, Chris, but I'm very likely to win. Is that okay?"

"Are we in competition here too?" Chris laughed and Bryan scowled. "I rather think the squire might best us both!"

"Oh, I don't know about that!" Tarquin gave his riding crop a nonchalant swing, then tutted at Bryan. "You really ought to be polite to the joint masters of the hunt, Mr. Reeve!"

"You think I *wasn't?*" came Bryan's blustery reply. "Just a little bit of schoolboy joshing with the new boy in the village, that's all, squire!"

"Oh, I'm not the joint master *yet,*" Petunia simpered, earning a quickly hidden smile of amusement from Chris. "Not until that ring's on my finger!"

"Won't be long, will it?" Bryan remarked. "But you look like the Queen of the Hunt already! You look stunning, Petunia. As ever."

Smarmy git, Tarquin thought. Although Petunia didn't seem to mind and was in fact absorbing his compliments.

"Are you *sure* you weren't at Leadbetter?" Chris peered very close now. "Never teased a younger lad and called him *Queen of the Riverbank* for out-rowing you?"

"No!" Bryan spluttered. "I told you, I was at Shillinglaw." He wore a forced grin as he said, "Really must find who this bally doppelganger of mine is before he causes trouble!"

"He was a Reeve too, must be a cousin." Chris shrugged. "But since it isn't you I feel no guilt in saying he was a cheating, bullying little rotter."

Bryan knocked Chris on the arm. "Was he indeed? What a bastard, eh? Not like me."

"Not like you at all!" Petunia agreed. "Bryan's the fairest, best man in our trade. So many shysters in antiques, but not him."

Bryan jabbed his thumb toward his chest. "Honest as the day is long, that's me. Not like this Leadbetter chap Chris keeps chuntering on about!"

Chris gave one of the most beguiling smiles Tarquin had ever seen as he turned his horse round and whispered, "I'm sure it's him."

Tarquin glanced back at Bryan, then said to Chris, as quietly as he could, "Good God! What's the man trying to hide?"

"Maybe he really *has* reformed," Chris remarked. "I'd better let it go, I suppose."

Tarquin patted Chris' arm. "Maybe it's for the best. Put it aside for today, at least. Anyway, I think we're about ready to begin the hunt, don't you?"

"Lead the way, squire!" Chris reached across and gave Tarquin's knee a matey, not-at-all intimate pat.

"Right, off we go, then!" Tarquin winked at Chris. He put his glass on the salver presented to him and took up the hunting horn. Tarquin tipped back his head and blew.

The drag hunt had begun.

The horses thundered down the lane after the dogs and off into one of Tarquin's own fields as the supporters gave a cheer of motivation. Chris was there at Tarquin's side as they retrod the steps of their steeplechase, the sound of barking and galloping hooves filling the air. He'd done it. He was Master of the Lower Bough Hunt and at his elbow was the most handsome man he had ever met, the man he wanted more than anything. And Christopher Hardacre wanted him too.

Dust kicked up by the horses' hooves stung Tarquin's eyes and pitted his face, but still he rode on, Vulcan more than equal to the task. They jumped over a fence and Vulcan didn't lose his footing, and Chris landed safely too.

If we can do this, couldn't we – Isn't there a chance that we –

Tarquin's memories of yesterday came flooding back and he forced the images away. He'd think about them later, not now, but still the temptation was there. The pull on the silk cords, the tensing of Chris' muscles and the joining of their bodies were distracting images that appeared in his mind unbidden.

Focus, Tarquin!

But Tarquin was sure that even the squire would allow his thoughts to wander into bedrooms and tack rooms if a man like the captain would be waiting for him.

The dogs suddenly gave a pack-wide chorus of excited barks and streamed off toward the trees. From somewhere behind him Tarquin heard Petunia bemoan, "Oh for a real fox to really *tear* into! I miss the good old days!"

"We could always set the dogs chasing you next time, Ms. Rudd," Chris called with guileless cheer. "If you're so desperate for live quarry!"

Tarquin cupped one hand around his mouth and shouted, "Tally-ho!"

He caught Chris' quick glance and in it saw such affection that it almost bowled him over. But he forced himself to focus as they sailed over hedge after hedge, chasing the hounds toward the horizon.

Tarquin was so happy at that moment, with Chris there beside him, and he turned his head to smile at him. Only to see Chris' horse rear up as Bryan came galloping by.

"I'm winning! I told you!" Bryan yelled.

His cry of jubilation was drowned out by Oscar's whinny as horse and rider were flung into the thorn-studded hedge that rose up on either side of the wooden gate which the horses were jumping, but Tarquin had no thought for the hunt. Instead he saw only his lover as Oscar bucked forward, sending Chris sailing into the fearsome tangle of branches.

Tarquin watched the dogs' whip-like tails up ahead, knowing they were nearing the hunt's end, but he couldn't leave Chris. He pulled up and let the other riders pass.

"Reeve!" Longfellow bellowed in fury as he galloped past in pursuit. "What the devil! Reeve, that's my bloody horse, you cheating bloody bastard!"

Bryan? He's done this?

Tarquin dismounted Vulcan and hooked his reins over the gatepost, then pulled at the thorny branches, trying to reach Chris. "Are you hurt, Chris? Answer me, please, for God's sake!"

"Only my pride and a few scratches," Chris gasped, emerging from the thorns with a wince. "How's Oscar?"

"In one piece!" Longfellow called from the other side of the hedge. He trotted to the gate and opened it, leading Chris' steed through. "Did you see what happened? Did you? The bloody little worm! Typical Upper Bough bastard! He'll not get my custom again at his bloody auctions!"

"Lean on me, Chris." Tarquin put his arm around Chris. He looked up at Longfellow. "What did Bryan bloody well do? I was ahead of him, all I saw was poor Oscar rearing up. Did he hurt the horse?"

"Oscar's a hardy lad, but he's thrown a shoe so he's out of the hunt for today." He patted the riderless horse on its neck. Chris sank against Tarquin and unbuckled his hat. "Bloody Reeve has to turn everything into a competition, always has. He let Oscar have it with his whip, right on the rump! No doubt he'll claim an accident, but I know what I saw."

"Oh, hell, I'm sorry, old boy!" Tarquin shook his head. "Some hunt master I am! I'll speak to him. Chris, do you want to carry on—you can have Vulcan if you like—or would you rather go home and clean up?"

"You go and rejoin the hunt," Chris said. "I'll be fine. Just need a hot shower to soothe away my aches. If I thought he was Aubrey before, I know it now. He holed my boat at school, nearly bloody drowned me!"

"I'll get Oscar home," Longfellow decided. "Reeve deserves a bloody good thrashing!"

"He bloody well does. Thanks, Longy." Tarquin sighed. "And, Chris—I'll help you home. I should've kept an eye on Bryan—this is my fault. I'll pop you up on Vulcan."

As Longfellow trotted away, Chris finally let out a long breath of relief and admitted, "That was a close shave. Few too many thorns in there for me."

"You've rattled Bryan, haven't you? He's a bloody idiot to do that—you and the horse could've broken your necks!" Confident no one could see, Tarquin kissed Chris' cheek. "Right, I'll give you a boost up into the saddle."

"The squire walking?" He shook his head. "You ride, darling, that wouldn't be right."

"I'm not the one with a twig sticking out of my collar." Tarquin plucked out the offending piece of foliage, then patted his saddle. "I won't hear a no, captain! Up you hop!"

Chris kissed Tarquin's cheek and let him boost him up into the saddle, giving Tarquin a front-row seat of his bottom as he did. It always paid to be helpful, one way or another.

Chapter Fifteen

Tarquin was glad to be back in Chris' house, although he'd have preferred it to have been a happier occasion.

"Do you need help getting your boots off?" he asked.

Chris closed the door and threw his hat onto the staircase, then stretched his arms over his head as though testing his bruises.

"You could give me a tug?" he suggested. "Or I could keep it all on and we could go upstairs and make the most of our unexpected moment? I'm only a *little* bit stiff from the fall."

Tarquin took in Chris' pose.

What a figure!

"I—I wouldn't say no to going upstairs. Are you sure you're not sore? No scratches from the thorns or anything?"

"I imagine one or two, but I'll survive." Chris grinned and reached to take Tarquin's hand. "Being alone with you is worth a few scratches!"

"Lucky old us!" Tarquin brought their joined hands to his lips and kissed them. "Gosh, I'm all dusty, aren't I? What a mess! I hope I don't ruin your new carpet."

Chris drew Tarquin closer and whispered, "What's a bit of dust between lovers?"

Tarquin brushed his mouth over Chris' then replied, "An excuse to have shower?"

"Sorry for dragging you away from your hunt, squire." Chris' voice shifted into that slightly more plummy tone, the bray that he had first heard from the hot tub in what seemed like another lifetime. "Took my eye off the horizon so I could have a good look at that arse of yours!"

"I suppose I should apologize for having a godlike rump, but by Jove, I refuse!" Tarquin guffawed like the squire. "Because you love it, captain."

Chris tossed his hair and said breezily, "It's nice enough, I suppose, for a rural arse! Very shapely considering you sit on a tractor all day chewing a piece of straw."

Tarquin slapped his thigh and the sound of hand against flank reverberated around the hallway. "I'll have you know I chew straw in a robust, manly fashion. You'd swoon away to see me do it, you Canary Wharf canary!"

"Sitting in your combine harvester," he teased, "counting sheep and baling hay!"

"And thinking about my next opportunity to tie you up and spank you." Tarquin nibbled Chris' earlobe, then dragged his lips over Chris' throat. "Then give you the best fuck you've ever had."

He felt the quickening of his lover's pulse beneath his lips. Chris tipped his head back a little and asked, "Upstairs, squire?"

"Yes — quick — before I burst through my jodhs!" Tarquin chuckled. He let Chris lead him up the staircase past those painted Hardacres, that gorgeous jodhpur-clad arse tantalizingly in his reach.

Off to the promised land again.

Naughty, forbidden, wonderful fun awaited, and Tarquin almost rubbed his hands together with glee. Once they were at the top of the stairs, he gave Chris' arse a slap.

"Into the bathroom with you, captain!"

Chris gave a wiggle of his bottom in reply and together they almost tumbled into the bathroom, the fall forgotten.

Tarquin pulled Chris into his arms, kissing him as deeply as he could as he gripped his buttocks through his jodhpurs. Was there anything better for framing a perfect bottom than the clinging fabric of jodhs?

Chris groaned into the kiss, pressing his hips to Tarquin's. His hands slid down over Tarquin's back, possessive and fierce. Tarquin reached between them and roughly unbuttoned Chris' jacket, then pushed it off his shoulders. He plucked the pin from Chris' stock then kissed his way around Chris' exposed neck.

There was something almost forbidden in the curve of Chris' throat when he let his head roll back, his arched neck a perfect, classic line for Tarquin to explore and enjoy. And he knew then that he could happily spend a lifetime exploring the planes of Chris' body, not to mention sharing dishes of homemade crumble in bed. He had been enchanted.

Chris' cologne seemed to fill the room — that and the scent of their warm skin. Tarquin unbuttoned Chris' shirt and let it fall to the floor before he stroked the muscles of Chris' back and those strong shoulders.

How had they ended up here? How was he, a pillar of village society, standing fully dressed with a half-naked man in his embrace? A half-naked man whose jodhpurs were even now straining to contain his erection, in fact.

"Boots off, captain," Tarquin ordered, his voice thick with desire. With just a touch of studied insouciance Chris sank to sit on the edge of the gleaming bath and lifted one leg.

"Give me a tug, squire?"

Tarquin took the boot and slowly pulled it from Chris' leg. Then he bowed his head to kiss Chris' toes.

"Oh, Tarks," Chris sighed happily. "You're bloody lovely."

"I try to be." Tarquin grinned as he set the boot aside. "Next foot. Chop-chop, captain!"

He swung his leg up, gripping onto the edge of the bath as he leaned back. "Yes, sir!"

Tarquin crouched down in front of him, knowing full well what that would look like as his jodhpurs stretched against his thighs. And his groin. Tarquin captured Chris' leg and pulled the boot free with a deliberate grunt of effort. He kissed Chris' toes again.

"You better not be wearing anything under those jodhs, captain!"

"Nothing," he breathed, gazing unashamedly at Tarquin's jodhpurs. "And you, squire?"

"Not a thing!" Tarquin pushed aside the squire for a moment to remark, "And it doesn't chafe at all!"

Chris laughed and lifted his foot until he could stroke his elegant toes down Tarquin's chest.

"Would you like me to stay dressed a little bit longer?" Tarquin circled his fingertip against Chris' ankle. He cocked his head to one side and gazed at Tarquin for a long moment.

"I want whatever you want," he said eventually. "Is that very soppy of me?"

Tarquin kissed Chris' foot. "I want to get into that shower with you and give you a good scrub. And make sure you haven't got any horrid scratches or bruises."

"So let's get you out of those gorgeous clothes?" Chris lowered his feet and stood. "And let's get into that shower."

* * * *

The warm water cascaded down over them as Tarquin caressed Chris' body, examining him for any sign of injury, even the slightest, from his fall. It wasn't exactly an arduous job, but Chris' fall had really worried Tarquin. The thought of any harm coming to Chris terrified him. Yet there wasn't a mark on his lightly tan skin, not a scratch or blemish. Even so, he would have stern words with Bryan Reeve.

But for now, Tarquin would enjoy their stolen moment together. "Captain, your body is as perfect as ever. Your insolent nipples and your eager cock are hard and ready, I see!"

"My nipples were never more insolent than they are right now." He grinned, reaching back to slide his arm around Tarquin's waist. "What're you going to do about it, squire?"

"Give you a good, hard fuck." Tarquin pressed his erection against Chris' buttock. "You'd like that, wouldn't you?"

"I'd love it," Chris purred. With a moan he ground back against Tarquin's cock while his fingertips teased between Tarquin's buttocks. He turned his head and sighed. "You know how to keep a demanding captain like me *very* happy."

Tarquin kissed Chris' cheek then, because he was a little embarrassed, whispered, "I want you to beg me."

Perhaps there was something ironic about begging to be begged, but Tarquin couldn't help asking.

And Chris paused. It was only for a second but to Tarquin it felt like hours, an interminable interlude as he waited for his lover's response. Had he misunderstood their relationship so badly?

But as Chris reached out for the bottle of shower gel, Tarquin's anxieties melted away.

"You want me to beg, squire?" Chris opened the lid and squeezed the bottle, pouring a sensuous slick of gel over his chest. Then he began to massage it into his skin, lathering thick bubbles over those contoured muscles. "Is that what you'd like?"

"Yes — please." Tarquin's voice was hoarse with need. "Beg me, captain, please beg me."

"Take me," Chris begged. He took Tarquin's hands in his own and ran them through the bubbles, tensing his muscles beneath his palms. His voice was breathless with need, low and heated. "Please, squire, I need you. Fuck me, please."

Oh, God.

Then Chris glanced back and, every inch the frustrating city boy that he played so well, asked with feigned insolence, "Would you like some more?"

A jolt of desire ran through Tarquin. "Yes, more, please, more!"

"You're so big," he sighed, sliding Tarquin's hands over his nipples with a moan of desire. *This* wasn't an act, Tarquin knew, it was only the city boy's insolence that was part of the game. "I want you to take me. I want you to fuck me as hard as you can, to hold me down and have me."

"Captain, I will!" Tarquin reached for the condom that he'd sensibly brought into the shower with them and discreetly placed on the soap tray with a tube of lubricant. "Hands on the tiles while I ready myself."

Chris reached out and put his palms flat on the tiles. Even as Tarquin prepared himself, he could see that his lover was peacocking again, making the best of his water-slicked skin as he subtly tensed for him. *It's fair to say Bryan hadn't intended this when he sent Chris flying into that hedge.*

"You're a splendid sight, captain! The perfect man for your squire!"

Tarquin held Chris around the waist with one strong arm and wrapped Chris' erection in his other hand as he slowly entered him. Tarquin closed his eyes, overcome by a rush of affection and longing as their bodies joined once again, with lust roaring in with Tarquin's first thrust.

Chris gave a hoarse cry of delight and pushed his body back to meet Tarquin. Then he arched his neck and kissed him in a glorious tangle of sighs and moans. At that moment, Tarquin seemed only to exist to pleasure Chris, to bring the gorgeous man in his arms exquisite joy.

"Hold my wrists." Chris flexed his fingers against the tiles. "Please…"

Tarquin took Chris' wrists and held them tight, pressed to the tiles, while thrusting as hard and deep as he could. How amazing it felt to have this muscular man relinquishing his strength to him, wanting pleasure in return. Every stroke and thrust drew a fresh moan of abandon from Chris' pouting lips and he drove back against Tarquin, their bodies so closely joined that it seemed they had almost become one, sharing the same needs and pleasures, a connection that positively blazed.

"Do you want to come?" Tarquin held Chris' wrists even tighter. Chris arched his neck, catching Tarquin's lips for a fevered kiss before he managed to gasp his reply.

"I need you..."

"I need you too..." Tarquin blinked away the water that had fallen into his eyes, then in a deep voice, he said, "Beg me for permission to come."

"Please," Chris moaned, driving back onto Tarquin's cock. "Please, squire, let me come."

"Beg harder," Tarquin purred.

"You delicious bloody bastard..." Chris dropped his voice to a low, lustful plea. "Please...I need to come. Tell me I can come...you know you love it too."

Tarquin nibbled Chris' earlobe, then whispered hotly, "You have my permission. Come, captain!"

It was like having the most remarkable and inappropriate magical power imaginable, because before the words had left his mouth, Tarquin felt the telltale tremors in Chris' body. He gave a cry of pleasure and bucked hard against Tarquin, consumed by his orgasm.

"Christopher Hardacre, bloody *hell*!" Tarquin cried as his own climax shot through him. He slapped the tiles with the flat of his hand, then held Chris tight as they leaned against the wall of the shower together, their entire bodies softened with answered pleasure.

"Wow..." Chris' voice was dreamy with happiness. "Tarks, you're wonderful."

Tarquin covered Chris' neck with affectionate kisses. "Let's have a lie down. But I can't stay too long. Sorry, darling."

"The Master of the Hunt has to be there for the boozy lunch." Chris smiled. "And I'll be there too, but I'll try not to just *gaze* at you all afternoon."

"Shame I can't have you sitting on my lap!" Tarquin gave Chris' bottom a slap.

This is how a couple of fellows should spend a Sunday. What could be better?

Chapter Sixteen

Tarquin glanced at Chris' bedside clock. "Should head off to the lunch now, I suppose?"

But he didn't want to go. It was so snug and lovely in Chris' bed, with his lover wrapped around him. Who would want to walk away from that?

One last kiss.

He ruffled Chris' hair and kissed him. "My gorgeous captain."

"I'll arrive ten minutes behind you," Chris murmured. "And pretend I'm not desperate to kiss every bit of you."

Tarquin stroked Chris' jaw, mesmerized by the ocean depths of his blue eyes. "We can slip away for a couple of minutes if we can't resist each other."

"Tarks…" Chris sighed with contentment. "I —"

The door, which had been ajar, suddenly flew open and there, her eyes wide and dark with fury, stood Ms. Petunia Rudd. For a moment she was silent, then she said in a surprisingly calm snarl, "We're waiting for you at the pub. Get dressed *now*."

Tarquin stared. He was quite possibly having an out-of-body experience, because it seemed as if he were watching from somewhere against the ceiling, looking down on the scene below. He wasn't scared, but oddly detached. As if he'd been waiting for this moment to come. And now that it had, he could relax.

"You *could* knock," he said as he began to turn back the duvet. "I was just on my way. I've checked Chris over and he's fine, but Bryan—oh, he's in one hell of a lot of trouble."

As are you, you damn fool.

"Petunia—would you give me a moment? I need to find my jodhs."

"I think they're in the bathroom," Chris said helpfully, then addressed Petunia. "I'm sorry, we didn't—"

"I *really* don't want to know." She stalked into the en suite, and a moment later Tarquin's discarded clothes came flying out, hurled with the might of the sixth form medal-winning shot-putter Petunia had once been. "Mr. Hardacre, you're too sore to come to the hunt drinks this afternoon, I think."

"He has every right to come to the hunt drinks if he wants to." Tarquin rolled his eyes at Chris as he got out of bed. He hopped about on one leg as he put his jodhs back on, hoping he wouldn't discover they were inside out once he'd squeezed into them.

Chris looked mortified though, a look that only grew worse when she called, "He's just another typical, lying, faithless, dirty Hardacre! You could do a lot better if you must have your final fling."

Tarquin tucked his shirt into his jodhs and peered around the bathroom door. He flinched back. Now his fear hit him.

Oh my fucking bloody God, she's going to murder me in my bed.

"Not in the man's own home, Tuney! Chris is..." *Gorgeous and sexy and he needs me.* "Is a...an excellent chap!"

Petunia pushed past Tarquin and strode back into the bedroom. She came to stand beside the bed, where Chris appeared to have frozen in guilt-stricken horror, and put her hands on her hips.

"Your pig won't be coming home," she said in a low, menacing sneer. "And on the day you're kicked out, I'll serve her with apple sauce and throw the party of a lifetime. Tarquin, pub, now!"

Tarquin hobbled across the room after her, wedging his foot into his boot as he forced his arm into his jacket.

"She's joking, Chris, just having a laugh!" His voice was tight and strained, a terrified squeak that was a world away from the squire's confident boom. "I'll see you soon — come round for a drink one evening!"

"God, I hope you used protection." Petunia grimaced. "You never know with Hardacres, they could've been anywhere. All the money in the world, no class."

"Tarks," Chris called weakly, looking like a man who was suffering from shell shock, "I'm sorry."

"He isn't sorry at all, Tarquin," Petunia informed him as she seized his hand and dragged him from the room like an unruly child at playschool. "Come along, people're waiting. Can't let the village down."

"No, indeed, can't let the good people of Bough Bottoms down. Duty calls."

Tarquin smoothed down his jacket. At least he'd showered.

* * * *

Can anyone tell?

Tarquin had spent the drinks party smiling when all he wanted to do was hide in a corner and cry. What the hell could he do? He'd never wanted Petunia to find out, never set out to hurt her, but hadn't he realized that she'd find out eventually?

Idiot, idiot, what a fucking idiot.

He chuckled and shook hands and smiled in photos, all the time knowing that inside that shell of bonhomie was a failure of a man who had blundered about in the shadows because he couldn't be himself.

Petunia should never have said what she had about Chris in front of him, but his uncle had been a dreadful man. What if Chris was just as bad? All that sighing and moaning, and that party with his dreadful mates — he was a hedonist.

A rogue.

Bryan had told everyone that his arm had spasmed and he'd accidentally hit Chris' mount, and Tarquin had nodded but he had no idea anymore — what was true? Was everyone concealed behind a false exterior, just like him?

And Chris was so good at assuming his role of captain, the city-slicking canary from the Wharf, the man who *had* to charm his way into the village because he had nowhere else to go. What if it was all one big act? He stood to inherit a fortune if he could convince the Oracle of Delphi to come home, and what better way than seducing the man she trusted?

He wouldn't.

But what if he had?

He looked at Petunia standing among an adoring crowd of her friends, the village ladies hanging on her every word as she discussed the plans for the wedding next year, the petunias in the church, the petunias in her bouquet, the ivory gown with its eight-foot train and the family pearls that would be stitched into her veil. Petunia was normality. She was respectability and safety and a life without surprises or silken cords or the squire. As Mr. Petunia Rudd, he would wrap that fearsome fellow in newspaper and pack him safely away in a forgotten attic, a memory of what had once been.

A memory of what could never be.

Tarquin hung his head. How could he have done all…all those things? The spanking, the tying up, the sex?

My word, the sex.

Tarquin drained his glass in one go. No, he would be *good ol' Tarks*, and he would behave from now on.

Petunia didn't need a squire, after all. She wasn't that sort of girl.

It wasn't until members of the rowing team began to depart for training that Tarquin realized there *was* something worse than being at the pub with Petunia. It was the prospect of going home and being alone with her in her silent, stoic fury. And Chris next door, equally alone, that last sentence unfinished.

I…

What was he going to say?

"Tarquin." Petunia was standing before him, her car keys clutched in her hand. "We have to pop off."

"Righty-ho." Tarquin shook hands with the stragglers who were left and, shoulders hunched, followed Petunia to the car park. She unlocked her shining silver Range Rover, the one that Tarquin had watched her pay cash for just a few months earlier, and waited for him to climb in. Once she was in the driving seat she hit the central locking and turned on the engine.

"We're going down to the river," she told him in businesslike tones. "And you're going to tell Christopher that it's over between you two."

Tarquin lost the protective glass layer he'd shielded himself behind since being dragged from Chris' bed. A shudder ran through him as he shook his head. "I — no. You can't make me. I don't want to!"

"We all have to do things we might not like," was her reply. "You've had your fling. God knows why you didn't choose a woman but your family always were a bit odd, weren't they? I think the best thing will be to pretend this never happened. I blame that filthy collection of yours. We can look into getting it valued and listed. Let's just be sexually *normal*, shall we? Well, not *we*, *you*."

Even as Petunia attempted to crush him, Tarquin folded his arms like a truculent teen and spat, "Any sex *at all* might be nice."

"Well, there'll be none of that until you've been checked over," she replied. "You never know what someone with his lifestyle might be carrying. You could be *riddled*."

"Don't do this to me, Petunia, please," Tarquin begged. "We can work something out. I know we can. Erm...remember the three little words? Centre Court tickets?"

"Work something out?" She giggled, but it was hollow. "Do you want me to pimp you out to Christopher for Centre Court tickets, Tarquin? You're lucky I still want you at all since you've been — I don't even want to think about what's been where. You should thank me for forgiving you, not bleat at me."

"I'm sorry, all right. I'm sorry." Tarquin twisted his hands in his lap, then forced himself to grip his knees and stop fidgeting.

If I don't make Petunia happy, she'll tell everyone in Bough Bottoms. She'll tell the world she found me in bed with a man.

Finally, Tarquin's words flooded out. "I shouldn't have gone behind your back. I should have told you about my...my urges. And I didn't, and I should have, but no one can know. I've kept it hidden for so long, and I never thought I'd end up engaged, I thought I'd be a confirmed bachelor for life, but...but.... Please don't tell anyone, Tuney! I'm sorry. All right? I'm sorry."

"Here we are," she said, as though he hadn't spoken at all. Before them the river glittered and the Bough Bottom Blues toiled, carrying their boat from the shed toward the pontoon as Shobna bellowed into her megaphone on the riverbank. There was no sign of Chris, and for a moment Tarquin dared hope that he was being given a reprieve, that Chris wasn't here and Petunia might change her mind.

"Shobna!" Petunia rolled down her window with an electric hum. "Sweetie, where's Christopher hiding? Isn't he here?"

"Boat shed!" Shobna announced through the megaphone, disturbing a family of ducks. She lowered it and added, "He's on the phone."

"Off you go," Petunia instructed. "Like ripping off a plaster."

Tarquin got out of the car and took a huge lungful of riverside air. He'd throw up if he wasn't careful.

He headed over to the boathouse, aware of how ridiculous and out of place he looked there in his pinks. He would have to tell Chris it was over, but one solitary voice pestered him, telling him he could be with Chris, that it wouldn't be the end of the world.

Maybe.

The door was ajar, and Tarquin was about to push it open, but he could hear Chris talking.

A chap can't barge in on another chap when he's on the phone.

Tarquin glanced back to Petunia's car. He couldn't run off and hide either. But he'd be a gentleman and give Chris a minute.

"It's a lifesaver, if I'm honest," he heard Chris say. "And I think Great-Uncle Beardsley would approve, don't you? Working in the family firm at last, or something like it!"

The family firm.

Hardacre Books, with its glittering London headquarters.

Chris was leaving, then. Back to the champagne and the exchange, away from Bough Bottoms and the tattered remains of their failed affair.

"No, thank *you*," he went on. "I can't wait to get started. Have a lovely Sunday, bye-bye."

Tarquin tried to swallow the bile that was rising up his throat. He knocked on the door.

"Christopher?" His voice was high-pitched, as if someone was standing on his foot in hobnailed boots. "It's Tarquin. I need to have a word."

"Tarks?" Chris sounded so full of hope. He pulled the door open. "Oh God, Tarks, I thought —"

He was silenced by a sharp toot from the horn of Petunia's Range Rover. She gestured to Tarquin as though to say, *hurry up.*

"Goodbye, then." Tarquin held his hand out to Chris to shake.

"What?" He looked down at Tarquin's hand, as though he had no idea what was expected of him. "You can't tell me— Didn't it mean anything? It did to me, didn't you feel— Do you mean it, really? Goodbye?"

"We can't... I'm a dreadful bounder, Christopher, can't you see that?" Tarquin dropped his hand and plunged it into his pocket. "I went behind Petunia's back, and us two—we shouldn't have, but we had an affair, and I've behaved awfully. To both of you. I'm a bloody cad!"

"Please don't do this," he whispered, shaking his head. "It's not just— *Please*."

The horn sounded again and Petunia called through her open window, "Tarquin, come along now, it's time you let Christopher get on with his rowing!"

Tarquin took a step away from Chris. He forced himself to stare at Chris' knees, because it was easier than looking into those wonderful blue eyes and reminding himself of everything he had lost. "You've got a life to live, Christopher. You'll leave Bough Bottoms and...and I have to stay here, Chris, don't you see? I can't be the local village gay chap. I *have* to marry Petunia. And you're...you're a Hardacre, for God's sake! We should never have—it would never have worked, never!"

"I was falling in love with you," Chris admitted, the words landing like a stone in Tarquin's gut, a rock of despair that he already knew he'd never shift. And Petunia tooted that damn horn again. "Petunia's waiting, you'd better go."

Tarquin glanced outside, then back at Chris. "I couldn't have given you what you needed, Christopher. I'm so sorry. I couldn't give you what you deserve. You would never have been happy living in secret—all you Hardacres, you're hedonists. And I'm just a sad chap with other people's perversions hidden in his attic."

"A perverted hedonist," Chris murmured. "Well, that's a hell of a comeback to *I was falling in love with you*. Go home, Tarquin. I won't make your life difficult, don't worry. Hardacre's just a name. We're not the devil incarnate, whatever you may think of us."

I was falling in love with you too.

Tarquin's mouth was dry. He wanted to speak, but no words came. He nodded, then, without saying another thing, he walked back to the car.

"All done," Petunia announced with a look of amusement. "Let's go home and I'll throw a salad together. We want you trim for the wedding, don't we?"

Bloody wedding.

"Whatever you say, dear," Tarquin said.

Chapter Seventeen

Animals always know when you're sad. Better than people do.

The Oracle had nudged her snout against Tarquin's knee as he had stood in the orchard with brandy in his hip flask. He shouldn't be drinking, not before the wedding, not if he was to be trim, not if he was to do as Petunia wished.

But how else would he get to sleep?

It hadn't worked through. Even with brandy and the Oracle's sympathy, Tarquin couldn't sleep. He lay there in the guest bedroom, waiting for the hours to pass, hating himself for hurting Chris. Hating himself because he couldn't tell the world that he loved another man.

Petunia thought he was dirty. That was why he was lying there, banned from his own bedroom. And she'd reminded him, before sending him to the guest room, of everything she had done for him.

And that played on his mind as he lay there in the dark. As soon as news of his father's ludicrous death had spread around the village and the surrounding countryside, Petunia had arrived, armed with a casserole and homemade bread.

Hadn't she been kind?

Helped feed him up. Get him back on his feet. Then one day, she was holding his hand, and saying, *What a shame, such a lovely house, it needs a family in it!* And she had kissed him, and Tarquin had been taken by surprise, and she'd said she loved him, and before Tarquin knew it, they were engaged and Petunia had moved in.

He'd felt so raw after his father's death. Mourning hadn't been easy when he'd kept thinking of that giant cock and bursting out laughing. He'd been vulnerable, going about with a layer of skin missing, like a barely healed wound.

And Petunia…

Tarquin opened his eyes wide. He saw it now, clear as if the noon sun were pouring in.

Petunia had taken advantage of him.

She didn't love him now, and she had never loved him to start with. Tarquin was an eligible bachelor, and with his family gone as if by a finger-snap, she had swept in with her Nigella Lawson cookery books and presented herself as the perfect wife.

But she wasn't. She didn't really know him, didn't appear to like him very much, certainly didn't love him, and hadn't given him time to grieve.

Tarquin threw aside the twisted, sweaty bed sheets and announced to no one in particular, "I can't marry her."

Perhaps it had been the brandy, but as Tarquin scrubbed at his pillow-flattened hair, the squire revived inside him.

"I want my captain. And I shall have him. And I'll bloody well bring him ice cream."

* * * *

Tarquin stood by Chris' French windows, the tub of ice cream softening in the warm summer night. He rapped his knuckles against the frame again, hoping Chris didn't sleep too deeply.

If he can sleep at all.

His heart began to hammer against his ribs as he saw an oblong of light spill under the closed door into the sitting room. A moment later the door was opened and he saw Chris framed there, looking at him across the length of the moonlit room.

Tarquin held up his melting offering. Through the glass, he called, "Can I—would you like some ice cream, old boy? It's so very hot tonight, I *cannot* for the life of me get to sleep."

Chris stood unmoving and Tarquin wondered what he'd do if he turned away and disappeared back into the house. But as the thought of it entered his head Chris crossed toward the French windows and turned the key.

"Promise me," he was saying as he opened the door, "that you're not here to say goodbye."

"I promise." Tarquin hovered on the threshold, not sure if Chris would want him in the house. "I'm so sorry for what happened earlier. I'm not sure I can make it up to you, but…it's luxury vanilla, by the way. With caramel swirls."

"You'd better come in." Chris stepped back, scrubbing his hand through his tousled hair. "Sorry about the paint smell. I couldn't sleep so… The hallway needed a last coat."

"You…you do look a little painty." Tarquin realized he was smiling and stopped himself. But it was hard not to look happy, seeing Chris barefoot in jeans, his shirt fastened with only a couple of buttons. Tarquin stepped into the house. "Got a bowl, or shall we just attack it with spoons?"

"I'll grab some spoons," Chris replied, offering the ghost of a smile of his own. "Make yourself at home."

He turned toward the hallway and flicked a switch as he went. Soft lamplight illuminated the room, bathing Tarquin in its glow. At the doorway Chris glanced back before disappearing into the hallway. Tarquin wondered where to sit and plumped for the sofa. Claiming an armchair seemed presumptuous, somehow. Sofa—that seemed friendly. He put the tub down on the coffee table and hoped the melting ice wouldn't leave a noticeable ring.

"So, how are you?" Chris padded into the sitting room, two spoons in his fist. He held one out as he sat beside Tarquin. "I look a sight, but let's pretend I don't."

Tarquin took the spoon. "I thought…" Tarquin wrestled with his words, but in the end decided it was high time to be tell the truth. "I thought you looked quite rumpled and lovely."

Chris smiled. He leaned forward and picked up the ice cream, giving a jokey tut of disapproval. "Not homemade, Mr. Bough? I'd expect that from a Hardacre, but never from you!"

"It takes a while, that homemade stuff! Days, if you want to do it properly." Tarquin wagged his spoon as he imparted his hard-won knowledge. "Much easier just to nip to the shop!"

"The ice cream I served you with my scrumped-apple-crumble was handmade." Chris dipped his spoon into the tub and popped it between his lips. "By me."

"It *was*, by jingo?" Tarquin grinned. "It was bloody good."

"In the interests of honesty," Chris said, filling his spoon again, "the affair... If you're here to ask if we can pick up where we were, I can't. I'm too selfish to share you, Tarks."

"Ahh, *that*." Tarquin blinked rapidly, before saying, "I don't want to rekindle the affair. That wasn't why I came round."

Chris nodded toward the tub, indicating that Tarquin should take his share. He said nothing though, but skittered his gaze away. Tarquin took a spoonful. He was regretting his choice of ice cream now, as he wobbled the soft mound to his mouth. He swallowed it, then said, "I was thinking. About...things. And I... Christopher, I can't imagine being without you. But I can't...this whole affair business, I can't do it."

And you've got a job in the family firm. In London.

He nodded again, then said, "We're not doing it, Tarks, so it's fine. And whatever I said down at the river... I was emotional, shook up from the fall."

"Oh." Tarquin took another spoonful of the ice cream. *So you don't actually love me.* "That's all right, we were very emotional. I...erm..." So Tarquin decided to make conversation. "When are you off then, or will you commute?"

"You're keen to pack me off!" Chris dug his spoon into the ice cream again. "I might still win the old girl over, but if you'd rather— Look, I care about you. If you want me to move on I'll talk to Driscoll, see if there's any leeway in the will. I don't want to make things rotten for you by hanging around."

Tarquin's hand shot out and clutched Chris' knee. "But I *like* you hanging around. I really do! And I've made a decision. Not that it matters now so much, but... I'm not going to marry Petunia. I lay awake thinking, and I realized something—she's never loved me, Chris. She appeared on my doorstep almost as soon as my father died, and you see, everyone in my family, and all my friends, have only been ever so nice, and... I had no idea that someone would even dream of turning up at one's house, after one's father—well, has met his untimely end under a large phallus, and would take advantage of one being a shambles. And I thought she really liked me, but she didn't. And I can't live a lie. I can't have an affair. I need you, Chris. It's in *here*." Tarquin took his hand from Chris' knee and pressed his palm against his chest.

"I want to be with you." Chris blinked his large eyes, then took his spoon out of the ice cream and gently dabbed a blob of the cold dessert onto Tarquin's nose. "You've got ice cream on your nose."

Tarquin smiled as he stroked Chris' cheek. "Oh dear, will you wipe it off?"

"Maybe." Chris leaned forward and very gently kissed the ice cream from Tarquin's nose. "How's that?"

"I liked that." Tarquin retaliated with a blob of ice cream for Chris. He aimed for his nose but only succeeded in getting it on Chris' lips. "Oh."

"Are you going to kiss me?" Chris ghosted his fingertips over Tarquin's jaw. "Or just cover me in ice cream?"

Tarquin leaned closer and brushed his lips over Chris' ear. "I'd love to cover you in ice cream, but first things first—I want to kiss you."

When he touched his lips against Chris', a rush of memories hurried through him. Every heated embrace and husky sigh, and when he thought of every laugh they'd shared he realized he couldn't go through his life without Chris.

With one kiss, Chris' lips were clean of ice cream, then Tarquin held him and kissed him deeply. For a second Chris didn't respond, then Tarquin was in his arms and Chris' fingers were clutching at his shoulder as if he feared Tarquin might be swept away on the tide, their kisses breathless with passion and need.

And love, he realized.

Tarquin stroked Chris' hair, desperate to feel it against his hand one more, trailing his fingers through it as if counting every strand. The smell of paint vanished and in its place was the scent of Chris' skin, heady and exciting, but comforting too, like coming home. Familiar and thrilling all at once.

And he tastes like ice cream.

"I've never had a home, not really. Boarding school, traveling, trading floors… I want *this* to be home." Chris pressed his cheek to Tarquin's, clinging to him. "I've fallen in love with this village just like I've fallen in love with you."

"Oh, Chris!" Tarquin gave him a squeeze. "I'm so glad you said that. When you told me that earlier, I…I love you, too, you darling man. I can't—I don't bloody want to imagine being without you!"

"And not only am I one pig away from getting a home... I got a job," he admitted, relief and excitement mingling in his tone. Somehow Tarquin knew then that he had been wrong, that whatever this new job was, it wasn't going to snatch the man he loved away. "One of Great-Uncle B's animal charities is based in Brighton... He was pretty hands-on with it right to the end apparently, chief exec on the sly. Turns out they rather like us Hardacres for some unknown reason and they'd like yours truly to take his place! *Continuity*, they reckon. So it'll be a little bit of a commute now and then — maybe an hour on a bad day — but I've always rather liked the idea of working from home."

"Bravo!" Tarquin said. "And do you know, if you can't convince Driscoll that you've won round the pig, come and live at the Towers! I don't even know if that's the right thing to say, but it feels right, so...there we are."

"So, what about Petunia?" He kissed Tarquin again, stealing a quick smooch. "Have you told her?"

"No, not yet." Tarquin winced. "I got out of bed and I...I grabbed the ice cream and came straight over here. I'll speak to her tomorrow. She's put me in the guest bedroom. Not even letting me sleep in my own bed now. But I'm not having that. I know it was wrong of me, to go behind her back, and I should've been brave enough to tell her that women aren't exactly my thing. But... Well, it's over now. She doesn't know it, but it is."

Chris studied Tarquin's face, catching him in that irresistible blue gaze. "Stay the night?"

"I'd love to." Tarquin patted Chris' knee. "And I mean it. I'm not just saying this, then tomorrow I decide it's easier not to get Petunia's hackles up. I'm serious. I love you, Chris, and I'm not going to hide from myself anymore."

"Ice cream, bed and the man I love." Chris kissed his cheek. "Let's go up and snuggle, darling. It's been an emotional day."

Chapter Eighteen

Tarquin woke early, as he always did, and left Chris sleeping. In the early dawn light he was able to finally admire the man he loved and who loved him in return, who even now slumbered with a soft look of happiness on his face, sunlight picking out the golden tones of his thick hair.

But Tarquin had a farm to run.

He scribbled a note — *Farm duties – back soon! T xxx* — and went off to see to his cows.

Would Petunia realize he hadn't slept in his bed?

I don't bloody care!

Tarquin strode toward the house, only to hear Petunia's voice coming from the back garden.

"All that money," she was sneering. "All that money for a bloody pig! After all that I did!"

With the squire in his veins, Tarquin headed through the gate, and —

"Petunia, what the hell are you doing?"

"I should've put a bloody bullet in you the first time you waddled through the bloody door," Petunia snarled as she lifted Tarquin's shotgun up to her shoulder, bracing it against her floral-print blouse. Standing before her the Oracle of Delphi squealed, held in place by a dog lead that was looped through her harness and tied to the fence. "Bye-bye, you ugly sow, hello, *my* inheritance!"

Her *inheritance?*

Not…not the last fancy.

Tarquin's heart raced, but he steadied himself, his hands in his pockets, his stance wide. He shone the terrified Oracle an encouraging look.

Don't worry, old girl, I'll get you out of this!

"Petunia, a word if you wouldn't mind?"

"I'm going to shoot the pig," she announced. "The pervert next door will lose his inheritance and you'll give me the money that the will says you'll get for her ridiculous funeral. That should tide me over until I get *my* inheritance."

Tarquin shook his head. "First of all, the man next door is my boyfriend. Secondly, if you shoot the Oracle like this, I'll make sure you're prosecuted for animal cruelty, and thirdly, *what* inheritance?"

"Animal cruelty?" Petunia pouted, her face crumpling as tears began to trickle down her powdered cheeks. "The pig got loose and I was *so* frightened, Officer. I didn't know what else to do, I adore animals, I feel *so* guilty." Then she smiled. "Beardsley *swore* he'd leave me something!"

But she couldn't be the *last fancy*, not if she'd been the one who wanted the Prince Albert. Petunia was far too sensible to offer thousands for something that was already under the same roof.

Besides, her finger was already tightening on the shotgun trigger.

Tarquin crouched and picked up a fallen apple, which he tossed nonchalantly from hand to hand as if he was limbering up for a game of cricket. But inside, Tarquin was fuming. At least she had confirmed for him his doubts about their relationship. A person who could do this was not someone he wanted to have in his life.

"Petunia, there's something we need to talk about, and I can't do that while you're holding my shotgun. Pop it down and we'll have a chat."

"You leave my pig alone!" Chris called as he hopped the fence. He didn't catch his trousers, of course. Then he held up his phone and told her, "You're on camera, I'd listen to Tarks if I were you."

But she wouldn't, Tarquin knew, because she never had.

The Oracle struggled against the harness and stared wide-eyed in fear at Tarquin, then at Chris. Tarquin didn't like violence, but by trying to murder a pig in the back garden, Petunia had crossed a line and had to be stopped.

He lobbed the apple he'd been toying with at Petunia. Its soft, rotten flesh burst apart as it glanced off her shoulder. That seemed to break the spell and Petunia gave a cry of disgust, then lowered the gun. In two strides, Tarquin was at her side and took the gun from her. He slid out the cartridges and put them safely in his pocket before hanging the shotgun over his arm.

"Chris, would you untie your pig? Petunia's going to be busy now, packing her bags."

"I can't wait," she spat as she stalked away toward the house, leaving them alone. Chris quickly unknotted the lead then sank down beside the pig, softly stroking her head.

"Come on, old girl," he soothed. "No harm done."

The Oracle snuffled against him, her squeals now replaced by contented grunts.

"She likes you," Tarquin said. "She certainly doesn't like Petunia!"

"That's understandable on both points," Chris decided. He ducked his head until his nose was level with the Oracle's delicate snout. "And if your late daddy was *really* carrying on with Petunia, Orry, his taste in women fell far short of his taste in best friends. Don't you worry, Miss Hardacre, because I'm not going to let you out of my sight from now on."

"Petunia carrying on with Beardsley. What a thought!" Tarquin shuddered. "She didn't seem at all sad when he died, but I suppose she was thinking of her dratted inheritance. All she cares about is money. I wish I could have seen through her earlier—and now…"

Tarquin stroked the Oracle's floppy ears and beamed at Chris. "You and me, lovely boyfriend, have a pig to charm!"

Chapter Nineteen

As the days of summer wore on and the Upper Bough versus Lower Bough rowing grudge match grew nearer, Tarquin and Chris embarked on not one project but two. Every free moment was spent together, exploring the loving bonds that they had forged in the guise of the squire and his captain, indulging not just the physical desires that had drawn them together in the first place, but the emotional pull that thrummed between them like a shared heartbeat. Sometimes it was romance and roses, candlelit dinners and long walks through the meadows, and others it was a trip to the farmers' market to gather Sunday lunch, the Oracle trotting alongside them or lazing in the sun beside their table as they passed a balmy evening in Bough Bottoms' beer garden.

Of Petunia, precious little seemed to be said. She was simply gone, disappeared from the life of Bough Bottoms as though she had never been there, and though Tarquin had girded himself for unwanted commiserations and whatever poison she spread about him, it seemed that Petunia Rudd wasn't much missed at all. Perhaps it had been Chris' video that had silenced her before she started, perhaps she was ashamed or even heartbroken, but somehow Tarquin thought not. She didn't seem like the sort of woman who knew what shame was.

But with each minute that ticked away toward the boat race, another minute passed on Chris' deadline to tempt the Oracle home and safeguard his inheritance. The inheritance that might well end up being Petunia's if he was unsuccessful. The elegant pig certainly liked her new guardian and she listened happily to his spirited readings of PA Pierce's legendary *Madam Fanny's Floral Pomander*, squealing in scandalized merriment at the *busting breeches* and *swelling bosoms*, the *delicate buds* and *muscular thrustings*. She and the dogs dozed as he sang to them too, a look of utter delight on the pig's gently sleeping face with every rendition of Sondheim or Berlin, Hammerstein or her particular favorite, Gershwin, and there was nothing she liked more than joining Tarquin and Chris in the garden as the moon rose over the Sussex countryside, snuffling lazily in the grass with her pack of hounds as they shared a bottle of something nice.

Yet for all of that, whenever the Oracle needed a little me time, it was to Bough Towers that she repaired. Whatever drew her there, Tarquin knew, he and Chris had to find it fast and save the Hardacre inheritance from *his last fancy*, whether it was Petunia or some other, possibly even worse, prospect.

"Who's a lovely girl in her crown? You! That's who!" Chris cooed at the Oracle of Delphi, snapping a photo of her in the floral crown he had crafted as they bobbed lazily down the river together in a thankfully sturdy rowing boat one Sunday afternoon. "Don't you think, Tarks? A natural elegance and poise that few can match!"

"She's a beauty, our girl!" Tarquin smiled as he pulled on the oars. "I just wish she'd stop faffing and go back to your house."

She lifted her gaze and grunted at Tarquin, causing the floral crown to slip just a little. The Oracle's snout sniffed the air and, with a toss of her head, the handcrafted headpiece fluttered up into the air and spiraled back down into her waiting mouth. Chris patted her shoulder as she chewed thoughtfully on his creation, watching her as though he might be able to intuit what it was about Bough Towers that had so enchanted the Oracle.

"I'm counting on you, Orry," he said as he settled back in the boat, lounging with a decadence that Tarquin knew would never cease to make him melt. "Unless you want Petunia Rudd living next door and spending *your* inheritance, you need to charm Mr. Driscoll just once and tell him that the Hardacre place is the best place in Bough Bottoms. After that, if Bough Towers is where your snout leads you, Bough Towers it shall be." Chris ruffled his hand through his hair and said casually, "Besides, Tarks, I've been thinking thoughts about the absurdly big Hardacre place. Future plans, and all that."

"Really? What sort of —?" At the sound of a familiar voice barking down a megaphone, Tarquin winced. The Upper Bough rowing team were speeding along the river, Petunia Rudd, would-be pig murderess, as coxswain. "Wait, I'd better get us out of the way — they're going at quite a clip!"

Tarquin maneuvered them toward the bank.

Petunia.

Petunia, who'd slept with the hundred-year-old Beardsley Hardacre just to get into his will and who, he now suspected, might be more than business partners with Bryan Reeve. Why the suspicion occurred to him he wasn't quite sure, but it seemed all too cozy that she had somehow ended up in the front of the Upper Bough boat.

They're welcome to her.

"Let's be having you, you miserable bunch!" she bellowed, hardly needing her megaphone. "Come on, you're supposed to be men! You're not men, you're pathetic little girls! Row! Row! Put some muscle into it!"

"Bloody hell, imagine being married to her!" Tarquin chuckled. "Maybe Bryan will find out one day?"

"Do you think…" Chris' mouth fell open and he watched the boat approach, amusement dancing in his eyes. "If he *is* Aubrey Reeve, it couldn't have happened to a nicer bloke." The boat was steering toward them and Tarquin could see Bryan readying himself for some quip or other, but Chris got there first with a chipper call of, "Morning, Aubrey, nice day for it!"

"Hold water!" Petunia roared and the boat slowed to a gentle glide, the better to allow Bryan his moment in the sun. "You're a bloody shower!"

Bryan, whose face had been red with effort, blanched to a horrible gray. He stared at Chris as the boat skimmed slowly by, then, with a shake of his head, turned back to Petunia.

"He *is* Aubrey, isn't he!" Tarquin whispered.

"We're working very hard here, Petty, darling!" Bryan replied. He was sitting right in front of her and leaned in, his lips puckered to kiss her. Tarquin's stomach roiled with nausea.

"So nice to have a real man," she cooed, pressing her lips to Bryan's. Chris rolled his eyes and the Oracle paused in her chewing to give a snort of distaste at the woman who had tried to blow her brains out. Petunia waved one hand and said, "Too late, Tarquin, this ship has sailed away!"

"Keep an eye on Aubrey in that case," Chris said helpfully. "He's got form for sinking boats when he doesn't get his way."

"Got to shoot off, Petunia? What a shame!" Tarquin called after her. "The bloody cow. Good riddance." He looked up at Chris. "Sank a boat? What the hell happened? You said before something about Aubrey trying to drown people. Sadly, that wouldn't surprise me from Bryan."

"We'll settle this once and for all." Chris took out his phone, tapping at the screen as he spoke. "Aubrey Reeve was a couple of years above me and whatever I did, he was there. My father's very keen on competition, so I was put into every team you can think of at school, and when it came to a choice between studying and training, I was expected to focus on the latter. *Bring home the gold*, Dad would say. And I did. Archery, rowing, shooting, whatever you can think of. And silver was always this bullying bastard called Aubrey Reeve. The boys were all terrified of him — he was a rotten bit of work even then."

He pocketed his phone and stroked the Oracle's back as she went back to her chewing. "And Leadbetter has this annual solo boat race, bloody punishing, and Reeve just couldn't *quite* best me. So after three years of it, he holed my boat. Not enough to go down in one, but enough to cause me serious trouble in the middle of a fast-moving river. I finished it though, came in silver. Dad was furious. Then a miracle happened. One of Aubrey's cronies got caught stealing exam papers from the headmaster's study on behalf of Aubrey and in a last blaze of glory the thief gave up the Godfather in return for the chance to take his final exams before they kicked him out. And one of those he gave up was Aubrey Reeve, who he'd helped hole my boat. Reeve got expelled, I got my gold and my bloody dad never apologized. But rich dads rarely do."

Tarquin had nearly lost his oars, so intensely had he been listening to Chris' story. He gripped them at the last moment before they could splash into the water. "What an absolute rotter! He *is* certainly competitive. I must admit it washes over me somewhat, but he'd always come round the house and tell me how his car was better than mine, his house was better than mine, his kitchen was better than mine, and... He would, wouldn't he? He would've gone behind my back with Petunia just to win her from me! What a load of hypocritical twaddle—she demanded I give you up, she made me sleep in the spare room, and she'd been boffing your uncle *and* Bryan bloody Reeve while taking over my home and forcing me to marry her! Bloody hell."

Tarquin slapped his forehead. He'd been played like an idiot.

"I don't approve of Beardsley's immoral dealings at all, but I hope I've got even a quarter of his stamina when I reach my centenary," Chris said dryly. "All of my old school pics are still boxed up until I know if the house is mine. I've just emailed a few old Leadbettian chums though. One of them might have a picture of

Aubrey they can send our way. Until then it's just you, me, our girl and the river. And that suits me."

"And me as well." Tarquin paddled them back into the center of the stream. "Hmm… Bryan did say he wasn't at the same school as you, but I wouldn't be surprised if he was sent to Shillinglaw after he was expelled. That's Bryan for you — or Aubrey. You don't buy a Porsche from selling old books without primping the truth somewhat."

"And how did I *ever* waste time with an Aston when there was a crazy old homebrewed Land Rover just waiting for me? It's great fun, like being a lad again." Chris laughed. "So, I didn't finish telling you my plan. I think, if everything turns out all right, I'd quite like to try my smallholding. I'm going to have a silly amount of land and there are a silly amount of animals who aren't as lucky as the Oracle, and I think they might like to have a sanctuary filled with show tunes and questionable literature. But if you're my neighbor, I really think you should have the right to say no. Animals can be noisy and if a hungry goat got into your orchard… Well, we could have chaos!"

"I think that's just what old Hardacre Grange needs! I can't wait!" Tarquin grinned. "Now look here, Orry, your fellow beasties have a lot riding on you moving back to your old house. I know you like Bough Towers and the dogs, and I've loved having you to stay, but you show Mr. Driscoll that you're great chums with Chris and all will be well."

She looked up at him then, with a snort, went back to her crown as Chris gave a cry of triumph when his phone beeped.

"Look at the sixteen-year-old oik!" He held up the screen to Tarquin. "What do you say? Was I right about Reeve or was I right about Reeve?"

Tarquin recognized the expression before the face. That tight-lipped sneer, the self-important stare. It was Bryan to a tee. Albeit with a more freckled nose. His face was undistinguished, and, if Tarquin was feeling unkind, somewhat resembled a potato. The hair was cut shorter — school regulation length, perhaps — and a blazer replaced the pinstripes.

But it was definitely Bryan Reeve. Or Aubrey, as he'd once been.

"Bloody hell. That's him! *Definitely* him! What a small world, eh?"

"Squire!" A voice bellowed from the bank and there was Longfellow, his dogs milling around his wellingtons. "Bough! I say, Bough, steer your way over here, man!"

"Oh heck, what does *he* want?" Tarquin mumbled. With only a few strokes, he brought the boat up to the bank, then shielded his eyes with his hand as he blinked up at Longfellow. "Afternoon, old bean! What can I do for you?"

"Afternoon, Hardacre, afternoon, pig!" Longfellow lifted his flat cap for a second. "I was along at your former lady friend's auction house this morning, picking up some odds and ends of brass for Mrs. Longfellow's chimney breast, and what should I see but a little chap with a member you could lose an eye to!"

The mind boggles.

A chap and his member at Rudd Reeve?

"Now, I thought he'd go down a storm in your little collection of naughty whatsits so I picked him up on your behalf." He reached down among the dogs and produced a shoebox-sized parcel wrapped in bubble wrap. "I'd say it's a gift but it isn't. Three hundred quid, Bough, you can drop it round any time before tomorrow. No need to thank me or add a little finder's fee, though I imagine you'll insist. You're a decent sort, after all."

"Oh." Tarquin struggled with the oars, trying to bring them into the boat before nearly losing them again. He stretched his hand out to Longfellow. "Antique, is it?"

If anything, it'd make a brilliant Christmas present for the boyfriend.

"Probably not, but it'll be a talking point." He handed over the surprisingly weighty parcel. "They were keen to see it go. No provenance beyond *Eastern*, but you're the expert on tumescence around these parts."

Chris stifled a laugh, turning it into a cough with no small amount of skill. He hastily cleared his throat, holding up his hand by way of an apology. With the box on his lap, Tarquin squeezed Chris' knee, fully aware that Longfellow would see.

"Chris would know all about that!" Tarquin said.

"Mrs. Longfellow was right!" the farmer declared, triumphant again. "Well, no doubt you gentlemen shall both appreciate the contents of that box then, and I'll say no more on that. A Bough and a Hardacre, is it? Wonders will never cease."

"Is that the only bit of this unexpected development that's taken you by surprise?" Chris asked with a chuckle. "Not Squire Tarks falling for a man, but a Bough and a Hardacre?"

Longfellow shrugged as though it happened all the time. "Well it's not unheard of. Even in Sussex. How do you think Bough Bottoms got its nickname?" Then he gave a nod of farewell and turned, matching off across the field with his dogs at his heel.

Tarquin burst out laughing. "No? That can't be true. Although... Shall I open the box? God knows what sort of tat I'm now the proud owner of."

He unwound the bubble wrap from the box and levered off the lid. Several layers of tissue paper divided him from his quarry, but after some help from the Oracle, who decided Tarquin required the aid of her snout, he finally reached the object.

He held it up to show Chris — a tiny soapstone figure with an enormous cock.

"Erm...this seems familiar, but I've never seen it before."

Chris was staring at it, apparently dumbstruck. He sat up, leaning closer as he murmured, "This is the Nepalese artifact I was talking — Three hundred quid? It's about as close to priceless as it gets. This must be a copy, it can't be!"

A cold shudder went up Tarquin's spine. "How the balls does a priceless Nepalese statue end up in an auction house in rural Sussex? You don't think... No, Petunia wouldn't. Maybe they just didn't know what it was. Someone offloading it, no provenance, looks like something a lad brought back from his gap year backpacking in the Himalayas for a jape?"

"I can't see Petunia being into international relic theft," Chris decided. "But whoever's on the top must be desperate to offload the pieces they've got left, just to be rid of them. When we get back I'll call the coppers and let them know. This could be really important, Tarks. Not just for me but for those communities who were robbed. We could finally be onto the boss!"

* * * *

The police hadn't seemed all that surprised when Tarquin opened the front door and the Oracle trotted up to greet them. They had, however, looked very surprised by the artifact that Chris presented them with.

"Obviously couldn't find trousers that fitted him," Tarquin quipped. Quipping seemed to suit him, and he'd never really thought of trying it before. Chris' influence, he decided.

He rather liked Chris' influence. Loved it, in fact.

Once the police had gone, Tarquin said, "It's a shame that little — or should I say *rather big* — chap had to go. Would've fitted into my collection very well! But I won't have stolen artifacts under my roof."

"And it really means something to the people it was stolen from," Chris told him. "It's their history, and to think somebody just took it and passed it off as a bit of tat— I guess it's better than ending up in some oligarch's secret stash. At least this way they'll see it again one day."

"If there's any justice in this world, Chris, they will." Tarquin twined his fingers with Chris'. "Don't suppose the captain would like to go upstairs for a private view of the squire's collection?"

"Darling, I would love to." He quirked one eyebrow. "And just for the squire, the captain will slip into his jodhs."

Chapter Twenty

Tarquin unlocked the door and his collection greeted him.

"Here we are, captain. My very special private museum."

Chris strolled into the room, dressed for his squire in jodhpurs and riding boots, a pale blue shirt buttoned *just* enough to be decent tucked in at his trim waist.

"I've been looking forward to this," Chris told him, looking around. "The squire's pleasure palace?"

"Oh, yes. All sorts of sordid items live up here." Tarquin pointed out the cabinets as he wandered the room. "Casanova's silk dressing gown, Christine Keeler's false eyelashes—one bat of them could bring down the government—the Hellfire Club cravat with the skulls embroidered onto it, the Duchess of York's tiny jeweled slippers. But I'll show you my most special artifact—Prince Albert's Prince Albert!"

"Can I see the dressing gown too?" Chris drew the tip of his tongue along Tarquin's jaw. "I've always had a thing for silk."

Lust stirred in Tarquin's blood.

In a soft, deep murmur, he remarked, "Why am I not surprised, you outrageous popinjay? It's wrapped up safely to preserve it from fading...but I'll let you have a look."

Chris' hand stole down Tarquin's tweed-clad back and settled on his bottom, squeezing softly. "*Your* outrageous popinjay."

"Come over here and bring that insinuating hand of yours too." Tarquin beckoned him over to a drawer under one of the cabinets. He pulled it open and took out what looked like a flat leather valise, which he placed on top of one of the glass cases. "You may do the honors, captain. Draw back the wrappings and admire."

With great care, Chris opened the valise and peeled back the wrappings that preserved the delicate garment. Below those unassuming sheets was a blaze of orange silk, as bright now as it must have been all those centuries ago. Chris leaned closer and peered at the robe, then met Tarquin's gaze.

"Casanova's robe," he whispered, his eyes wide with excitement. This was Chris, he knew, not the careless captain. "Safely in the care of *another* great lover."

"Oh, I...I don't know about that." But the squire soon reasserted himself, and Tarquin winked. "Of course! It's very delicate, but what a piece to own! Imagine the boudoirs this gown has visited? And imagine the toast crumbs he spilled down it!"

"I wonder if it ever saw a rump as fine as yours?" Chris turned, the captain once again. He grinned and added, "Or mine, even? Unlikely, but you never know!"

Tarquin gave Chris' bottom a hearty slap. "Rumps like ours aren't ten-a-penny, that's for sure!"

He gave a saucy wiggle and peered down at the robe again, his bottom rather prominent. Deliberately so, Tarquin knew. Wonderfully so.

Tarquin grasped Chris' buttock. "You're teasing me, captain... You're getting my dander right up!"

"Are you going to give me what for, squire?" Chris' voice was low and breathless. "How *stern* are you feeling? Plenty of stamina, I hope, old thing?"

"Bloody stern." Tarquin spanked Chris' arse. "And bloody energetic!"

As though Tarquin hadn't laid a finger on him, Chris took his time wrapping the silken robe again. He began to whistle a carefree tune, wiggling his bottom again as he closed the valise and fastened it safely. Then he glanced back at Tarquin and asked, "Did I feel a tap?"

Tarquin put the precious garment back in its drawer. He stroked Chris' bottom, then said, "You'd feel it sting properly if I yanked down your jodhs."

"Maybe," he teased. With a wink for Tarquin, he sauntered across the room and rested one elbow on the conspicuously grand fireplace. It was an impressive feature for an unassuming room tucked under the eaves, but somehow entirely in keeping with Tarquin's decadent collection. The iron grate was surrounded by black marble, which had been carved on one side to show a muscular man in a loincloth holding up the mottled marble of the mantelpiece, and on the other side a woman swathed in a flimsy gown that was very close to slipping off. There was a hint of lust in their expressions as they just about caught each others' eyes across the grate.

"Hands on the mantelpiece. Grip it." Tarquin held Chris' waist firmly. "Came from the bedroom of a royal mistress. Imagine what this has seen—but that's nothing to what it's about to."

"And me in my jodhpurs just for you." Chris pouted then turned and gripped the mantelpiece just as Tarquin had instructed. He squared his broad shoulders, putting on a little show of strength for his lover.

Tarquin stroked Chris' shoulders. "Very nice. Hold tight, captain." He stroked down Chris' back, then brought his hand to the front of Chris' jodhs and cupped Chris' erection through the fabric. "You're straining against the fabric again. I like a keen lover."

"And I like a hard squire," Chris purred. "That must be why we get on so well."

"Indeed it must." Tarquin pressed his hips to Chris' side, knowing he would feel him through the corduroy. Then he tugged down the zip on Chris' jodhs and carefully brought them down to his knees, revealing Chris' firm bottom. "You're a fine sight, captain."

"I know. Aren't you lucky?"

Tarquin gave his buttocks an appraising stroke, as if Chris were a choice horse on sale at the market. "Mmm...firm." Then he drew back his hand and gave Chris a solid spank. The reply was a low moan of pleasure and Chris threw back his head, tossing his dark blond hair.

"How was that, squire?" he asked. "Did you like that?"

"Moan again for me, captain..." Tarquin spanked him once more, a little harder this time. Just as Tarquin guessed he might, Chris bit back the moan, his lips tight together even as his body arched with unspoken need.

Tarquin kissed Chris' neck as he closed his hand around Chris' erection and stroked him back and forth. "I can't hear you moan, captain… Louder!"

"You've got to earn it," he sighed. "Come on, squire, put your back into it and I *might* let you put your cock somewhere too!"

Tarquin caught Chris' earlobe between his teeth and teased it as he released his erection. "Somewhere you bloody well love me putting it, too!" Then he gritted his teeth and, with a grunt, gave Chris a spank.

"I won't…moan…" he breathed out, long and low. "Until you've really earned it."

Tarquin grasped Chris' buttock and gave it a firm squeeze. "Hmmm… Could you take a riding crop to the arse, captain? A priceless antique one at that?"

He glanced over his shoulder at Tarquin, his eyes flashing. "Try me. You might *just* get your moan."

With great care, Tarquin took a gold-handled riding crop from its cabinet. The metal was cool against his palm as he brought it back to show Chris.

"This riding crop was once owned by Skittles, a Victorian courtesan who brought crowds to Rotten Row as she rode." He walloped it against the mantelpiece. "And she rode many a famous cock in that century of petticoats and lace!"

"She sounds like a fun sort of girl." Chris grinned, his blue gaze flirting between the crop and Tarquin. "I bet she was never at a loss for a story."

"Oh, yes, I'm sure of it." Tarquin flexed the crop and stood back. "Ready, captain? Prepare yourself for quite the rasping!"

"Come on, squire," Chris told him, his voice alive with excitement. "Give old Skittles something to be proud of!"

"Too bloody right I will!"

Tarquin drew back the crop, then swished it through the air to land with a *crack* against Chris' arse. He still didn't get his moan but instead Chris gave a groan of excitement, his sculpted back arching. He drew the tip of his tongue over his lips and said, "Again, darling!"

Tarquin pressed the handle flat across Chris' buttocks. "I don't believe I heard a moan, captain! *Again!*"

Drawing his arm back farther, Tarquin streaked the riding crop through the air with a cry of "Huzzah!"

"Yes!" Chris exclaimed. "Bloody hell, yes! I love you, you bastard!"

Tarquin's blood fizzed. "Another, you delectable bounder?"

Chris nodded, gripping the mantelpiece so tightly that his knuckles were white, the muscles in his forearms taut beneath his rolled sleeves. He looked at Tarquin, panting, then begged, "Another."

"All right, but first…" Tarquin crouched behind him, stroking the pink marks on Chris' buttocks before gently kissing them. And that was all it took for him to tempt one of those beguiling moans from his lover's lips. Then Tarquin rose to his feet again. He popped his cuffs, drew back the crop and spanked Chris firmly.

"Tell me how much you want me," Chris gasped, pushing his bottom toward Tarquin's hand. "I know you're desperate for me."

Tarquin pressed his lips to Chris' ear and told him, "I want you more than oxygen." Not something the squire would necessarily say, but Tarquin didn't care. The air seemed suddenly very still and Chris looked back over his shoulder, his eyes filled with nothing but love.

"I love you, Tarks," he said gently. Then he beamed a devilish smile. "You got your moan, squire, I'm all yours."

Tarquin kissed Chris on the lips, then broke away. He put the riding crop aside and his hands fell to the hem of Chris' shirt, where he toyed with the fabric. "I'm glad to hear that, captain. Keep holding tight to the mantelpiece… I want you, captain, I want you so much I—"

Tarquin was never sure afterward if he had meant to do it or not, but whatever his intentions, he had gripped Chris' shirt and with one almighty rip had managed to tear the shirt in two, all the way up to the collar. Tarquin stared at Chris' exposed back and shoulders, and at the handfuls of cloth that he still held.

"I…I appear to have torn you out of your shirt."

"You appear," Chris began, looking back over his shoulder, "to be *entirely* in charge, squire."

Tarquin brushed the remains of Chris' shirt down his arms. "Let go of the mantelpiece…let the shirt go."

He obeyed, letting the tattered remains of the shirt whisper onto the wide hearth. Then he replaced his hands on the mantelpiece, tensing for Tarquin's benefit.

The excitement Tarquin felt whenever he was with Chris seemed amplified somehow, naughtiness burning in him. He brushed his fingers over Chris' lips and commanded, "Suck them."

Chris took Tarquin's fingers into his mouth, caressing them with that ridiculously talented tongue of his, and there was the promise of that perky erection that had stolen Tarquin's breath in the tack room on a bright morning at the start of summer.

"That's it," Tarquin murmured. "Nice and wet, that's it."

Then he withdrew them and pressed them between Chris' buttocks. With a little push, they slid inside, and Tarquin kissed Chris' shoulders as he stroked him from within. Now there was no shortage of moans as Chris tipped his head back, seeking a kiss from his squire.

Tarquin kissed his way to Chris' mouth, and their lips met in a sloppy snog, passionate and careless and free.

He loved everything about the man in his arms, his Chris, his captain, who took advantage of Tarquin's distraction to give full expression to his studied, deliberate insolence. As their kiss went on Chris took one hand from the mantelpiece and began to stroke himself in what Tarquin knew was a very deliberate challenge.

We seem to get more wild with every passing day.

Tarquin brought his free hand to Chris' erection and stroked him too. "Are you ready for your squire? For a good old seeing-to?"

"You have very, *very* talented fingers," he sighed, his perspiration-sheened body pushing back against Tarquin's hand. "God, you have..."

"You're lovely to touch," Tarquin said, his voice soft. "I can't help myself...but now..."

Tarquin withdrew his fingers. In his pocket, he'd brought everything he needed from the bedroom to ensure the two of them enjoyed what remained of the afternoon. Within moments, Tarquin had kicked aside his trousers and he was ready.

He pressed against Chris and with one thrust and a deep sigh, their bodies were united. Chris moaned his name in a hoarse whisper then thrust back against Tarquin, joining them as close as they could be. Tarquin was breathless for a moment and paused, savoring the sensation of their joined bodies. Then he began to move with strong thrusts, the hearthstone beneath his feet creaking with every buck of his hips.

"I love you." Chris groaned, jerking their joined hands against his own erection. "Tarks, I really do."

"I love you too, Chris. Have you ever been happier? I haven't...I haven't..." Tarquin's voice vanished into a sigh.

"Never," he breathed. "Tell me when you — I want us to come together, darling, I love you."

"You saucy thing." Tarquin pressed himself close to Chris' back, his eyes half-closed. All he saw was Chris' dark blond hair and his sweat-sheened nape. The floor was creaking rather badly, and Tarquin made a mental note to get it looked at. But for now, the room seemed rather stuffy and the clouds must've rolled in as the light was dim, but still Tarquin thrust, making love to his captain against a mantelpiece. "Soon, soon...this is fantastic, you're fantastic! I'm on the verge, darling, any moment... Chris, darling, *now*!"

In that moment, as pleasure swept through them, he felt as though they were soaring, weightless, toward heaven. It was the most wonderful, overwhelming experience Tarquin had ever known and to share it with the man he loved made it more perfect than he could ever have imagined.

Tarquin held Chris tight. "That really was something. Could do with a cup of tea now, couldn't — *what the hell has happened to my room*?"

Tarquin had glanced up from Chris' shoulder and come face to face with — where could he start? The wallpaper had vanished. The window had gone. The cabinets had disappeared. The room was a third of its size. Weak light came in from above through a dingy, unwashed skylight.

"Erm… Chris…."

"You're all that's holding me up, Tarks," Chris said dreamily. "Don't move too fast."

"You know that bit in *The Wizard of Oz*, when Dorothy realizes she isn't in Kansas anymore?" Tarquin asked. "Well…I sort of know how she felt."

"I don't— Oh." Chris lifted his head and blinked. "Where's the room gone?"

"And our clothes!" Tarquin chortled nervously. "I've lived in this house all my life and I have no idea… What's that, over there?"

Tarquin nodded toward a table. Now his eyes were accustomed to the light, he could see what looked like an ancient wooden table, piled high with paper. And on it, an old-fashioned portable writing desk, like a school desk without any legs. A rickety chair, fit for the lumber room, was tucked under the table. "Are we inside a cupboard? How did we…?"

"Looks like we're due a half-naked explore." He laughed. "Together we've got a full outfit at least!"

Tarquin brought his arm away from Chris' waist and took his handkerchief from his pocket in an attempt to tidy themselves both up. "There. We're almost decent, with a torn shirt and a whole shirt, jodhs and a jacket between us!"

"You should always wear nothing at all," Chris told him as he pulled his jodhpurs up. "But then every man would be jealous and I'd be fighting off hordes of your adoring fans."

"At least it's quite a long shirt. Sort of like a nightshirt." Tarquin tugged at the hem. "Erm… I had no idea this room existed. What is it, an office?"

He stepped carefully from the hearth onto the dusty wooden floorboards, and picked up one of the papers.

Tarquin sneezed, which fortunately cleared the dust off the elegant, faded handwriting. "A receipt! For… for… something bought at auction. It's very old…must be from my grandfather's time. Blimey, it's for Sir Francis Drake's codpiece!"

"God, I love a secret room!" Chris gave Tarquin's bottom an opportune tap. "But how the hell did we end up in it?"

"The fireplace is the same, look. It must've rotated." Tarquin put the receipt down on the pile. "I don't remember pressing anything. The only secret button I've come into contact today was on your person! And you were holding on to the mantelpiece, so no pressing secret buttons for you."

"My hands were definitely otherwise engaged!" He patted Tarquin's behind again. Then he went back to the mantelpiece and gripped it, testing the strength in the structure. He stooped and peered beneath, as though there might be something on the underside. "Seems solid enough."

Tarquin squinted in the half-light and shuddered. "Oh, God — there's only a bloody snake hanging there! Right next to the fireplace! How the hell did —" He chukled awkwardly. "It's a bell pull! At least we might be able to call for help, although quite frankly I'd rather be wearing trousers in front of our rescuers."

"Something must've triggered it, there has to be a switch." Chris braced his hands on the mantelpiece again, approximating the position he'd been standing in when the fireplace moved. Then he shrugged. "Half-naked exploring first, we'll figure out how to escape after."

Chris stepped back on the hearth and, with a loud creak, the chimney breast, fireplace and the man standing on it suddenly began to move. The whole structure turned and rotated, leaving a dumbstruck Tarquin in the small room alone.

"Found the switch!" Chris called, his voice muffled by the wall that divided them. Then the hearth began to rotate again and there was Chris, one elbow resting on the mantelpiece and Tarquin's trousers thrown over his arm like a tailor. "And your trousers."

He stepped carefully from the hearth then gestured to it with the polished toe of one boot.

"Try putting your weight just there. You have to step hard into it, but that's where the switch is."

Tarquin tried his heel against the spot, but not hard enough to set it off. "Well, someone was very ingenious! But why? What's so special about this room that it needs a revolving fireplace? Maybe there might be something in those receipts that needed to be kept secret."

Leaving Tarquin to deal with his trousers, Chris began to leaf very gently through the papers. Tarquin fizzed with a collector's excitement at the thought of what he might find. Had the mysterious PA Pierce ever found this room, when he stayed here all those years ago? Had the notorious advocate for sexual freedom and unashamed pleasure, whether man or woman, straight or gay, stood where he was standing now? Tarquin liked to think so—there was a certain romance in it.

Tarquin took a handful of the papers and flicked through. "Receipts...receipts... For a delivery of coal, newspapers, an auction catalogue..." Tarquin smudged away the dust from a receipt from a stationers to read it more clearly. "Interesting... My grandad was buying a lot of typewriter ribbon for some reason. What have you got there, Chris?"

"Receipts." He shrugged. "Maybe he was buying the ribbon for Pierce during his stay here back in the day? Just think, one of these ribbons might've been used in the creation of England's most saucy and controversial book. *The book that shocked the world!*" Chris laughed then held up a sheet of paper on which an immaculate copperplate script could be seen in dark red ink. "Look at this, it's from *The New Statesman* in 1954. *Received from PA Pierce via Beardsley Hardacre. The Secret Study number five, pertaining to the pleasures of pleasure itself, for publication in November.* That sounds like a fun read to me!"

Tarquin slapped Chris' bottom. "We could write the sequel! I wonder...what's in here?" He tugged the lid of the writing desk, but it was stuck fast. "Might be some PA Pierce stuff in here, you know! Could be worth quite a bit, but don't tell *you know who!*"

"Locked?" He peered down at the desk, one arm round Tarquin's waist. "I always had this little dream that there *was* no Pierce. That it might even be Beardsley. No one ever saw him, did they? He went overseas when they summoned him to the obscenity trial, after all. But I've found so much stuff between him and Bea that he had to have existed. Beardsley *was* just a money man, not a secret artist with a poetic way of writing filth!"

"But then, who was he? You know pen names and aliases are often similar to the person's own name, or mean something to them in some..." Tarquin's words trailed away, his attention fixed on what might be the desk's keyhole. Except it was small and round, not shaped like an ordinary keyhole at all. Shaped, in fact, rather like a — "Prince Albert Pierce, perhaps?"

"You don't think…" Chris looked thoughtful, then widened his eyes and looked around them at the unassuming room. "*The Secret Study?*"

Tarquin blinked. "It…it could well be, couldn't it? An actual, secret study, that one can only find behind a revolving fireplace that once belonged to a royal mistress. The perfect place to hide away and write about terribly saucy things!"

"We need to know what's inside that desk, Tarks."

"We do." When Tarquin lifted the desk from the table, something shifted inside it. It was so plain and unassuming, a little scratched here and there and with ancient ink smudges on its wooden surface. "Let's get out of this room and see what's inside here. I think I know what might open it."

Together they returned to the fireplace and, with much mutual amusement, Chris deferred to Tarquin when it came to having the honor of operating the concealed switch. He felt almost giddy even without the slow revolve of the chimney breast, the writing desk held before him like an ancient relic and at his side his topless lover, a little reminder of what they had just done.

Not that Tarquin was likely to forget in a hurry!

As it turned, Tarquin admired the workings — someone had gone to great effort to construct the secret entrance to the secret study. His grandfather or someone else in the family must have known about it. Had Tarquin's father?

Tarquin laid the desk on one of the cabinets. "Chris, you're going to think I'm bonkers, I know — but… I think the key to this desk is Prince Albert's PA."

Saying it aloud made the idea sound ridiculous and Tarquin grimaced, waiting for Chris to tell him he was a great big daftie.

"So long as nobody has to wear it, that's fine by me!" Chris squeezed Tarquin's shoulder. "Let's see if you're right, Scoob!"

Tarquin pecked Chris' cheek then, after a steadying deep breath, he took the PA from the safe. His hand trembled as he lifted it from its box. "Someone wanted this PA badly. Beardsley did, and his *last fancy* still does. If I'm right…"

Tarquin closed his eyes and slid the little piece of metal into the hole. He wriggled it and turned it, then it got stuck. "Oh, hell, I was wrong. Let me just—" As Tarquin tried to pull it free, he heard a click. He glanced at Chris and saw excitement dancing in his large eyes.

"Chris, would you like to lift the lid?"

"Okay, I'm going to sound really silly but…let's do it together?" He pecked a kiss to Tarquin's cheek. "It feels right."

"Righty-ho!" Tarquin held the lid with Chris. "If all we find in here is an old bus timetable— Ready? After three."

Together they counted down then, as one, lifted the lid.

It was full of paper.

Tarquin leaned down to look. The edges had been nibbled by a creature of some description, but the typewritten pages seemed to have more or less survived. The same could not be said for the ancient, vulcanized rubber band which held it all together.

"It's…it's a manuscript. A PA Pierce manuscript!" Tarquin stared at it in amazement. "Look at the title— *The Ripening of the Swollen Wheat*. I haven't heard of that one! Maybe *Madam Fanny's Floral Pomander* started life under a different name?"

"Great-Uncle B *did* mention a planned sequel in his papers, but I'm not going to kid myself this is it." Chris turned the first page. His eyes scanned the words and his smile slowly vanished, replaced by a look of disbelief. He turned the second page and gasped. "This isn't *Madam Fanny*, Tarks. This is *not* what I've been reading to Orry every night before she goes to bed."

"My word, Chris...this has been moldering in my attic all this time, and I had no idea! Is there anything else in here? Let's lift it out *very* carefully."

Tarquin placed the pile of typescript on the cabinet, hoping it wouldn't slide off and spread across the floor. Handwritten notes lay underneath in the desk, and Tarquin picked up the top one. "This is Grandpa's writing. It's a challenge to decipher, but... *You're quite right, PA Pierce sounds better than Bunbury Bough.* Yes — his name *was* Bunbury! Granny called him Bunny, although not in company, you understand."

But Chris was reading the typewritten pages again. He blinked and murmured, "If *Bunny* was PA Pierce, then Bunny had a thing for riding crops. Just like Tarkers."

"Wait — Bunny was PA Pierce?" Tarquin shook his head in disbelief. "Grandpa? But he was a lovely old chap, he — well, he had quite a filthy laugh after a few brandies, but... And Grandma was a dear old lady. She..." Tarquin read over the letter again.

"Dear Beardsley, I'm glad you enjoyed Madam Fanny as much as I. What a thing for a quiet country squire like me to write! Can't have all that thrusting nonsense published under my real name though. Wouldn't like to shock the

locals! You're quite right, PA Pierce sounds better than Bunbury Bough."

Grandpa Bunny had written raunchy stories. And no one except Beardsley had ever known.

"So…" Chris' smile grew into a grin. "All those investigative journos, those explorers and nosey parkers who've spent thousands chasing PA Pierce sightings across the tropics… He was here all along? PA Pierce didn't flee the obscenity trial at all, did he? He just got that bloody old shyster Beardsley to put it about that he *had*! And the coppers went to the Caribbean to winkle him out while Bea and Bunny drank champers and congratulated themselves on a con well done in Bough Bottoms!"

"What a bloody pair!" Tarquin said. "Do you think Beardsley knew about this writing desk opening with the PA? Hence the pen name. I don't wish to call your late uncle a thief, but when the PA vanished from the collection…do you think it could've been Beardsley? That he'd need it to open the desk, if a chisel and screwdriver weren't to hand, so he took an opportunity — and there would've been many, seeing as he was only next door — and nabbed it. Maybe someone stole it from *him*, which would serve him right — one of his many mistresses — and *that's* how it ended up at auction?"

"And that's when the Boughs and the Hardacres *really* fell out?" Chris tipped his head to one side. "Because Bea, who was interested in sex and cash and not much else, wanted to publish the sequel and Bunny preferred the anonymous, quiet life? So he took to his *Secret Study* essays and left Uncle Bea so near and yet so far from the sequel he *knew* existed. It would've made him even richer than he already was! That's why Bea hated you and your dad and your grandpa, the nasty old bugger!"

"It all makes sense now! And Beardsley must've told his *last fancy* about it, too. Well, they won't be getting hold of it now." Tarquin stroked the cover page. What a saucy old chap his grandfather had been. "This novel must be worth a fortune. I'll have to get some advice...confidential... There might be other Pierce writings among those receipts. But I'm not asking Bryan, the dodgy git. And we have to keep it a secret, we have to keep Bunny's pen name if someone wants to publish this—he didn't want anyone to know what he wrote, and we should respect his wishes."

"Absolutely," Chris assured him. "Don't worry, Tarks, I'm not Great-Uncle Beardsley."

Tarquin slipped his arm around Chris. "He'd never have looked that good without his shirt on!"

Chapter Twenty-One

Tarquin held Chris' hand as they headed to the boathouse. "Lovely day for the race!"

"Sure you're all right about coming out like this?" Chris squeezed his hand. "I got the impression at training this morning that Longfellow's put the word around. A few knowing looks, nothing nasty."

"I can cope with that." Tarquin beamed. "I'm not going to announce it over a loudhailer, but I love you, and I want to hold your hand, and if we get strange glances from people, that's their lookout, not ours."

They strolled along the riverbank, greeting the villagers who were beginning to gather and who, if they were surprised to see the squire and the captain hand in hand, thought better of saying it. But perhaps it had been obvious from the start. Mrs. Longfellow had seen it, so maybe she hadn't been the only one. Behind the couple trailed the Oracle. A ribbon in Bough Bottoms' blue was tied around her neck, and she paused now and then for photographs, as gracious as she was fondly received.

"Right." Chris took a deep breath as the boatshed drew closer. "This is where I have to say adieu!"

Tarquin kissed Chris' cheek. "And this is where I say, *Give Aubrey Reeve a pasting!*"

"I intend to. He won't nobble me again!" Chris put his arms around Tarquin and held him close. "Love you."

"Now that's *adorable!*"

Tarquin and Chris both looked round to see Shobna, waiting with her hands on her hips and a smile on her face.

"No smooching before the race, captain!" She gave them a wink. "But you've got as much time as you like afterward."

"When we win, you mean?" Chris grinned. "Let's go and get the team whipped into shape, shall we? Bring that trophy home."

Shobna clenched her fist. "It's *ours!*"

"Look after your dad, Orry." Chris stooped to pat her head. "And give us a cheer as we go past."

With another hug for Tarquin, Chris followed Shobna into the boatshed and a moment later, Tarquin heard a cheer go up as the captain arrived. The sound warmed his heart and he beamed at the Oracle, who gave a happy oink. Now all there was to do was amble and wait and no doubt indulge in a bit of squirely chat with the locals.

He was just a few minutes into his happy patrol when a hand landed on his shoulder and a horribly familiar voice said, "Tarquin?"

Oh God, no – not you!

But lo and behold, it was Petunia. Tarquin tightened his hold on the Oracle's harness and gave his former fiancée a curt nod. "Petunia. How do you do?"

"Can I have five minutes?" She fluttered her eyelashes. "Somewhere quieter? I just need a little chat."

"I don't see why not—although do I need to frisk you for firearms?" Tarquin raised an eyebrow in warning, and the Oracle gave an annoyed squeal. Petunia's smile looked almost painful and she led them away from the throng, many of whom were already beginning to unpack tasty-looking picnics, ready for the big moment.

"We've had some artifacts at the sale room, from overseas," she explained. "And one of them was sold to Mr. Longfellow. And he gave it to you and you called the police. Why would you do that?"

"Because it was stolen," Tarquin replied, his tone matter-of-fact. "Chris identified it, and we called the police."

"They've been questioning us, Tarquin, it's *very* unpleasant." Petunia tossed her red hair, haughty even as she seemed to be aiming for vulnerable. "Something about a city scam? And Bryan has interests in the city, it's getting rather thorny for him too! They're digging around in everything, asking questions about this and that, looking at all our business interests!"

Interests in the city.

He seems the sort.

"If you've done nothing wrong, what do you have to worry about? It's coppers dotting the i's and crossing the t's." But there was a sour taste in Tarquin's mouth as he thought of Bryan and his business interests. Could he have been involved in the investment that Chris blew the whistle on?

"Tarquin." She smiled again. "I know you love your collection so…if Chris could perhaps realize he'd misidentified the artifact or somehow point the police elsewhere... Well, we could even give you a little thank-you gift? Just a little something between friends so you could buy a few more bits for your display cases? Bryan and I are happy to discuss the finer details but cash flow is a little tight until this is all resolved."

Frozen assets?

Does Bryan really have it in him to try and ruin the boy who'd had him expelled?

Either way, the police would no doubt be interested in this conversation.

Tarquin shook his head. "It's in the hands of the police. They're looking into it. All you have to do is tell them where that lewd little soapstone chap turned up from and you'll be fine!"

"Do you know what I love about Bryan? He sees things through, even expulsion." The false bonhomie was gone. She leaned close and whispered meaningfully, "Christopher Hardacre had it coming since school. Enjoy the race, Mr. Bough."

A cold shiver trembled through Tarquin, but he put on a brave face. "I'm sure I will. And may the best captain win."

"Oh, he will." She turned and strode away, no doubt off to bellow at some unexpecting rowers.

It struck Tarquin as he wandered back down to the riverbank that saddest thing about this new development was the very fact that, in many ways, it didn't surprise him. Petunia knew how to manipulate and when that failed, she knew even better how to bully. And Bryan... Well, anyone who could change his own name and blatantly pretend he hadn't done so when faced with his childhood nemesis was really capable of anything. But looting the cultures of indigenous people and selling their treasures on the anonymous black market?

If anyone could, it was probably Bryan Reeve.

I hope they chuck the whole bloody book at him.

By the time he made his way along to the starting line with the Oracle, Tarquin was sure that the good folk of Bough Bottoms had no intention of burning either him or Chris at the stake. In fact, all they seemed to really want to do was offer him cupcakes and sausage rolls, Buck's Fizz and flask-warmed cuppas. There was a party atmosphere in the world and Tarquin was ready to join in, especially since he'd be cheering on the finest man ever to don a rowing vest and shorts.

My lover.

And Tarquin felt a thrill for the race that had long been absent, ever since Bryan had appointed himself captain of the Upper Bough Blues and set about bleaching any fun there might have been from it, replacing it with stone-cold competition. Perhaps today they might show him what it meant not only to be a winner, but to do so graciously.

Tarquin had already plotted his own route, and once the boats were away he would speed home and be at the foot of the garden waiting for them to pass by again. Another short hop in the car would take him to the finish line. The only man, other than those on the team, to literally see the race from the starting line to its finish.

And he'd be cheering every step of the way.

The teams paddled toward the starting line. Tarquin gazed at Chris, so handsome in his rowing club gear, his golden hair glowing in the sunlight. He glanced at the other boat and saw Bryan, glowering at the boy who'd managed to get him expelled. Chris didn't give him a second glance, instead offering Tarquin a wave and a kiss from the palm of his hand. Petunia, seated in pride of position as coxswain, shook her head and sneered, but she alone showed anything but enthusiasm.

The rival clubs' flags flew from the pole above the starting hut and Bough Bottoms' mayoress, Mrs. Longfellow, waved from the hut to the waiting crowd. She held the hunting horn aloft, and silence fell.

Then she blew.

Small children clapped their hands over their ears, and somewhere several dogs started to bark, but the race had begun.

A roar went up and Shobna and Petunia lifted their megaphones, shouting instructions to the crews. With an almighty pull on the oars the boats pulled away along the river, leaving a spearheaded wake as they went. The Oracle snorted happily and tossed her head, adding her own cry of encouragement to her friend.

Tarquin patted his knees. "Come on, Orry, home we go—let's go and cheer Uncle Chris on!"

The locals parted, making way for Tarquin and the pig as he hurried to his Land Rover. He put the pig in the footwell, but she climbed onto the passenger seat anyway, apparently enjoying the breeze through the open window as Tarquin drove home. Then once he'd arrived at Bough Towers, the Oracle galloped through the garden down to the river, with Tarquin panting behind.

"There they are, Orry! Look! Can you see—they're coming around the bend!"

And for the first time in too long, Bough Bottoms was easily in the lead, with Upper Bough but a speck on the horizon. Yet even as jubilation seized him, Tarquin could see that something was wrong. The rowers weren't at anything like full power and — *No.* He held up his hand to shield his eyes as he watched half of the team throwing water over the side of the boat.

They were bailing out water, lots of it.

"Bloody Reeve did it again!" Chris shouted to him as they drew nearer. "Something corrosive, we didn't know we were in trouble until we were *really* in trouble!"

"Don't sully Bryan's reputation!" Petunia called through her megaphone as the pursuing boat began to gain ground. "Bad maintenance *and* bad sportsmanship, typical bloody Hardacre! See you at the finish — or the bottom of the river!" Then she grinned and, if there had been any doubt that Bryan was once Aubrey, added, "Queen of the Riverbank all over again, Christopher! Enjoy coming last!"

And she was right, Tarquin knew, because as far as he understood it, boats didn't come with handy plugs that one could just wedge into unexpected holes.

"Should've checked your boat before the race!" Bryan jeered as the boat skimmed by. "You never know who might get into your boatshed overnight! Hope you can all swim!"

"You bastard, Reeve!" Tarquin shouted, impotently waving his fist at the departing boat. All of that training, that dedication, that...*hope.* So much skill shoved outside by a rotten, cheating trick.

Bough Bottoms needed something to fill the gap. A bung, a plug, *something.*

Tarquin blinked as an idea came to him. It was no way to treat an artifact, he knew, but needs must.

"Don't worry, Chris! I'll be back in a jiffy!"

Tarquin ran to the house, the Oracle close on his heels. He hurried up to the collection room and grabbed the

Tudor dildo from its case. He was about to run downstairs with it again, when he remembered the pig was just outside. Flinging open the window, Tarquin called, "Take it to Uncle Chris!" and threw the dildo down to the Oracle.

His dignified porcine assistant scooped the wooden member from the grass in her mouth with admirable delicacy. Then she turned and set off at a spirited gallop to save the day. She scooted away across the lawn toward the riverbank, snorting and squealing as she went, causing every person on the stricken vessel to turn her way.

"Orry!" Chris exclaimed. "And Queen Elizabeth, saving the day!"

But the intrepid pig stopped dead still a couple of feet from the edge of the riverbank. And it was there that she remained, her head extended as far as she could possibly reach but Tarquin had a feeling that it wouldn't be far enough. Chris balanced carefully on the sinking craft and reached out but he couldn't quite span the distance. Even at full stretch an inch or so of air remained between his fingertips and Queen Elizabeth I's favorite dildo.

"Come on, girl," Chris urged, beckoning to her gently. "Just a bit closer, Orry, you can do it."

The Oracle looked down at the bank but remained unmoving, apparently unsure about taking that one extra step that would carry her trotters to the very edge of the grass and the incline into the water.

"Come on," Chris urged again then, as the rowers began to bail ever more frantically, he started to sing. It was the most bizarre tableau Tarquin had ever seen but if anything could work, it was this. Yet still the Oracle of Delphi hesitated until, as they bailed, the Bough

Blues joined their captain in a rousing chorus of *Anything Goes*.

And the Oracle edged forward.

Chris took the wooden dildo from the pig's mouth with a cry of, "Good girl!" Then he dropped to his knees, wedging the feted monarch's favorite companion into the hole that Bryan Reeve had created.

Will that be enough?

It has to be.

Tarquin hurtled outside, skidding over the grass to get back down to the riverbank. The rowing boat didn't seem to be as low in the water as it had been.

"Chris, has it worked?" Tarquin shouted to the boat, which was now picking up as it sped along the calm surface of the river.

"It's perfect!" Chris shouted in reply. "We've got some serious work to do, but we can still win this race! Come on, Blues, let's show those Upper Bough cheats how we do it in the Bottoms!"

His fellow crew cheered and as one they pulled on the oars with renewed vigor, heading off after their cheating opponents.

They can do it, Tarquin knew. *With a captain like Chris, how can they fail?*

The Oracle squealed and Tarquin waved until the boat had rounded a bend and vanished out of sight.

"Orry — to the finish line!"

Tarquin drove through the lanes to Upper Bough, the Oracle resting her snout on the wound-down window as if she was trying to detect the cheating Bryan's scent.

From a hill, Tarquin could see the two boats, neck and neck. And once he got down to the finish line, the boats had very little distance to go. The Upper Bough crowd were tense with silence. Tarquin was almost holding his breath as he watched, hearing the pull of the oars, the shouts of the coxswains and the occasional yell from the gathered spectators. In the bows of their respective boats Shobna was all encouragement, but Petunia was more like a woman supervising a chain gang, sneering and barking at her prisoners. It looked like hell on Earth, and from the annoyed look on the faces of her teammates, Tarquin got the impression that she probably wouldn't be asked to repeat the experience.

Turning from the sight of his former fiancée, Tarquin fixed his gaze instead on Chris, watching the pull and thrust of his muscles, the expression on his sweat-sheened face one of absolute, concentrated focus.

They can do it, Tarquin told himself silently. *Chris can do it.*

"Come on," Chris called to his team, as though Tarquin had spoken his thoughts aloud. "Give it one last push over the line!"

Tarquin couldn't imagine where they found their last burst of energy, but mere meters from the line, the Bough Bottoms' boat shot forward and was over the line first, a whole boat length ahead of Upper Bough.

"They did it! They won!" Tarquin cheered.

Oh, how I'll enjoy giving Chris a celebratory rubdown later.

"We did it, Tarks!" Chris shouted. "*You* did it! And Queen Liz and Orry too!"

Tarquin had never heard a roar of excitement like that given by the winners. It seemed to fill the very heavens and beside him the Oracle turned in excited circles, squealing merrily as she celebrated a victory to savor, a victory for the ages. Yet there was no celebration on the losing boat. In fact, it sounded more like a mutiny.

"We don't need to cheat," someone was shouting, and it wasn't someone in the crowd, it was a member of the crew. "And we don't like people who do."

"Cheat! Bastard! Cheat!" The cries of dissent seemed to be coming from everyone on board, souring the happy atmosphere. The crew turned on Bryan, shouting, their arms waving and their fingers angrily stabbing at the air.

Then Petunia lifted her megaphone and bellowed, "Sit bloody down, you bunch of losers!"

"Yeah, you bloody useless oiks!" Bryan bellowed. "You can't even beat a sinking boat! I'm sacking the lot of you!"

As the Bough Bottoms Blues came ashore, the Upper Bough boat began to rock and somehow, Tarquin wasn't sure exactly how, Petunia and Bryan were suddenly in the water, spluttering and choking as their disgruntled former teammates jeered at their cheating captain. Only then did the Upper Bough Blues turn to the victors and applaud, apparently more gracious in defeat than their captain and coxswain.

"Tarks!" Chris threw his arms around Tarquin. "We won! We bloody won!"

Turning his back on Petunia and Bryan, Tarquin covered Chris' face in kisses. "You're wonderful! Oh, darling, what a triumph over adversity!"

"Trophy time." His lover beamed. "Then back to Bough Bottoms and all up to Hardacre Grange for the party of the year!"

Chapter Twenty-Two

And it really was quite the party, with champagne and music, and this time no furious squire with torn trousers. As the evening wore on and the drink flowed, the Oracle finally left her public and retired to bed in Bough Towers, but as the evening slipped into the night, still the team and the village partied. How lovely it was to have such life and light back in the neighboring house, where once all had been overgrown and crumbling.

Apart from the ancient late resident of course, who had apparently had *fancies* by the dozen.

Bryan and Petunia hadn't gone to the party, although their teammates had. And Tarquin knew that even if Chris' team had lost, he would still have thrown the party to celebrate his rivals' win. And that was why Tarquin loved him.

Once the last few stragglers had gone, Tarquin started to tidy up.

He yawned. "Don't know how you're still awake, Chris—you've had quite a day!"

"Adrenaline." He was smiling more brightly than even the surface of the silver rowing trophy. "And tomorrow my month is up, so fingers crossed the Oracle agrees to come over and at least pretend she likes it here!"

Tarquin crouched down and diligently loaded the dishwasher. "I'll have a serious word with her over breakfast, don't worry! But the offer still stands— you're more than welcome at Bough Towers if you lose this place."

"And I'm gainfully employed now." Chris scrubbed his hand through his lover's hair. "An honest man! With a gorgeous boyfriend and a secret dirty book to read in bed, thanks to Bunny Bough!"

"All's well that ends well." Tarquin got back up to his feet and kissed Chris on the end of his nose. "Back to mine for words with Mrs. Oracle?"

"Shall we take a bottle of fizz?"

Tarquin surveyed the carnage of the party's aftermath. "If there's any left!"

With a bottle of chilled champagne clutched in each hand, Tarquin and Chris sauntered over the garden and neatly hopped the fence into Tarquin's garden. Yet despite the celebrations of the night, something seemed off as soon as they reached the house. Even though the world's worst guard dogs still slumbered there was a certain sense of unease in the air, like the rumbling of a distant storm.

When Tarquin opened the door, he could hear the Oracle's squeals, but from somewhere deep inside the house.

"Orry?" he called. But she didn't come. Tarquin glanced at Chris. "She sounds very upset—she made a racket not unlike that when Beardsley shuffled off this mortal coil. Maybe a draught caught one of the doors and she's shut herself in somewhere?"

"Orry!" Chris put the bottles down on the side and reached for Tarquin's hand. "Let's go and let the poor old girl out!"

They headed into the hallway. Her cries were louder now and Tarquin tipped up his head. "Sounds like she's gone upstairs! Come on! Keep calling to her, Chris! Or sing!"

Tarquin took the stairs two at a time. Why the pig had chosen the day before Mr. Driscoll was due to arrive, he couldn't fathom. The Oracle was clever, but surely she hadn't been ticking the days off on a calendar. To the sound of Chris singing a medley of Gershwin they ascended not just to the bedrooms but beyond, heading up to the eaves where the collection was housed.

It was a hell of a climb for a Gloucester Old Spot.

"I didn't think pigs could climb stairs," Chris admitted.

"She's a pig, not a Dalek," Tarquin told him with a chuckle. "Stairs hold no fears for pigs! I just wonder what she's doing up here. She's making a right old row! Unless taking you the dildo has given her a great interest in saucy artifacts!"

Chris laughed. "It seemed to survive its dunk in the river, didn't it? I know how much your collection means to you, yet you did that for us."

"Of course I did! That thing has survived all these years, a little trip in a boat wasn't going to hurt it." Tarquin winked. "Right, let's find out what the Oracle is up to in my collection room!"

As soon as they reached the landing Tarquin knew this wasn't a simple case of porcine mischief. The troubled pig trotted back and forth in front of the revolving fireplace, squealing with agitation just as she had on the evening that Tarquin had heard an intruder in the house. She was a better guard dog than his dogs, it seemed. Not surprising, really.

"Oh, I'm a bloody idiot, I must've left the door unlocked after I'd thrown the dildo out of the window!" Tarquin watched the Oracle's progress and noticed something. "What's that — piece of cloth in her mouth? Someone's in here — they're in the Secret Study!"

"Is that —" Chris peered at the scrap of material, frowning. "Royal blue and red?"

"That's the Upper Bough colors." Tarquin folded his arms, his jaw jutting in squire-like fashion. "Take a wild guess, Chris, as to who entered my house *uninvited*?"

"No!" Chris whispered. "They *wouldn't*!"

"Help! Is someone out there? Oh, at bloody last! Help!"

Tarquin pointed at the mantelpiece. "Unless my fireplace can suddenly speak, that sounds a lot like Bryan Reeve!"

"Oh, God, no!" Chris gave a bark of amusement and called, "Is that Aubrey Reeve or is Santa very early this year?"

"Let us out!" Bryan pleaded. "And don't call me bloody Aubrey! That mad pig tried to eat me! We're not coming out until the pig's under control, or better yet, barbecue!"

"Christopher!" It was Petunia, Tarquin realized. "Tarquin! Let us bloody out! She bit Bryan in the arse!"

The Oracle squealed, presumably incensed all over again at the sound of Petunia's voice, and scratched against the wall with her trotters.

Tarquin banged his fist on the chimney breast. "Neither of you has yet explained what you're doing up here. Hunting for Prince Albert's PA again, were you? And how'd you get behind my fireplace anyway?"

"Beardsley told me about this bloody manuscript and said it was behind a fireplace so we've tried them all and — well, we thought he meant in the chimney but as soon as Bryan knelt on the hearth it spun round," Petunia admitted. "He said we'd need that gross Prince Albert to get at it, *that's* why we tried to convince you to sell it, because I didn't know your bloody combination!"

"You're well rid of her," Chris said, earning a nod of agreement from Tarquin.

"And Bryan's stupid bloody stock market scheme was shut down thanks to Christopher and we *need* that manuscript because it'll be worth a fortune!" she went on. "You should be proud, Christopher, you made such an impact on Bryan at school that he set it up just to ruin you. And to make us rich, of course, but they've frozen *everything*. I couldn't even rely on getting that inheritance even though I *was* the last fancy!"

"No, you weren't!" Bryan spluttered. "*I* was! *I'm* in line to inherit a fortune, not *you!*"

"You?" Petunia and Chris chorused as one. It was possibly the strangest thing Tarquin had ever heard. Bryan Reeve and Beardsley Hardacre? What was the world coming to?

"Yes, *me!*" Bryan spat. "*Me!* He took a shine to me in my rowing gear, I went round his house, and I knew very well what a rich old bastard he was — and with my knowledge of first editions and all that twaddle, I charmed him! *I* was his last fancy, and Driscoll knows it. *He* tried to winkle the PA from Tarquin, but Tarks is such a dimwitted magpie surrounded by all his crap, he had no idea what he was sitting on."

"My arse, Bryan. That's what I've been sitting on." Tarquin shook his head. "So you came into my house, uninvited, to rob me. And now you're insulting me. How terribly charming, Aubrey."

"Don't call me that," Bryan whined. "Do you know what they called me at school? *Aubrey Strawberry*! I won't be called bloody Aubrey — and get us out of this bloody hellhole!"

"Shut up, you sound like an idiot child," Petunia sneered. "I'm going to slap you, you're hysterical."

From behind the wall there came the sound of a hard, furious slap landing followed swiftly by a cry of pain. Tarquin winced as he remembered Petunia and that shotgun, ready to do some damage.

"Right!" Petunia spat. "Christopher Hardacre, let us out right now! I know everything there is to know about his sordid little relic scam and I'm ready to tell! *Two* men going gay behind my back? Bloody hell! I've got receipts, evidence, messages! Tell your copper friends that I'm happy to talk!"

"It's very...*rural*, isn't it?" Chris teased Tarquin. "Everyone having it away with the mad old millionaire just to get in the will?"

"Isn't it just?" Tarquin chuckled. Then he called through the wall, "Hold tight, Tuney, hold tight, Aubrey Strawberry — we'll go and get the coppers. And the Oracle will stand guard outside. She hasn't quite finished eating your shorts, Aubrey, and, Petunia — she's really pissed off about you trying to shoot her in the head, so watch out, she's got a hell of a bite. Hasn't she, Aubrey?"

"Stop calling me bloody Aubrey, you moronic country bumpkin!"

Tarquin turned to Chris and laughed again.

"No hard feelings," Chris called merrily. "We'll even get you a plaster for that bite on your bum!"

Chapter Twenty-Three

Tarquin decided that he would never grow tired of waking up with Christopher Hardacre in his arms.

"Good morning, darling." Tarquin kissed him and ruffled his hair. "Sun's up, and I've got an hour until it's time to milk the cows!"

"And I'll spend the morning convincing the Oracle to play along with Mr. Driscoll." He grinned, snuggling sleepily against Tarquin. "And admiring my trophy, obviously. I might come along with Orry while you're doing the cows. I'd like to be helpful if I can, it's more fun than standing about in a noisy office like the old days."

"If you can help me get the milking cups on the ladies, we'll have more time to have words with Orry before Mr. Driscoll arrives." Tarquin chuckled as he ran his hand down Chris' side. He was all warm and soft with sleep. "Sorry. I shouldn't talk shop while we're in bed."

"It's not the cash or the house, it's the thought of one of those two getting their hands on Bea's inheritance, even if they *are* in prison. And who knows how many *other* fancies are going to come swarming out of the woodwork?" Chris sighed and shook his head. "And if I'm honest, I rather like being the Hardacre of Bough Bottoms. It's a home. In every sense of the word."

"You suit Bough Bottoms. You belong here, darling." Tarquin kissed Chris' forehead as under the covers he caressed Chris' buttocks. "And you especially belong in my bed, captain!"

"And you belong in my arms, squire," he murmured. "So you can make love to me every single morning. Or whenever you fancy, really."

"How about—" Tarquin kissed Chris' cheek. "Right—" Then he pecked his lips. "Now?"

Chris draped his arms around Tarquin's neck and told him, "Right now is always best of all."

Tarquin touched the tip of his nose to Chris' and gazed at the sparkle of his blue eyes. Then he kissed him, soft and teasing to begin with until, responding to the heat in Chris' kiss, it deepened. However today went, it would bring huge changes to Chris' life, but they had each other, and Tarquin knew that whether Chris inherited a fortune or nothing at all, he would always love him.

What had happened to the man who started the summer, the curmudgeon with a wedding to plan who had been so very ready to leap a garden fence in pursuit of the new fellow next door? Tarquin wasn't sure exactly *how* that grumpy fellow had become the squire, but he had an idea that it had happened in the tack room where he had stood thousands of times before, but in one wild morning, had become the portal to this new world. The world where he had always dreamed he might one day find himself.

As they made love, every tender caress heated into passion, just as it always did. Tarquin wanted for nothing with Chris in his arms, the man who had shown him how to accept himself, and how to love and be loved in return.

What sauce they could enjoy as the squire and his captain, filled with heat and wildness, but what tenderness too when they were joined like this. No man could ask for more and Tarquin knew that he never would. He had everything he could ever want. Whatever happened to the house next door, the boy next door would always be his.

They were made for each other, a Bough and a Hardacre, and Tarquin couldn't think of anyone he'd rather share his life with. Such a man as Chris, loving and silly, handsome and extremely saucy, and who looked amazing in jodhpurs, and —

"I adore you, Chris," Tarquin whispered against Chris' neck. His lover repeated the sentiment back to him, a tender gasp close to his ear as Chris tightened his arms around Tarquin, stroking his foot down the back of his leg.

"Oh, Tarks," Chris cooed gently, "I love you, you gorgeous bloody farmer."

"I love you, you Canary Wharf canary!" Tarquin kissed him. "My handsome neighbor."

"Your man," Chris sighed, his eyelids fluttering as their shared pleasure grew. "Love you…"

Tarquin twined his fingers with Chris' and together they tumbled into bliss. Tarquin soared in Chris' embrace and everything in the world fell away apart from his man, his lover. His Chris.

They lay together in the sunlight, listening to the gentle sounds of the village awakening as they drifted through the open window on the summer breeze. Tarquin didn't want to move, but the farm wouldn't wait and the cows, ready for milking, certainly wouldn't appreciate any delays. Yet even that wouldn't seem like work if he had Chris at his side.

And Chris doesn't want to be anywhere else.

Together they fed the dogs and settled the Oracle with her own breakfast out in the paddock, in the cool shadow of the barn. Demure as ever, she waited a few seconds to begin eating, just long enough for Chris to tell her, "Just one day, Orry, then you can live wherever you like, but neither of us wants a convicted con merchant living next door."

The Oracle blinked up at Chris, her head tilted to one side. He met her look with a smile before ducking lower to kiss her pink head.

"Right," Chris said to Tarquin then. "Onto those cows, squire!"

* * * *

Tarquin was banging the mud from his wellies when he spotted the sun glint off Driscoll's shiny car. He was heading to Chris' house.

The moment has come.

"He's early, the annoying git!" Tarquin muttered. He looked up to see Chris dash around the corner of the house, and from the look on his handsome face, Tarquin knew before he spoke that there was a problem.

Please not the Or –

"The Oracle of Delphi!" Chris stooped, resting his hands on his thighs as he caught his breath. "She's gone, Tarks! Paddock's empty!"

Tarquin's heart plummeted. *Not now. Why now?* "Oh no… Maybe she's gone upstairs again? At least we know Bryan and Petunia haven't done a number on her, but what if—oh, hell, no, do hitmen bump off pigs?"

"Whatever happens, we don't tell Driscoll, okay?" Chris stood up straight and put his hands on Tarquin's shoulders as though steadying himself. "We keep smiling, and we tell him that everything's perfect and… Let's say she's sleeping and we can't disturb her! I don't even know how she got out—pigs might be able to do stairs, but they can't unbolt bolts. My gut says she's safe, but I promise you we'll find her as soon as we've charmed Mr. Driscoll back to town. Love you, darling."

"And without Petunia around to conveniently leave the gate unlatched…the Oracle's a damn clever pig, though!" Tarquin arched an eyebrow. "Right, let's pop over to yours, make him a cuppa, and while you charm him, I'll do some pig-wrangling."

Tarquin's dog pack appeared in a crowd of wagging tails, but there was no curly pink tail among them. "And there's no point asking you useless bunch to help find her, is there?" But he fussed them all the same. Chris joined him, looking for all the world like a man about to face a judge and jury rather than a line solicitor whose fee today was entirely dependent on the decision made by an opinionated, escape-artist pig.

"Mr. Hardacre, Mr. Bough!" Driscoll's voice was cheery as he made his way through the yard, his navy pinstripe suit entirely incongruous amid the trappings of rural gentility. "I'm sorry to be a little early but I'm keen to discover the outcome of this most unusual last will and testament! Mr. Hardacre, you've certainly settled into the ways of the countryside. You both look very well for it, I must say!"

"Mr. Driscoll!" Chris beamed and shook the solicitor's hand. *Nobody would know anything's amiss,* Tarquin told himself. *We might still be able to pull this off.* "I'm definitely settled into my new home, thanks to Tarks and the Oracle of Delphi and her doggy pals. It's bye-bye, London, hello, fresh air and early-morning milking."

Chris winced just a little, no doubt hearing more than one meaning in his own words.

"Good morning to you, Mr. Bough." Driscoll extended his hand again. "I hope your new neighbor hasn't proven too much of a trouble, eh? No loud music at ungodly hours!"

Tarquin tried to focus on Driscoll while trying not to look over his shoulder for the pig. "No loud music, but he's been keeping me entertained!"

"Typical Hardacre." Driscoll rolled his eyes. "Well, where is she? Where does the lady in question now reside?"

"Hardacre Grange." Chris grinned, charming and easy as ever. "But it was a late night yesterday after the boat race celebrations and we wondered, is there any chance that you might be able to come back this evening, perhaps? Orry's fast asleep and we wouldn't like to wake her."

"Oh, I won't wake her," Driscoll assured them. "But I must see her in the Grange of her own free will, and clearly displaying a willingness to be there."

Chris darted Tarquin a rather worried glance and asked, "Would you really disturb a lady's beauty sleep?"

This time Driscoll's face grew a little sterner and he asked Chris with deceptive levity, "Would you willingly give up the Hardacre inheritance rather than mildly inconvenience a pig?"

"Well." Chris beamed and this time it was Tarquin's turn to wince, because the smile looked as though it hurt. "Well. Right. Shall we — How about a cup of tea before we —" But Driscoll shook his head slowly, a sure sign that he suspected *something* was afoot. And Tarquin couldn't help a slight admiration for Chris as he plowed onward with his pantomime, as though hope alone might conjure the Oracle of Delphi into being in the cherished home he was surely going to lose.

To Petunia.

Or Bryan.

Or God knows who.

"Right." Chris nodded and set off walking at a torturous pace. "To Hardacre Grange and the Oracle of Delphi!"

As they walked he began to sing a medley of Orry's favorite show tunes just a little too casually, as though he always strolled very slowly around farmyards singing eleven o'clock songs and showstoppers. Yet of the Oracle of Delphi there was no sign, and all too soon they were at the door of Hardacre Grange, waiting to face their fate. Chris stood politely back, allowing Tarquin and Driscoll to enter ahead of him.

"She loves it here," Tarquin promised the solicitor, trying to disguise the note of desperation in his voice. If Petunia and Bryan were in police custody, then...then perhaps someone else who considered themselves *the last fancy* had nobbled the poor pig. "Absolutely delights in the place. Doesn't she, Chris?

Gambols about on the lawn just as happily as when old Beardsley was alive. Adores Chris. She's quite fond of me, too, but it's Chris who's her daddy now."

"She really does love it." Chris beamed. "As the saying goes — well, it doesn't, but the Oracle of Delphi has *two* daddies now!"

"I had heard something to that end," Driscoll admitted. "But where is she? Surely she doesn't have her own room? A pig climbing the stairs?"

"She's a pig, not a Dalek," Chris told him, just as Tarquin had reminded him last night. "She's certainly not downstairs or she would've come running. Let's have a look upstairs. I hope she hasn't taken herself out for a constitutional!"

At the top of the stairs, however, Driscoll held up his hand to halt them. He cleared his throat and said, "Mr. Hardacre, I believe you are leading me on a wild goose chase. If the Oracle of Delphi has come to some harm or has met with another fate, it's best that you tell me now. I believe, at best, you have lost her. And that means, I'm afraid, that you have also lost your great-uncle's inheritance. It will be forfeit as laid out in his last will and testament."

Tarquin swallowed, his throat dry.

No, no, this wasn't meant to happen!

"Please, Mr. Driscoll, as a farmer I have to tell you that animals can't be beholden to instructions written on bits of paper. Dogs are meant to guard houses — did mine the other day when Bryan and Petunia broke in? No. Could you demand a cat to arrive through the cat flap at exactly a quarter past twelve? No. And the same goes for a pig. The Oracle is highly intelligent and most definitely her own boss, and she hasn't a clue about wills and all that jazz. It simply won't do — it simply isn't *fair*—to turn up and declare poor old Chris destitute thanks to an impossible clause in a will!"

Yet Driscoll clearly wasn't listening. Instead he was looking at the door of Chris' bedroom. It stood ajar and from behind it came the soft sound of snoring grunts, like those that might emanate from the snout of a slumbering pig. Chris seized Tarquin's hand and whispered, "Mr. Driscoll, if you'd care to lead the way, I think you'll find that Orry is *definitely* at home."

Had Chris had the foresight to plant speakers playing a recording of the Oracle asleep? Or was it—could it be—?

Tarquin took the initiative and pushed the door open. There, in the newly refurbished bedroom, was a pig.

The Oracle was snuggled on Chris' bed, with her blanky that Tarquin had given the orphaned creature when she had first run in squealing circles across his garden. And beside her, the gnawed end of a turnip. She lifted her head and blinked at the trio, then gave a satisfied snort and laid it down on the pillows again, returning to her happy dreams.

"Well." Mr. Driscoll nodded, then took Chris' hand and pumped it vigorously. "Since she is clearly under no duress and a pig can hardly open a front door, let alone be settled on a bed and bring her breakfast and blanket with her unless she is in agreement with her domestic arrangements, I declare that to my satisfaction that the esteemed Oracle of Delphi is indeed a *very* happy resident of Hardacre Grange. Congratulations, Mr. Hardacre, you have satisfied the conditions of your great-uncle's will and the inheritance is *certainly* yours!"

"We did it." Chris laughed, gazing at Tarquin. "Me and you and the most wonderful pig in England! We're home at last!"

Chapter Twenty-Four

A year later, that same pig stood in the large garden that had been opened up behind Bough Towers and Hardacre Grange, munching the floral crown she had worn to Tarquin and Chris' wedding. Her two fathers, however, were more than willing to be indulgent on this of all days. Besides, wrestling the Oracle's crown from her gently chewing jaws would mean they'd have to let go of each other's hands.

And that would never do.

The garden was filled with locals from both Upper and Lower Bough, with a celebratory row planned along the river as it wound along the banks behind the two houses. The city kids who were staying at the Grange on a farm holiday had been invited too, and Tarquin's pack of dogs ran to and fro between them all, evidently hopeful of scraps falling from the tables.

And at the center of the party were the two men, husband and husband, Bough and Hardacre, who had started out as neighbors and ended up as lovers. And as they danced beneath the sun of the late summer dusk, there could be no happier couple. Nor none so handy with a vintage riding crop.

And what else mattered but that?

Want to see more from these authors? Here's a taster for you to enjoy!

Captivating Captains:
The Captain and the Prime Minister
Catherine Curzon & Eleanor Harkstead

Excerpt

Tom lay sprawled on the beanbag between the two small beds — one shaped like a car, the other shaped like a boat. He'd nearly sent himself to sleep with the twins' bedtime story, but finally it seemed, from the sound of their gentle breathing, that they'd dropped off. He sat quietly in the dimly lit room, the elephant nightlight casting its gentle glow. And in that glow, he re-read the text from Stuart.

Hey good lookin', ya miss me? Through with Barca and heading home - you shud SEE my tan lines babe. Get ready Laaahndaaaan! x

Stuart wasn't high on the list of people who Tom wanted to talk to. Their break-up had been acrimonious, Stuart furious at one too many dates being canceled at the last minute because Tom had to look after the twins. *'You love that family more than you love me!'* And off Stuart had gone to Barcelona.

Except, apparently, Stuart was back.

And that list of Tom's was rather brief. It'd be rude not to reply, wouldn't it?

Tom lifted his head and glanced at the children. They were both sound asleep, so Tom carefully got up from the beanbag and tapped his reply.

Hey Stuart yeah I'm still in London. Maybe I'll see you sometime? T.

They'd been through a lot—both ex-army, both gay, although Tom's career had taken an unusual turn when he'd decided to become a nanny. Or *manny*, as the press had christened him. But it worked. Captain Southwell had transformed into Tom, but he still dealt with crises before breakfast, and marshalling small children was just as challenging as directing a company in a warzone.

The reply took seconds.

Believe it manny Tom. I'll be knocking on door of no 10 and sayin' where's my man ;) xx

Tom worked on the principle that being hostile to exes wasn't the mark of a gentleman but equally, dealing with someone who thought Tom was his *man* after all this time, wasn't a task that filled him with joy.

I thought your man's in Barcelona? T.

And his phone rang, vibrating silently in his hand as Tom heard the flat's front door opening and closing softly, so as not to disturb the sleeping children. The prime minister was home.

Tom stuffed the phone into his pocket. He wasn't going to answer it—he had a family to look after.

Before Alex had reached the kitchen doorway, Tom had poured him a glass of wine. It sat there on the worktop when Alex appeared in the doorway, his hand already loosening the knot of his tie.

"All the way from the House I was thinking about diving into a *huge* glass of red wine." Alex chuckled, widening his eyes at the sight of it. "And there it is!"

"You look like you could do with one!" Tom said.

"The thought of cuddling Al and Mad and a little sniff of red is what's kept me going through the last two hours of paperwork," Alex told him, slapping a matey hand to Tom's shoulder and letting it linger there. "As soon as I hit the bottom of the despatch box I made for home. I don't suppose there happens to be any supper left over, or am I raiding the fridge again?"

Tom passed him the glass across the marble worktop. "There's a shepherd's pie waiting for you if you'd like it?"

"If anyone finds out about this, they'll be tempting you away with a pay rise," Alex teased. "I already have to tell them you're like the anti-Mary Poppins to throw them off the scent."

Tom checked the pie in the oven, then turned it on to warm.

"I don't have a magic carpet bag, and I'm not into chimney sweepers," he said. "I have no intention of leaving, tempt me all they like!"

"If any chimney sweeps *do* come along, I want to know about it," Alex told him. Then he raised his glass to his lips and took a grateful drink. "I can't lose my shepherd's pie whisperer."

"Do you want to eat in here, or in the lounge?" Tom hoped he'd say the lounge, because if Alex put the television on in the kitchen and discovered that the last channel Tom had watched was BBC Parliament, it might be rather awkward.

It's because the children wanted to see you when they came home from preschool. Honest.

"Lounge, sofa, general couch potato of a night?" He nodded, apparently satisfied with his own suggestion. "Did you eat with the kids?"

"Well, I tried! We had sit-down dinner time together but Madeleine wanted to draw at the same time, so I had my hands full." Tom dragged his hand back through his hair. "I think I got all the sweetcorn out of my hair, but I'm not sure!"

"I'm going to nip in and see them before I eat," Alex decided. "I hate that I missed them tonight and I know they're asleep but it's really for me, not them. But you know that."

"I know." Tom patted his arm. "They'll know you're there. You'll suddenly pop up in their dreams."

"Oh, God help them! Then you have to be off the clock, Tom, you know that. Much as I love coming home to you and your shepherd's pie, you must be cursing my name?" He assumed a grumbling mutter to say, "Bloody Alex keeping me bloody working all bloody hours."

"It's not really *work*, though," Tom assured him as he got a tray ready for Alex. "We're like housemates!"

"I couldn't ask for a better fellow to share with." Alex laughed and brushed Tom's shoulder as he headed for the door. "I'll be back, Captain!"

Tom leaned against the kitchen cupboard, flicking through a recipe book. He heard Alex's footsteps through the baby monitor and saw the night-vision version of the prime minister on the screen. Tom should have gone back to his book to give Alex his privacy, but he couldn't resist a glance at Alex crouched beside his child's bed. He was such a kind father and it brought a lump to Tom's throat. Thank God Stuart hadn't rung again and shattered their peace. He didn't need it tonight, and Alex certainly didn't.

Tom heard Alex's voice, as gentle now as it had been commanding in the chamber earlier, wishing his sleeping children sweet dreams. Then, as he always did on the rare nights that he didn't make it home in time for supper and bedtime with the twins he adored, Alex remained in the room for a while. He settled onto the beanbag where Tom had sat just a few minutes earlier and became part of the peaceful scene, soaking up the calm in that sometimes rather busy room that his son and daughter shared. And though the two children slept on, surely they sensed that protective presence watching over them until, with a whisper of, "I love you," Alex rose to his feet and made his careful way toward the door.

Alex was such a lonely figure sometimes, and during those moments Alex shared with his children, Tom wondered if he was thinking of his late wife.

He shouldn't ever be lonely. Gill wouldn't have wanted it, and Tom certainly didn't. Alex deserved to be loved.

"I see the permanent marker has *almost* washed off of Alastair's cheek," Alex observed cheerfully as he padded back into the kitchen. He returned to the serious business of unknotting his tie and added, "You must have magical skills that I lack!"

The sound of the silk rasping against Alex's hand very nearly sent a tremor through Tom, but he pushed it down.

You can't think those things about your straight boss.

"We had a game at bath time — I made them beards and moustaches out of bubbles, then rubbed them off. Al didn't notice a thing — he was too busy laughing."

"See, I learned the hard way that saying *don't scribble on your face* is the guaranteed way to get a little monster like my son to scribble on his face." Alex threw his tie onto the worktop. Then he unfastened his silver cufflinks and tossed them with only a little more care atop his discarded tie. Tom knew what was coming next even before Alex rolled first one immaculate sleeve to his elbow then the other, because he knew Alex's routine as well as his own. *And his arms are to die for.* "He's joining a long line of Hart boys who never did as they were told!"

Tom chuckled. "Were you naughty, then?"

You wish he still was naughty, Tom.

"I was a terror." Alex leaned forward to peer into the glass door of the oven, his hands braced against his knees. "But I went one better — I drew on my sister's face while she was asleep. Gave her a moustache to be proud of!"

"And having met your sister — !" Tom tried not to notice how the fabric of Alex's suit trousers strained pleasingly across his bottom as he leaned down. He was a fine figure of a man — Tom would be an idiot not to notice. "Bet she was pleased!"

"Oh she loved it, you can imagine how thrilled she was!" Alex stood straight again and turned to face Tom. "You don't have to hang around if you don't want to, you know. Honestly, I can't imagine this is how you want to spend your off time."

"If I worked in an office all day, I'd be chilling at home just like I'm doing now, so… It's fine, honest." Tom slipped the recipe book back on the shelf. He liked being part of a family, too. In some ways it made up for the lack of his own. "I should apologize for these jogging bottoms though. I don't think I've even jogged in them. But then…you wouldn't want to see me in my pajamas, would you?"

Although I wouldn't mind seeing Alex in his again.

"This is your home, Captain Southwell. If you have to see me bleary eyed in my bath towel now and again, I wouldn't complain if you wanted to wear your pajamas after a long day trying to keep my children in line!"

Alex in a bath towel. That was a thought to ponder.

"I *say* pajamas, I actually sleep in —" *My boxer shorts. Oh, God, he doesn't want to know that.* "Do you want to see what the twins got up to at preschool today?"

Tom was already delving into the satchels that Alastair and Madeleine carried about as proudly as the chancellor wielded his briefcase on Budget Day. Alex gave an impromptu drumroll, pounding his hands on the worktop, and asked, "Go on, show me."

"Ta-da!" Tom produced a sheet of paper from Madeleine's bag and handed it over. "They had to draw their families so she's done you in the House of Commons. She's even got the green seats right, although she's only given you three strands of hair."

"But what excellent strands they are." Alex laughed, brushing his hand back through his rather more generous head of *real* hair. "But who's the terrible threesome watching from the benches? Alastair's hair's looking rather bluer than I remember but she's got Gill's curls right and as for *you*… How is it that I look like a balding head teacher and you look like a film star?"

With a deliberately camp flourish, Tom said, "Oh, just my fabulous good looks! I suppose I'm the minister of tidying up the toybox?"

"A deserved gold star for Mads." Alex beamed proudly. He took the picture and placed it on the fridge, where it joined a gallery of his children's artistic efforts. "At least she drew it on paper, not on her brother's face."

"And that's why I suggested wipe-clean paint on the walls in this house!" Tom said. "You never know when a pen or a crayon'll go rogue. Face, walls, clothing — if it's a surface, it can and *will* be drawn on."

"The question is, will Tom's shepherd's pie win a gold star of its own?" Alex peered at his reflection in the silver fridge door. "And will my hair survive the last year of its first Downing Street term?"

"You're not doing too badly. Not like some former PMs I can think of who start off with a full head of dark hair and end up with hair as white as Father Christmas." Tom peered into the oven. "That smells good, doesn't it? It's bubbling like a lava flow."

"I don't know what we'd do without you," Alex admitted, swirling the wine in his glass. "Honestly, Tom, I really don't."

PUBLISHING

Sign up for our newsletter and find out about all our
romance book releases, eBook sales and promotions,
sneak peeks and FREE romance books!

About the Authors

Catherine Curzon

Catherine Curzon is a royal historian who writes on all matters of 18th century. Her work has been featured on many platforms and Catherine has also spoken at various venues including the Royal Pavilion, Brighton, and Dr Johnson's House.

Catherine holds a Master's degree in Film and when not dodging the furies of the guillotine, writes fiction set deep in the underbelly of Georgian London.

She lives in Yorkshire atop a ludicrously steep hill.

Eleanor Harkstead

Eleanor Harkstead often dashes about in nineteenth-century costume, in bonnet or cravat as the mood takes her. She can occasionally be found wandering old graveyards, and is especially fond of the ones in Edinburgh. Eleanor is very fond of chocolate, wine, tweed waistcoats and nice pens. She has a large collection of vintage hats, and once played guitar in a band. Originally from the south-east, Eleanor now lives somewhere in the Midlands with a large ginger cat who resembles a Viking.

Catherine and Eleanor love to hear from readers. You can find their contact information, website and author biographies at https://www.pride-publishing.com.